THE WINDS OF HEAVEN

THE WINDS OF HEAVEN

MONICA DICKENS

THE BOOK CLUB
121 CHARING CROSS ROAD
LONDON, W.C.2

PRINTED AND BOUND IN GREAT BRITAIN

BY THE HOLLEN STREET PRESS LIMITED LONDON WI

To PAMELA

CHAPTER ONE

WHEN the winds of Heaven blow, men are inclined to throw back their heads like horses, and stride ruggedly into the gusts, pretending to be much healthier than they really are; but women tend to creep about, shrunk into their clothes, and clutching miserably at their hats and hair.

To Louise Bickford, on this late April day, the wind that iostled through the London streets seemed a bitter personal enemy, turning to meet her whichever way she turned, beating against her small figure on the open stretches, and calling in reserve cohorts to attack her afresh at every corner.

She had intended to walk to the Park and look at the spring flowers, but she was soon so tired of fighting the wind's fiendish determination to pluck her clothes and hair awry that she turned into a teashop to resettle her hair and recover her breath, until it was time to meet Miriam and the children at Marble Arch.

Miriam was Louise's eldest daughter. She had borne three daughters, to her surprise, for her husband had set his heart on a son, and Louise was in the habit of giving him everything he asked for. That she failed to give him a boy, with a long conceited nose like his own to look down on the world, had not helped to raise his opinion of his wife's usefulness to society.

Miriam was buying school clothes for the summer term. She would not let her mother come to the shops with her, because Louise talked too much to the salesgirls and confused the issue with irrelevant suggestions. To-day they had parted after a restaurant lunch, and Louise, who could not afford to buy clothes for herself, had then walked about and looked in shop windows, until the truculence of the untiring wind had driven her into the universal haven of Lyons.

It was that hour in mid-afternoon, when those who are on

the early lunch and tea break come forth among the exhausted shoppers to get themselves a bite of something to keep them going until five-thirty. When she had stood in line and paid for her cake and cup of tea, Louise could not at first see anywhere to put down her tin tray. Being a Londoner, it did not dismay her to stand holding a tray among a crowd of people with similar trays laden with unlikely food for the hour of day, and women stacking dirty dishes and wiping off tables with damp cloths.

She walked about determinedly, turning her feet outward in the narrow, old-fashioned shoes she had been buying at the same shop for thirty years, until she saw an empty chair at a table by the wall, and gained it easily ahead of a vacillating man in a raincoat. Two girls were talking earnestly across the remains of their tea, and opposite Louise, a fat elderly man in clothes slightly frayed at points of friction was eating biscuits and reading a paper-backed thriller.

When she had finished her cake, Louise lit a cigarette and smoked it with quick, naïve puffs. Dudley had not liked her to smoke, and although she had been widowed for more than a year, and had been smoking since she came back from her husband's funeral, she was still inexpert at it.

She reached for the ashtray, for she wanted to tap off the ash frequently, as she had seen highly-strung, busy people do. Louise was neither highly-strung nor busy, but when she was in London, among people who all seemed to be doing something important in a hurry, she liked to try and keep the pace.

Perhaps the fat man and the seriously gossiping girls would think she ran a dress shop, or was the key woman in a travel agency, or a writer of significant memoranda in Whitehall. Louise was always much concerned with how people were thinking of her and summing her up; not knowing that a small, middle-aged lady with stubby features and hair no longer brown and not yet grey usually goes unnoticed.

She reached for the ashtray with a purposeful gesture, and knocked the remains of her tea over the fat man's book, which he had just closed with a breathy, contented sigh. A small puddle spread over the grotesquely pointed breasts that upheld the swim-suit of the murdered girl on the cover, and the glossy paper began to sag and pucker.

' I'm so terribly sorry. I don't know how I could have done such a thing,' Louise gasped, although she spilled things every day, being naturally clumsy.

' Don't give it a thought,' the man said, in one of those surprisingly soft, inadequate voices that sometimes come out of fat people, like a small puff of air from broken bellows. ' It doesn't matter a pin.'

'Oh, but it does. We must get a cloth——' Louise looked round for one of the wipers of tables, but the man said: 'Please don't bother. It's a worthless thing.' Nevertheless, he blotted the book meticulously with a torn silk handkerchief, drying the blood and sex and tea-soaked girl on the cover with almost loving care.

The two girls had glanced across when Louise spilled the tea, then looked at each other with faint, withdrawn smiles, raising themselves with a lift of the eyebrow to a higher plane, where people were not so silly. The accident had disrupted their conversation, so presently they dabbed at their mouths with face tissues, and left the table. Louise saw one of them turn back on her way to the door, and knew that they were talking about her.

'Don't look so distressed,' the fat man murmured, so much like a friend instead of a stranger, that Louise, whom even marriage to Dudley had not taught circumspection of speech, was encouraged to say: 'If only one knew what people were thinking and saying about one behind one's back! How much less mysterious and difficult life would be.'

'Why should you mind?' the man asked. 'People say all manner of unpleasant things about me at my place of business, but what of it?'

Louise leaned forward. How wonderful that instead of drawing back, as most people would, from her blurted, too confiding remark, he had answered so naturally, as if there were nothing odd in suddenly starting a conversation in Lyons about the mysteriousness of life.

She gave him one of the broad, sweet smiles that were the prettiest things her face had to offer. 'I'm sure they don't,' she said.

'I know they do, because other people sometimes obligingly repeat them to me. But I don't get bothered. I daresay it's because I'm so stout.'

It was no good saying: Oh, but you're not, because he so obviously felt stout, from the way he sat in his chair, and puffed a little when he spoke; so Louise said: 'But I get bothered, although I'm a bit plump. I always have been.'

'Bothered or plump, madam?' he asked courteously, like a grocer asking: 'Back or streaky?'

'Both. My late husband used to call me Tubby.' She could hear Dudley saying it now, looking down at her from his enormous height, as if she were a teddy bear.

'If that was the nicest thing he ever called you,' the fat man said, so quietly that Louise barely caught the words, 'you were not fortunate.'

Although, now that she thought of it, that was about the nicest thing that Dudley had called her in the later years of their life together, Louise was not offended. This chance tea-shop conversation had started off so stimulatingly, so unlike the flippant meaningless talk to which she was accustomed with the people she met at Miriam's house. She warmed to the fat man with his pouchy skin and mild, half-hidden eyes, and his faraway, murmuring voice, like a priest in the confessional. She hoped that he would not get up and go away.

He stayed, refolding the handkerchief to polish the cover of the trashy book as if it were a first edition.

Louise apologized again. 'I'm afraid I spoiled it. Is it a favourite of yours? I like thrillers, too. Miriam, my daughter, is trying to remould my taste. I have to keep books like that in a drawer, because if I leave them by my bed, she takes them away and substitutes a biography she thinks I should read, or one of those novels they write nowadays about uneasy people who think things for pages and pages.'

'You like these things?' The man leaned back and pushed the small book across to her, his swollen hand more than covering it. 'Have you read this one?'

'I don't think so. *The Girl in the Bloodstained Bikini.* That sounds fascinating. Is it any good ?'

'You mustn't ask me.' He lowered his pouched eyes. 'I wrote it.'

'*You!*' Louise stared at him, amazed. His soft lips trembled slightly and he put out a fumbling hand to draw the book back.

'I'm so sorry,' she said. 'I didn't mean to be rude. It was just that—well, you don't look like someone who would write books like that.'

'What do people look like who write books like this?'

'I've never thought about it.'

'Neither had I, until one day it chanced across my mind. I was on holiday, by myself, and there was nothing to do, so I hired a deck-chair and sat by the sea and read one of these every day for two weeks. Who writes them? I began to wonder. Aren't they perhaps just ordinary people one might meet every day on the street? And then I thought: Why shouldn't it be me?'

'How enterprising of you!' Louise was genuinely admiring. 'I'd never have thought——' All her life, she had believed that some people could do things and some could not; and that it was no use trying to do the things that other people were born able to do, like playing tennis, or the piano, or writing a book for that matter. She was so entranced by the fat man's revelation that she was barely aware of the cavernous man and the anæmic girl, who had sat down at the table meanwhile, and were also listening with interest.

'So when I got home,' the man went on, 'I locked the door against my landlady, who likes a chat, and wrote a thriller, putting in all the most shocking things, if you'll excuse me, I could think of. It still wasn't as shocking as some I'd read, but the publishers took it and asked for more.'

'How wonderful,' Louise said, and the man and the girl nodded admiringly at each other, and being caught at it by Louise, turned hastily to their food, pretending they had not been listening.

Louise looked again at the book and tried to reconcile the lurid cover with the docile mass of man opposite her.

'Lester Drage,' she read. 'Is that really you?'

'In a way. It's me and several other people. The publishers have six or eight authors' names, and several anonymous scribblers like myself supply the stuff they're supposed to have written. It's not fame, and it's not riches, and most people who know I do it think I'm a bit of an ass, but I enjoy it.'

'Of course.' Louise narrowed her uneven brows, because she was going to say something intelligent. 'It's creative. Everyone has to create things to justify their existence.' She had heard someone say that, and it seemed to her to be true. She could not herself recall having created anything except a hooked rug one winter when she was ill, and her three daughters, which she hoped was enough justification.

'Thank you,' said the pseudo Lester Drage, his smile pleating the lower part of his face into semicircular folds. 'You're very encouraging. I wonder'—he cleared his throat with a shifting of phlegm that made his voice husky—'I wonder if I might ask you to read this little effort? It's my sixth. My best, I think. I'd value your opinion.'

'I'm flattered,' said Louise, whose opinion was seldom asked. 'I'd love to read it.' She took the book upside down, so as not to appear to be looking too closely at the rude, sexy cover. 'What a pity it won't go into my handbag. Miriam won't be too pleased to see me with it. She'll think I've been hanging round the bookstalls again. And she told me to go to the portrait exhibition, and I haven't been. Oh dear! I'm afraid I must go if I'm to get to Marble Arch at the time we arranged.'

'So must I,' the man said, 'or Mr ——,' he named a big department store, 'will think I've died on him at last. I'm in beds there, you know.'

'In bed?' Louise frowned.

'I sell beds. For sleeping in.'

'Oh, yes, I understand. How interesting,' Louise said brightly, not knowing whether to be pleased or sorry for him at this news. 'I never met anyone who sold beds before. I mean, not socially. Of course, I've *bought* beds, but——' She was beginning to sound foolish to herself, so she stopped, and smiled at him so nicely that he leaned forward with a grunt, and said: 'Will you really read *The Girl in the Bloodstained Bikini?*' He brought the title out with no difficulty. 'You don't have to, you know, if you——'

'But I want to!' Louise was anxious to read it now, to see what a man who sold beds for fifty weeks of the year would know or imagine about crime and sex and violence. 'You must give me your address, and I'll return it. I'll give you mine, if you like. I'm staying with my daughter.' She found one of her old cards in her handbag, and altered the address on it to Miriam's faintly embarrassing address: *Pleasantways, Monk's Ditchling, Bucks.*

The fat man tore a page out of a pocket diary and wrote in a scrawl: *Gordon Disher*, and an address in West Kensington. Our Mr Disher, Louise could hear them saying in the bed department. Our Mr Disher will assist you, and he would roll forward, with thirty years' experience, knowing all about inner springs and overlays.

'My card,' he said, handing her the piece of paper, and she wondered if he was mocking her for having an engraved card. Heaven knows she seldom used them. She still had some of the cards that Dudley had made her order after they were married.

Louise and Mr Disher rose to go out together. The man and the girl at the table had finished their food, and were missing nothing. What do they think? Louise wondered. Do they think I have picked him up? I have, though. Or he me. This will be something to tell Miriam. Quite an adventure. It's usually so dull, what I tell them when they ask me what I've been doing.

Outside the teashop door, constantly on the swing now that the tea hour was at its height, the temporarily forgotten wind attacked Louise as if it had been waiting there especially for her.

'Oh, this wind!' she fretted. 'Don't you hate it?'

'It's healthy, they say,' Mr Disher observed mechanically. He had put on a smallish grey hat with a soft, flat brim, that looked as if it had been out in the rain. His hair was too long at the back and hung in a silky fringe below it. Although Louise guessed that he was about her age, he still had quite a lot of fine, soft hair, the colour of tarnished silver.

He lifted the hat rather high in the air. 'Please write to me,' he said, so softly that Louise could only wonder if she had heard the words before the wind took them away, and Mr Disher with them, breasting the gale with his coat blown open like a square-rigged ship.

At a telephone box near Marble Arch, Miriam Chadwick had parked the car with the children in it, bickering with shopping fatigue. She was telephoning to her sister Eva.

'Look here, Eva,' Miriam said, 'I wish you wouldn't be so indefinite.'

'Do you want your spare room for somebody?'

'Well, no, not exactly, but I just wish you'd give me a date.'

'It's so difficult. Honestly, Miriam, I don't want to be mean, but I'm reading this play, and it's exciting. It might really be something big for me. And the B.B.C. are starting a new series, and it's a bit hectic. And there are . . . other things, too, at the moment.' There was David. Sitting on the floor, Eva shivered suddenly, although she was wearing a polo sweater and tight black trousers. What was going to happen about David? She did not know herself.

'You know how it is, Miriam. Mother . . . God bless her. I love her dearly, but——'

'I love her, too,' Miriam said crisply. 'And I've had her for two solid months. When is she going to you?'

'Why are you never in the place we agree to meet?' Miriam asked in her clear, level voice, as they drove away from

Marble Arch, round which she had driven two or three times before she found her mother, waiting in the wrong place.

'I forget, dear,' Louise said placidly, trying to check the futile argument of: Where were you? and You know we said ——in which the children would join, and which was so pointless now that they were all safely come together.

'Oh, Gran-nee!' Miriam's two youngest children, Simon and Judy, were in the back seat, wishing they were in the front, which was where they rode when their grandmother was not with them. Their elder sister, Ellen, who was eleven, had been left at home with the daily woman. She went to a day school, and so did not need the variety of expensive clothes without which life at Simon's preparatory school was traditionally unsupportable. Small Judy went to the day school, too, but she was brought on these shopping expeditions, while Ellen usually stayed at home.

'How did it go?' Louise asked, turning to give the children the chocolate bars she had bought for them, which they examined critically before unwrapping.

'Oh, the usual,' Miriam said. 'They were out of most of the things in Simon's size, of course; but they've promised to send.'

'Isn't it maddening?' Louise entered happily into a discussion of shopping, which was a subject, she had found, that a mother could discuss safely with any of her daughters, without being cut short for getting hold of the wrong end of the stick, or saying something aggravating. Mothers were good for talking to about things like clothes and shopping, which would bore a husband or an intelligent friend. That was one of the things mothers were good for.

Miriam chatted pleasantly as she drove the car through the late afternoon traffic out of London towards the village where she and her barrister husband had made their home. It was not a village any more, but the Londoners who commuted to and from it called it one, and thought it was the real country.

Louise, who had lived her childhood on a Shropshire farm,

knew that it was not, and disliked the self-conscious perpetua-
tion of beams and thatch that housed the sophisticated shops
and clubs and stiffly tweeded businessmen. When she had
once referred to it, however, as a glorified suburb, Miriam and
Arthur had jumped down her throat with as much horror as
if she had accused them of living in the slums.

Sometimes, Louise looked at her eldest daughter, and tried
to believe that the tall, composed woman had once been curled
up inside her, helplessly dependent. It did not seem possible.
The girl, as Louise called her—she called all her daughters
'the girls,' and would probably still do so when they were long
past forty—the girl was so self-sufficient, so very much a
separate entity, who moved upright through life, without
needing props or pushes.

Miriam was red-haired; slim, elegant and rather expression-
less of feature. Everything about her—her hands, feet, nose,
neck—was long, slender and fastidious. She even looked cool
when cooking a meal for six, and her underclothes drawer was
a joy to behold.

Miriam's best feature was her grave, green eyes, which for
the last few years, she had hidden behind pastel-rimmed
spectacles. Louise had been sad for her when she first had to
wear glasses, but when you got used to them, you saw that
they actually suited her unemotional face in some complemen-
tary way. Miriam herself did not mind them. They were
another piece of armour behind which she could hide anything
that was soft and vulnerable in her.

'What have you been doing, Mother?' she asked, when they
had exhausted the subject of iniquitous prices and slapdash
shop assistants. Louise's daughters all called her Mother.
They had not called her Mummy since Miriam was eight years
old, when for some reason she had started saying Mother,
and the younger ones had copied it.

'Did you see the pictures?' Miriam asked, her gloved hands
light and capable on the wheel at the 'ten minutes to two'
angle advised by the Highway Code.

'Well, no dear. I didn't have time. The afternoon just

seemed to fly. And it was so windy. I couldn't stay out in the streets any longer, so I went into Lyons.'

'Oh, Granny.' Simon leaned over the back of the seat. 'You always go to Lyons. Daddy says it's your spiritual home. Did you have baked beans?'

'No, because we'd just had lunch, you see.' Louise answered even the children's silliest questions with serious consideration. She thought that Miriam and Arthur too often shut them up, or fobbed them off with a careless answer.

'So I had a cup of tea, and one of those cakes that look better than they taste. And I met such a nice man,' she told Miriam. 'He was sitting at my table, and we talked. He was fat and gentle, and looked rather neglected. He sells beds. He was charming, I thought.'

'Really, mother.' Louise had known that Miriam would say this, as if she had seen the words written on the windscreen, for Miriam to pluck off and use.

'Somebody has to sell beds, I suppose. But he does something else. He writes books.'

Miriam raised her eyebrows.

'Not what *you* would call books, I know, but the kind I like. These shockers.' She showed Miriam *The Girl in the Blood-stained Bikini*, and then turned the book upside down on her lap, so that the children should not see the cover.

'He gave it to me to read. He wanted my opinion of it. Now don't say: Really, Mother, because he was nice, and so friendly. He was a little common, I think, and I liked him.' Louise put on the slightly defiant tone with which she occasionally tried to remind Miriam who was the mother and who the daughter.

'Mother being democratic again,' Miriam said, to no one in particular.

Louise wanted to talk about Gordon Disher, and to try to describe the queer, reassuring excitement she had felt in being able suddenly to enter into quite an intimate conversation with a stranger; but Miriam was not interested. She started to talk to the children.

Louise fell silent and began to read the book, which had two
screams and a pistol shot on the first page. She would tell
Ellen about Mr Disher when they got home. Ellen would
listen. Ellen wanted to share in everything that happened to
her grandmother. The spindly young girl and the middle-aged
woman were comfortable allies in a household into which
neither of them fitted very well.

Miriam's house was on the outskirts of the village of Monk's
Ditchling, at the end of the road that ran past the neat green,
and the garages, and the antique shops and the cocktail bar
that was still called a pub, and the grocer who sold *foie gras*
and peaches in brandy. It was not the best house, because
there were so many expensive and beautifully tended houses
around, but it was pleasing enough in a trimmed and tasteful
way. It was an old house, so well remodelled that you could
not tell which were the original beams and which the new ones,
or just where the usurping Victorian slates had been ripped off
the kitchen roof to bring back the mellowed tiles, which had
been obtained at considerable expense when Arthur won his
first big case in the Criminal Court.

The garden was orderly, with the daffodils in rows in the
flowerbeds, instead of scattered about in the grass and under
the hedges. There was a thatched lych-gate over the drive
entrance. This was a mistake, since the house and garage and
stables were tiled ; but there was so much thatch weighing
down the other houses and outbuildings in the neighbourhood,
that you could not really feel you belonged unless you had had
the old man in the green bowler hat—'Positively the last
thatcher left in the country. We're lucky to get him'—with his
blowing straw and his shears and his despotic demands for
beer. Quite a character. He would have been surprised to
know what a gay conversational subject he was at the local
dinner parties, where people had started wearing dinner
jackets and long dresses again since the war.

When they drove in under the unnecessary thatch, Ellen
was waiting on the edge of the lawn. She looked cold.

'Where's your coat?' Miriam asked, as she got out of the car.

'Oh, pooh!—I haven't had it on all day. It's been lovely sun.'

'The wind was cold, though,' Louise said. But although it was still blowing, the wind was not as cold and rough here as in London. It was tamed and caged and clipped at the claws, like the rest of nature in this overbuilt part of the country.

Miriam was making the other children collect the parcels from the car, but Ellen went skipping away with her grand-mother towards the house, her rod-straight hair dancing at angles.

'Did you have a nice time, Granny? Did you go to the cinema? Mrs Match and I had a lovely time, although we couldn't find much for lunch. She told me all about when she was in the hospital, while we were cleaning the silver. "It's better out than in, Mrs Match," they said. What did you do?'

'Nothing much. But I had quite an adventure. I met a man in Lyons, and he was so nice. I felt as if I'd known him quite a long time, like you did with the dog that followed you five miles on your bicycle. We talked, and he told me——'

Before Louise could get into her story, Miriam called from the car : 'Come and help with the parcels, you lazy child! Why should everyone else do all the work?'

'It's *their* clothes,' muttered Ellen, and dawdled back, scuffling the gravel of the drive. She was given the biggest parcel. As the family came into the house, Louise, taking off her coat in the hall, heard Ellen say: 'I must tell you about Mrs Match, Mummy. Her operation. "It's better out than in, Mrs Match," they——'

'I am not interested in Mrs Match's surgical history,' Miriam said. 'And neither should you be. Now take that parcel upstairs and get your hands and face washed. We're going to have tea.'

At seven o'clock, with Judy preparing for bed, and Simon hunched over the stripped parts of a model aeroplane, Miriam had a twinge of conscience about Ellen, who never seemed to have anything special to do. The child had no hobbies. She should. All the other children Miriam knew had hobbies.

Ellen's idea of entertainment was to hang about and talk to anybody who would sustain a conversation with her. Mrs Match, the gardener, her grandmother, the man who came to put down poisoned bread for the mice, occasionally her mother, if she could catch Miriam in an unguarded, responsive mood.

'I'm going to fetch Daddy. Do you want to come?' Miriam asked, finding Ellen sitting irritatingly on the bottom step of the staircase. Not doing anything. Just sitting. Not reading, or playing with a piece of string, or waiting for a meal. Just sitting patiently, like a pavement artist expecting the world to come to him.

Ellen got up indifferently. She was not sure that she did want to meet her father at the station. She never knew whether to kiss him or not. Sometimes he seemed to expect it. Sometimes her proffered embrace was no more to him than a hedgerow cobweb unthinkingly brushed off. However, she appreciated Miriam's offer, and did not want to turn down the motherly overture.

Miriam began to regret having suggested it as soon as she had spoken. It might make an atmosphere with Arthur, who was often so tired when he got off the train, that he had to be treated delicately until he had had his dinner. They stood there, the mother and daughter, trying separately to decide what to do.

How thin she is, Miriam thought. Perhaps she will be slim, like me, but I don't think I ever had such knobs of bones at her age. I do hope she's not going to grow up to be one of these raw-boned, striding women who can never get a man and have to pretend they don't want one.

There had been two men in Miriam's life. Dark, solemn-faced Arthur, whom she had known in childhood and married quite young, because all her friends were doing it, and it seemed preferable to living at home, with her father putting on his airs, and her mother so sickeningly compliant. Then Colin, Arthur's scapegrace friend, who had brought such reviving glamour to the difficult days when Arthur was slaving and struggling, and with whom Arthur was not friendly any more now that he was successful.

No, that was not fair. It was not because Arthur was successful that he did not see Colin any more. 'Come on if you're coming,' Miriam said abruptly, and Ellen rose, and fetched her coat, because she thought that would please, and followed her mother out to the car.

But Colin had accepted it so peaceably, Miriam thought, driving to the station past the houses that were beginning to light up behind their barricades of evergreens and rhododendrons. That was what had hurt the most. Although Miriam would not have left Arthur if she had been asked to, she had not been asked, and that made her think at times that she would have left Arthur for Colin.

The whole thing had been so gentlemanly. Arthur had found out. He had been wearily sad. He had not offered to fight anybody. Colin had faded tactfully out of the picture, after a heart-wringing and rather stagey scene with Miriam, in which he had talked excessively about 'doing the decent thing.'

It had all been deftly arranged so that there was hardly a ripple on the surface of the marriage of Miriam and Arthur. Her parents never knew. No one knew except Eva, who had guessed, challenged Miriam with it once, and been for ever silenced.

It was a neatly ended affair. No one had asked Miriam what she wanted. She wanted to stay with Arthur, but at the same time, she did not want Colin to be already so tired of her that he welcomed a husband's intervention.

What were his feelings when he thought of it now? Did he have to fight down the wild memories? Miriam hardly ever had to now. With a successful husband, a comfortable home, three children and plenty of sociability, she had little time to think of the restless, seeking girl, who had stolen out of the house where her husband pored over his dusty briefs, to run in fearful joy to her unscrupulous lover, waiting for her at the corner of the square. Or did Colin ever think of her at all?

How could he not remember swimming together, and the night they saw the ghost?

Ellen played with the window of the car in the annoying way she had of never being able to leave things as they were, either up or down, or open or shut. She always had to fiddle.

Colin! Miriam said in her heart, trying masochistically to recreate the yearning. But it was dead. She could only imagine how she had felt. She could not remember. It was all so long ago. And then the war had come; man's war, in which a pregnant woman could have no part except to wait about and drink orange juice, while the husband and the lover sailed out of her reach in the purifying nobility of the King's uniform.

Arthur left the train at the little creaky station, and stood looking round for a moment, stretching his legs and craning his neck stiffly, in the habit acquired by a man who is slightly shorter than his wife. Miriam touched the horn, and he came down the steps, looking exactly what he was: a rising junior counsel, whose lunch had not agreed with him. His striped trousers, black hat, umbrella and brief-case hardly looked incongruous at the country station, where several other men had left the train in the same kind of clothes.

Arthur nodded to some of them, and waved his evening paper to Alice Cobb, who was waiting for Sidney in a grey Jaguar. Sidney had gone over to talk to Miriam. The Cobbs and the Chadwicks were friends, which is to say that they went often to each other's houses, combined for parties at the club, and knew very few fundamental things about each other. If either couple had died or gone away, the other would scarcely have missed them.

Ellen climbed into the back seat of the car, and Arthur got into the front. Miriam kissed him, and felt the prickle of beard already roughening his skin. Arthur often had to shave twice a day. He began to get blue about the chin by mid-afternoon. When he had been in court all day, and was tired, with reddening, shadowed eyes, he looked like a careworn but exceedingly intelligent ape.

He was very dark, with thick eyebrows and black hair on
the backs of his hands. He was forty. 'One of the cleverest
young chaps at the Bar,' said the older members of the profession, which houses so many dotards, that a man is young
until he loses his teeth and begins to have difficulty struggling
into his gown.

It was as much his dogged capacity for work as his quick
brain, which was helping Arthur to make a name for himself,
and a comfortable position for his wife and family. His boy
was at his old preparatory school, and was going to public
school and Oxford. His wife was well dressed, and went to
London to get her hair done, and had help in the house, which,
if it was only Mrs Match, with her depleted inside, was still
a maid by post-war standards. His youngest daughter was
pretty and bright, with nasturtium-coloured hair and engaging
ways. His elder daughter was bonily plain at the moment,
with teeth that were costing a lot in dentists' bills, but at least
she was giving no trouble, and was said to be doing quite well
at school. Arthur was content to pay the dentists' bills and
to let her pursue her gawky, aimless life about his house, as
long as she did not trouble him. But when all the children
together gave trouble, it was usually Ellen who emerged as
the scapegoat.

Arthur sighed and yawned and said he needed a drink, and
grumbled a little because Miriam had let the petrol run low.
This was clearly an evening when he did not expect a kiss, so
Ellen sat back in the car and watched the battle for supremacy
between the headlights and the dusk.

'How was London?' Arthur asked.

'You should know,' Miriam said. 'You were there.'

'In court! That's not being anywhere, except in a padded
cell. Old Fowler dithered and drooled and made his senile
jokes. They should never have made him a judge in the first
place, even when he had all his faculties.'

Miriam told him something of her day. 'I took Mother with
me,' she said. 'It does her good to get about a bit. But she's
like a rabbit. All she did the moment my back was turned was

to dive down into Lyons and have tea with a car salesman, or something.'

'He sells beds,' Ellen put in gently, but they did not hear her.

'Did you ring Eva?'

'Yes. She's maddeningly vague.'

'She give a date?' They talked cabalistically, remembering Ellen. Even when they were alone together, they did not often talk outright about Louise. When it first became apparent that they would have to house her for some months of the year, they had had a torturing argument, with Arthur pacing the bedroom floor in silk pyjamas, and Miriam at the dressing-table, desperately creaming her face over and over again.

After a night's sleep, Arthur had begun to see reason, and had accepted the situation with only an occasional protest. It was just one of those problems that was there, and they lived with it, referring to it only obliquely. Arthur was proud of his unselfishness, and Miriam added to her family duties the job of trying to prevent her mother impinging more than necessary on her husband's ordered life.

Louise liked Arthur. She did not feel entirely comfortable with him, but she admired him for being shrewd and reliable and clever all through instead of on the surface, and all the things that Dudley had not been.

'He has a fine mind,' she told Miriam. Miriam, who did not care to discuss Arthur, or any of the things that mattered most in her life, would say: 'I suppose so,' and change the subject before Louise could go on to: I hope you appreciate what a good husband you have, which might lead to talk about her father.

There had been too much talk about him when he died, although Louise always tried to be loyal. Miriam had been fond of her father in an undemonstrative, critical way. She had been the least shocked of anyone at the mess he had left behind at his death, because she had always suspected what he was really like. She had been his favourite child, if he could be said to have liked any of his daughters well enough to have a favourite. Like all bullies and boasters, he had despised those who believed his pretences, and he had favoured Miriam, because she saw through him.

She remembered childhood times when they had shared a secret against the rest of the family, and odd occasions when he had taken her off on some exploit in which the others were not asked to join.

When she married Arthur, her father had given her a fabulous wedding present, which had set her mother struggling between anxiety that they could not afford it, and pleasure that Dudley should suddenly be so generous.

Miriam did not know that the bill for her wedding present was one of the things her father had bequeathed to Louise.

Arthur tried quite hard with Dudley's widow, but he could not always be as nice to her as he meant to be. Like other small animals, she had a talent for getting underfoot; for being there when you had hoped she would not be.

Arthur was so tired to-night that he had hoped to sit quietly in the drawing-room with his drink while Miriam finished preparing supper; but Louise was there with her sewing. She showed him that she was mending his children's clothes, as if to justify her presence, and even he could see that she was making a poor job of the darning. It was amazing that such a capable, skilful woman as Miriam could have been raised by Louise, who was deficient in nearly all the domestic qualities.

Louise found it hard to sit without talking in a room with someone else, especially someone like Arthur, with whom she could never quite relax. She asked him about his case, an unimportant but unusual murder trial, which was receiving some attention in the newspapers. She had been looking forward to hearing Arthur's side of it, and to writing about it to her friend Sybil, at Ryde, who craved inside information about anything, from the royal family to sex murderers.

Arthur never talked about his cases at home, until they were long past and paid for, and then only when there had been wine and brandy at dinner, and he could expand to an audience. Louise had not learned this yet. She continued to bumble into ill-received questions, ascribing Arthur's terse answers to the fact that he was tired.

Louise wished that someone would come into the room; but Judy was in bed, and Simon and Ellen were in the kitchen having supper, since Arthur only allowed them to dine with the grown-ups on Sundays. Presently, Miriam came in, wearing a green silk dress with a choker necklace round her swan-like throat, and announced that dinner was ready, although she did not look as if she had cooked anything more arduous than a boiled egg. Arthur got up and went to the side-table to make her a drink.

'For you, Mother?' he asked, and Louise said: 'Oh, I don't know that I——'

This, or similar dialogue took place every night, except when there was company and Louise was automatically handed a drink with everyone else. Arthur was quite willing to give his mother-in-law a drink every night. His wine bills were so big that it would not make any difference; but Louise, although she loved a martini, sharp and dry the way he made them, felt bad about accepting it, when she could not afford to buy the household even an occasional bottle of gin.

So she demurred, and Arthur poured her a drink just the same.

'One of these days,' he murmured to-night to Miriam, when Louise had gone through the door before them to the dining-room, 'your mother won't get a drink, unless she learns to say: I'd love one. Just what I want.'

'How can she?' Miriam said. 'She feels it's charity.'

'My foot,' said Arthur. 'People who have got nothing can't be so proud.'

Ellen was waiting in the hall to say good-night. She listened to see if they were going to say any more; then, as they came out of the drawing-room, she slid into the dining-room, to kiss her grandmother and question her eyes to see if she had heard.

CHAPTER TWO

IT WAS Sunday. Once on a Sunday, Miriam had offered to drive her mother to the Catholic church five miles away, and once the gardener had taken Louise; but Arthur said it was not fair to ask the man to give up part of his free day.

Louise was almost glad that the matter of whether or not to go to church had been taken out of her hands. She knew that she ought to go to Mass, and then again, she felt that she should not. She had not been married in a Catholic church. Dudley had refused, and Louise had been so young and so naïvely in love that she had thought the only thing that mattered was Dudley's pleasure. She knew that in the eyes of the Church she had been living in sin with Dudley, which must make her children illegitimate.

Her parents had attended the register office wedding, although unhappily, with hurt eyes. They would not have liked Dudley wherever Louise had married him. He did not like them either. Over the years, Louise gradually saw them less and less; but when they died, she was lonely for them. They had been the last link with herself as a happy person. There seemed to be no one left who cared.

If Dudley was in a mood, he would go for days without speaking to her, except to ask for things he wanted. Even the girls grew away from her at a surprisingly young age. They had secrets, and private occupations, and found their own solutions to childish problems. They seemed to have decided that there were two opposing tribes in the world—children and grown-ups—and that the barriers must be maintained between them.

In her loneliness, the faith against which Louise had transgressed came back to her, tempting her with its consolations. She crept to church, half expecting to be struck down by a bolt

27

from heaven as she knelt in a back pew. Nothing happened, except that she felt better. She went again, braving Dudley's ridicule when he found out. He did not forbid her to go, however. He said he did not care what she did, as long as she did not drag the children into her God-bothering gambols.

The Catholic church was an easy target for Dudley's brand of humour. He was the kind of man who likes to make jokes about priests and nuns and to snort if anyone mentions the Pope. If Louise ever secretly tried to tell her children some of the things she wanted them to know, they would quote some irreverent denigration of their father's, with which he had primed them against possible seduction.

Louise went to church as a beggar, feeling that she had forfeited her right to be there. She humbled herself before Christ, knowing that if you only had sufficient humility, anything could be forgiven. Often she felt reassured, but then, was that being humble—to fancy that God could be influenced by your inadequate prayers?

When the problem became too much for her, she mustered her courage and went to a priest, expecting to be chided, and found that she was listened to with the first real compassion she had ever known. She even got a concrete suggestion for help. The thing to do, the priest said, as practically as if she were a contractor discussing blue-prints, was to work on the hope that as her husband grew older and mellower, he would eventually consent to join with her in a belated wedding ceremony in church.

'Yes, but you don't know Dudley,' Louise had said sadly.

'He's not the devil,' the priest said. 'More impossible things have happened. Look at Saint Paul. Tell you what'—he was a very boyish priest—'I'll pray for you like mad. It's a good cause.'

Louise believed that he did pray for her, and was grateful. But she let him down by her own craven failure to do her part. Although Dudley did eventually weary of the Catholic church as an object of derision, and stopped ordering meat for her if they went to a restaurant on Friday, Louise could never bring herself to broach the subject of a church wedding. She had never dared, and now it was too late. Dudley was dead, and her sin was still upon her, and, like the daughters of Jerusalem, upon her children; and she still did not know if she was doing more wrong by going to Mass or staying away.

Dudley had been ill for several weeks before he died. He was ill at home, and Louise had bought white overalls and nursed him, guiltily happy in his helplessness and need of her. He was much nicer when he was ill. He had not the strength to put on the interminable acts of self-importance on which he had relied all his life, and which made him so difficult to live with.

Before his illness, he had always boasted of being self-sufficient, of needing help from no man. Even the domestic services which Louise performed for him, he had received ungratefully, with the attitude that she could do them if she chose, but he could manage perfectly well without her. He imagined that he did half the work of the house himself, although in actual fact, he barely raised a finger, except to look for dust along the shelves.

After he died, Louise read his diary, half fearful that his ghost would come and catch her at it. She found that he had recorded all the most trivial events of his days, with the words I, My and Me scattered over the pages like mustard and cress. The diary was a masterpiece of egotism. Louise came across an entry which related to the time when she had washed a blanket —an unusual feat for her. She had struggled unsuccessfully to wring it out, and was finally forced to ask Dudley to help her. She could see now the face with which he had performed this short task, the face of a man martyred almost beyond endurance. In his diary that day, he had recorded: 'To-night I washed some blankets after a hard day's work.'

She also found the entries for the time when she had a bad attack of influenza, and was ordered by the doctor, who knew Dudley, to stay in bed and ignore everything else in the house but her care of herself. The girls were all away from home then.

Dudley had brought her one sketchy meal, groaning and panting up the stairs like a slave labourer. After that, he had stayed out of the house most of the time, and only brought her an occasional cup of tea if he was making some for himself. Louise had to stagger to the kitchen and forage for herself, to avoid starving to death.

The entries in Dudley's diary, however, stated: 'Now I am nurse, cook and maid-of-all-work, tied to the house with a sick wife, whom I must wait on hand and foot.'

When Louise was first married, she had looked forward to taking a part in her husband's business life; to listening to his problems, even advising perhaps, and sharing with him the ups and downs he met as he made his way forward to the prosperity he was always blusteringly promising her. But Dudley had locked her away from that side of his life from the start. She knew nothing about his work, except that he was in a shipping company, which did not appreciate his talents.

Long before he was due to retire, he came home one night and announced that he had resigned his job, because it was a dead end, and he was sick of working himself to death to benefit a lot of sharks and boneheads.

'But the money!' Louise said, aghast. 'They were paying you a good salary. How will we live now?'

'Don't you worry, Tubby,' Dudley said, wagging his head complacently. 'I've been making some contacts. I've got plans for myself. I'm going to get into the big money.'

What his new enterprise was, Louise barely knew, except that it was something to do with shares and companies, and necessitated his having lunches with mysterious-sounding men in places like the Savoy, which Louise did not think they could afford.

She did not really know what they could afford, for Dudley never discussed finances with her. He paid the bills for the house, and the children's clothes, and school fees and holidays. Louise had two hundred pounds a year of her own, which her father had left her, so she did not have to ask Dudley for money to spend on herself.

He always seemed to have enough to buy himself a new car, or an expensive suit, or another cigarette-case to add to his collection. Towards the end, when he began to grumble about the laundry and grocer's bills, and to tell Louise that she must cut down, or they would have to leave the house, he still seemed to have enough to buy himself a radio-gramophone and to fly to Le Touquet for the week-end.

Louise imagined that there was still money coming in ; she did not know from where, and Dudley would not have told her if she had asked. Braggart to the last, when he was ruined, he would not admit it to her. He was still seeing prosperity just around the corner.

'Dudley is a big shot,' his brother used to tell Louise. 'A big-time operator. He knows it all. No one can tell him anything.'

When the big shot lost his health, he lost some of his bravado with it. He had to rely on Louise for everything, although even towards the end, when he could hardly see, he still would not let her read his letters to him. They piled up beside his bed, and once one of the mysterious men arrived, to see why he was not getting an answer. Dudley was not allowed visitors, but he heard the conversation in the hall, and shouted weakly through the door. To quiet him, Louise admitted the man to the sick-room. He came out quite soon, looking concerned, and glanced at Louise for a moment with an odd look of baffled pity, before he put on his black hat and padded overcoat and went thoughtfully out of the house.

When Louise was nursing Dudley, she was happier than she had been for years. At last she had something really important to do. She bustled about, knocking over things in the sick-room, spilling soup on the tray, and bumping into Dudley's bed every time she walked by it.

Her happiness was short-lived, however. He insisted that he must have a nurse. The nurse was suave and secretive, and cost ten pounds a week. Louise did not think that they could afford it ; but only guessed that they could not, when the day after Dudley died, the nurse came back to tidy up, and brought her last weekly cheque, which had been returned to her with the letters 'R.D.' in red pencil across the top.

With a nurse in the house, Louise felt more redundant than ever. The nurse did everything for Dudley, including cleaning his room and cooking such food as he could take. She moved through the house like a narrow whirlwind, so quick and purposeful that she made Louise feel shamefully slow and useless. There was nothing for Louise to do except to telephone her daughters, and cook meals for herself and the nurse, which they ate mostly in silence, having no common interests except Dudley, whose condition the nurse would seldom discuss.

Louise did not realize that the end was approaching. She would have sent for the girls, but the night-nurse did not call her from her room until three o'clock in the morning, just before Dudley died.

He did not know her, and after he died, Louise barely knew him. The chill, resigned face, and the long ridge of body under the sheets had lost every trace of the bravado that had sustained his charlatan passage through the world.

For a few hours, Louise had the wild idea of having him buried in a Catholic cemetery, thinking that this might atone for the defection of their secular marriage. She found that this was impossible. He was technically Church of England, so in a Protestant cemetery, with the wind and rain blowing across the relentless gravestones, she sent him to his God, with whom he had never yet sought encounter.

Miriam came to the funeral with a new black hat, and a face that concealed whatever she felt about her father's death. Eva came in a black velvet beret, with a face that was saddened more by pity than by loss.

Anne, the youngest daughter, came looking defiant and untidy, with a pack of dogs in the car. She brought her husband with her. Louise had not seen Frank since he and Anne were married the year before. Dudley had fought against the marriage. He called it 'a tragedy,' and forbade it. When Anne defied him, he refused to see either her or her husband, because Frank was a smallholder and spoke with a slight Bedfordshire accent, and had committed the insulting crime of permitting Dudley's daughter to marry beneath her.

Louise thought it was magnanimous of Frank to come to the funeral, after the way Dudley had treated him. When she said: 'It was so nice of you to come,' he looked at her honestly with his bright blue eyes, and said: 'I thought maybe *you'd* like it.'

Louise realized that she was going to like Frank. She would be able to see him and get to know him now that she was on her own, with no one to tell her what to do.

Everyone said that Louise was 'wonderful' about Dudley's death, but she could not be anything else, because, shocking though it was to her, she hardly cared. She was free for the first time in thirty-five years. She could go where she liked, do what she liked, behave as she pleased, without having to face contemptuous censure.

She began to plan the life that she would make for herself. She was fifty-seven. It was not too late to start to live. Then Arthur, solemnly shouldering his position as the reliable son-in-law, came round to her house to check on her financial position, and she found that she was going to be lucky if she had any sort of a life at all.

Dudley had left her nothing. Nothing except his debts. He had lost everything in the maniac speculations about which Louise was completely ignorant. He had sold every share he possessed, mortgaged the house, and realized his life insurance. He had been owing income tax for so long that Arthur could not understand how he had kept out of gaol.

Louise wished that it had been anyone but Arthur who had to discover the catastrophe. Arthur was so impeccable, so efficient and respectable. Louise was embarrassed when he asked her where he could find Dudley's bonds, his policies and bank statement, and she did not know. She had never been near Dudley's desk. He had even dusted it himself. Her embarrassment turned to humiliation, when Arthur began to find the evidence of Dudley's ruin.

'You mean to say, Mother, that you didn't *know* all this

was going on?' he kept asking, and Louise could only shake her head, and feel hopelessly foolish, and weep for the first time since Dudley died.

'I did wonder a bit,' she stuttered, 'when the nurse came with the dishonoured cheque. But I thought it must be a mistake—that Dudley had another bank account, or something. I didn't know. He never told me. He went on spending——' She looked at the shiny radio-gramophone, which Dudley had hardly played.

Soon she had to sell it. She sold the house, the car, Dudley's pictures and gold cigarette-cases, even what little jewellery she had, to help pay off the debts. She had nothing except the money from her father, which had been poorly invested, and was now not even bringing in two hundred pounds a year.

What was she going to do? How was she going to live? The question troubled her daughters as much as it did Louise.

Louise had a girlhood friend, Sybil Vernon, who ran a hotel near Ryde, in the Isle of Wight. She and Louise had been at school together; unlikely friends, for Sybil was masterful and insubordinate, while Louise had always been cowed by authority, even in the shape of the physics mistress, whom everyone else sought to electrocute with one of her own experiments.

Louise had kept in touch with Sybil mainly through letters, but she had seen her off and on over the years, in spite of the fact that Dudley did not like her. In middle age, Sybil was still noisy and casual, and she needed gin as other people need water, but she was warm-hearted and impulsive, and when she learned of Louise's plight, she offered her a room for whatever she could afford to pay, during the winter months when her hotel was half empty.

But the rest of the year? There was nothing for it but that Louise should stay with her daughters in turn to pass the spring and summer months. It was all arranged at an embarrassing family conclave, when no one could say what they were thinking, and each tried to outdo the other in unselfishness.

Louise's tragedy was still recent enough for her daughters to feel magnanimous. 'She can't live alone,' they agreed, and who was Louise to say that that was what she wanted? She could not live alone without financial help from her daughters, and to ask for that would be a bigger imposition than the one she was now forced to make on them.

Miriam had only offered to drive Louise to church on that one occasion. This was not because she disapproved of her mother being a Catholic. She did not care what people were as long as they did not make a fuss about it. It was simply that she had not thought of offering again, and Louise would not dream of asking.

Miriam was always very busy on Sundays, when Mrs Match did not come. She was often entertaining, or going out to parties, leaving the children with Louise, who could not control the two younger ones, but at least felt that she was being some use to Miriam.

Monk's Ditchling was too near London to be full of retired people, who could see each other on any day of the week. Most of the residents worked in London all week, and so went the pace fiercely at week-ends. In many ways, the village life was more sophisticated than the life to which town dwellers had grown accustomed since the war. At Monk's Ditchling there was sitting in bars on a Sunday morning, and going home, rather cross, to a late lunch. There was dining out, with 'black tie' written on the invitation, and men going into corners with other men's wives after dinner. There were horse-shows in the summer, with precocious children dealing roughly with expensive ponies, and cocktails and cold chicken in the boot of nearly every car. There was a local dramatic society, which the London talent had completely taken over from the Women's Institute, who had run it during the war, and who were now forced to retreat into the unassailable spheres of weaving and tomato bottling. There were even fancy-dress parties, for which guests paid large sums of money to hire a better costume than anyone else. It all had a curiously old-fashioned flavour like a slice from a novel of the 'thirties.

Louise's Sunday started by getting up too early. She found that as she grew older, she began to need less sleep. She always woke early. This did not matter at Anne's, where Frank was up and about at cockcrow, and would brew her strong tea in the untidy kitchen. Eva usually slept late, but when Louise stayed in her flat in London, she could get up and do some housework, before Eva could tell her not to bother.

Week-day mornings at Miriam's were chaos, with getting Ellen and Judy off to school and Arthur to the train. Louise stayed out of the way in her room until she heard the car go down the drive. On Sundays, Miriam and Arthur stayed late in bed. The children got up when they liked, and disappeared until they sensed that it was breakfast-time. Louise never knew when it would be breakfast-time on Sundays. She did not like to go down too soon and bother Miriam. She did not like to go down too late and find everyone sitting at the table, and Miriam getting up with a barely perceptible sigh to fetch her mother's egg.

Louise stayed in her room, making her bed and tidying up, and going to the door from time to time to see if she could hear sounds of life, or smell bacon frying. She thought about the years when Miriam was a child, and it was Louise who prepared breakfast, and served it out, and gently criticized table manners. How odd it was, the way their roles in life had become reversed, the mother's and the daughter's. For what a short time, it seemed, had Louise been able to look after Miriam. Now it was the other way round. Miriam was responsible for her mother. Louise was the child, and absurd though she knew it to be, as anxious to be in Miriam's good graces as if her daughter had been an exacting parent.

'Granny.' Ellen stood in the doorway in a shrunken skirt, her dun-coloured hair untidily caught back with a vast hair grip. 'I think it would be about right if you came down now.'

The child knew how Louise felt about Sunday breakfast-time, and many other things. She was much closer to Louise than her daughters had been at any age.

At breakfast, Arthur announced that he was going to inspect the ponies and their equipment, which put Simon and Judy into a spasm of nervous delight, for Arthur had manufactured for himself the reputation of being a connoisseur of horsey matters, although he actually knew little more about them than his children did. The gardener, who had once looked after an undertaker's plumed black horses, was in charge of the ponies and the children's riding, but Arthur would come along from time to time and give a lot of noisy orders, and push the ponies about with the flat of his hand, and put the jumps too high, and stick the children straight back on the saddle when they fell off.

It was this violent treatment that had sickened Ellen with riding. Once she had had a pony of her own, as Simon and Judy did. If she had been allowed to ride it quietly, getting off whenever she liked to give it sugar, she might have stayed the course. She had been fairly happy with her ambling first pony, but much too soon, her father changed it for a more temperamental animal, of whom Ellen was terrified. She used to go to the stable, when no one was looking, and try to bribe it with food to like her and behave kindly, but it ungratefully continued to carry her off at speed in the wrong direction, or unload her on to the hardest piece of ground.

The gardener knew that Ellen would never ride well, and did not expect her to do more than sit still and keep quiet; but when Arthur came into the paddock, with a little switch, he would command Ellen to canter, and jump, and perform feats of which she was incapable, and mortally afraid.

Finally, she fell off on her head and was concussed. Arthur, disgusted, sold the pony and said that she could ride no more. It was too dangerous, he said, and a waste of money besides.

Lying in bed in the darkened room, Ellen knew that she had disgraced herself; but the day that the pony was sold was the happiest day of her life.

Simon and Judy were good riders, as far as the gardener's rough-and-ready tuition and their father's sudden bursts of intemperate coaching could make them. They trotted efficiently off to pony club rallies, and appeared at local shows, very self-possessed in crisply-cut jackets and jockey caps worn well down on the head. Most of the local children had ponies, for Monk's Ditchling had diligently embraced horses along with the other high-class country pursuits. They seldom won any-thing at shows, for the professionals came in impressive horse-boxes from hundreds of miles away to scoop up the money; but they rode jauntily about, giving imperious commands to their tweeded mothers on the ground.

Ellen had always been an awkward, lonely child, hating to have other children asked to tea, invariably chosen last in games where sides were picked. The fact that she was one of the few children who did not ride made her life at Monk's Ditchling lonelier than ever. The other children went about in gangs, whether they were on foot or on ponies. Ellen was often seen about by herself, walking without purpose, as if she had amnesia.

Simon and Judy, always busy about the stables, or with the constructive toys their parents bought for them, had little use for Ellen. She was delighted when her grandmother came to stay, and she had someone to go about with, who did not try to make her do things for which she was not inclined.

Together, she and Louise would potter up to the post office and buy small amounts of stamps, and have milk shakes on the way home at the Tudor Snack Bar. They would stroll down the lanes, peering into the hedgerows, and try to identify wild flowers and trees from the book which Louise had bought to give herself something to do at Miriam's.

This Sunday morning, Louise and Ellen went to the wood to see if the bluebells were out. They passed by the stables, where Arthur was putting Simon and Judy through questions on the points of the horse, which they did not know he had looked up in a book before coming out.

The ponies were standing in the yard. Louise gave them a

wide berth. She admired them, but she never went near them. Ellen was afraid of them, but they were still animals, with warm breaths, and she could not help being drawn towards them. She went up to Judy's pony, which was the smallest, and diffidently stroked its nose. The pony threw up its head, and she backed away.

'For God's sake!' Arthur shouted. 'How many times have I told you, never touch a horse like that? Get right up to it, and put your hand on its neck.' Ellen backed farther away.

'Come on now, let's see you do it right.' He grabbed Ellen and pulled her forward. She jerked up her arm. The pony rolled the white of its eye, and jumped sideways, pulling the halter rope from Judy's hand.

'Oh, my God!' Arthur cried. 'Go and get him, Simon, before he——' Simon ran, and caught the pony skilfully, and Arthur said, with bitter patience: 'You'd better clear off, Ellen. And another time, go round the other way, if you can't behave sensibly.'

Louise wanted to put her arm round Ellen as they walked away, but she was afraid that it might look as if she were siding with the child against Arthur. She tried not to interfere with discipline, although she often crept up with sweets to a child that had been sent in disgrace to its room.

At lunch, Arthur was still rather cross. He had spent a happy enough morning with his two younger children, who had been bright, and pleasantly appreciative, but the sight of Ellen, walking through the hall with a drooping bunch of bluebells, aroused him again.

'I've told you a thousand times not to pick them,' he grumbled. 'They don't last. Why can't you leave them where they are? It's so *trippery*.'

Ellen did not say that she knew it was no good picking bluebells, but that her grandmother had wanted to take home a bunch. Ellen and Louise never split on each other. She went into the kitchen without answering, and listened to an almost word for word repetition of Arthur's rebuke from Miriam, who was making gravy deftly, without lumps.

When the children had left the lunch-table, Arthur and Miriam drifted into an argument about some trifling household matter. Louise had to sit by and watch the argument quicken to a quarrel.

'Nothing in this house gets done unless I do it myself,' Arthur scowled. 'I have to see to every damned thing.'

He sounded so like Dudley for a moment, that Louise longed to interrupt and stand up for Miriam, but she kept silent, and looked at her coffee cup. She hated it when they quarrelled. If she interfered, or took sides, even the one she championed would make it clear that it was none of her business. If she sat quiet, and let the caustic storm flicker about her, she felt foolishly stiff and disapproving, although she was longing to cry out: 'Don't, don't! Please be nice to each other!'

Since she could not say it, she rose and left the table. She went up to her room, and spent the afternoon reading Gordon Disher's book. Ellen was out with one of her few friends, so no one came to call Louise down to tea. Perhaps they were not going to have tea. They did not always have it.

At five-thirty, Louise heard a car stop in the drive. Someone got out, with cheerful hails. Louise went to her window, which was at the front of the house, and stood behind the curtains to see who it was.

It was Sidney and Alice Cobb, in their Jaguar. Alice was in furs and stilted heels, which made the legs between look thinner and less serviceable than ever. Sidney was wearing a pork-pie hat with flies in the band, and a jacket with two slits at the back and shiny new leather at the cuffs and elbows.

Louise presumed that they had come for cocktails. She did not know whether she should go downstairs, and if so, when. Since she was accepting the hospitality of the house, she could not use it as a hotel. She must take her part. She felt, however, that her part was usually so small, and what she could offer in the way of conversation so inadequate, that Miriam's friends must sometimes think: What a bore to have to have your mother living with you.

She changed her dress, and was putting on the unevenly matched pearl necklace, which had belonged to her mother and was the only jewellery she had not sold, when Miriam called up the stairs: 'What are you doing, Mother? Aren't you coming down?'

Louise went to the doorway. 'I thought perhaps I'd wait until your friends left.'

'Even if you don't like them,' said Miriam, deliberately misunderstanding, although the impulse that had sent her to call her mother had been a compassionate one, 'you can at least come down and have a drink. Alice and Sidney are going to stay to supper, and play Canasta.'

The children were cheated of their Sunday supper in the dining-room. They were sent into the kitchen to eat. Louise felt sorry for them, but they did not seem to care. They were cooking eggs and chips. Louise wished that she could have been pushed in there with them.

The Cobbs were exhaustingly gay. They were always gay, even without cocktails. It was their stock-in-trade to be 'good fun.' They dared not let it lapse. Louise sat quietly through the meal, while jokes and allusions that she did not always understand were bandied about the table. Arthur and Miriam seemed to enjoy the Cobbs. Louise could never see why, but supposed that it must be some deficiency in herself that prevented her from appreciating Alice and Sidney's strenuous conviviality.

After supper, when the cards were brought out, Louise sat in a corner and listened to the humorous bickering and incomprehensible references to the play. Bored, she presently got up, waited for a second to see whether anyone would notice and ask where she was going, and then went into the kitchen to wash the dishes, which Miriam had piled neatly.

Miriam came out to get glasses. 'What on earth are you doing, Mother?'

'Just a little washing-up. There seems so much.'

'Oh, leave it.' The sight of her mother dabbing gently with a mop annoyed Miriam, who was already tired of both the

Cobbs and Canasta. 'Mrs Match will do it in the morning. You know she always does.'

'I thought I might get it started. She always has so much to do on a Monday. All the washing——" Louise said vaguely.

'Oh, Mother, you're living in the past. People don't do great big washes on Monday any more. And you know the laundry calls on Thursdays.'

'Well.' Louise scraped a plate doggedly. 'I just thought I could help her a little, anyway.'

'She doesn't like it, Mother,' Miriam stated, going to the door.

'Doesn't like it? How can she not like someone doing the dishes for her?'

'If you must know'—Miriam turned, and frowned at what she was going to say—'she says you put everything away in the wrong place, and she has to sort it all out.'

'Oh, I see.' Louise put down the mop while Miriam went out, and stared out of the uncurtained window, where a privet bush was moving stiffly in the night wind. So she was useless. She could not even do menial jobs in return for her keep. Setting her small, square mouth, she began angrily to pile the dishes into the sink. She was determined now to do the whole lot, if it took her all night.

An ache of self-pity pushed against the backs of her eyes. It wasn't her fault—she moved her lips to her thoughts—if she had to live like this. It wasn't her fault that her husband had left her to live the last kind of life she would have chosen, although one of her daughters, in an exasperated moment, had hinted that it was partly her fault for spoiling Dudley, and giving in to him, and letting him go his own disastrous way.

She broke a cup. Miriam heard it, and got up with a sigh from the card-table.

'Mother—*please!*'

Hurrying to put the broken china into the bin, Louise jumped, and turned around.

'I told you not to bother,' Miriam snapped. 'I wish you——'

She shut her mouth, to stop herself, Louise thought, from saying: Whose house is this, anyway?

Miriam stepped forward, and suddenly kissed her mother. 'Go to bed, there's a dear. I'm sorry I was cross.'

'I'm sorry I was stubborn.' Louise rested her head against her tall daughter's shoulder, and they stood for a moment in an unfamiliar embrace.

If it could only always be like this, Louise thought, warming to the rare offer of affection. If we could only always be close and understanding, because we are a family. She kissed Miriam gratefully, but she knew that by to-morrow they would be miles apart again.

Louise went to bed, and kept herself awake, with straining eyes, to finish *The Girl in the Bloodstained Bikini*. It was thrilling and shocking, with passionate embraces and savage blows on nearly every page. Louise did not understand how kindly Mr Disher, who had seemed as restful as his beds, could have written it. Escapism, she told herself, satisfied with the word. Before she fell asleep, she composed the letter that she would write to him, to tell him how much she admired his work.

It was Louise's birthday. Miriam had decided that it was time for a family gathering, and had persuaded Anne to come from Bedfordshire, and Eva from London.

Eva telephoned in the morning. Louise answered. When she had offered her birthday wishes, Eva said: 'I wanted to ask Miriam something.'

'Shall I get her for you?'

'Please. Or—no. Wait a minute, Mother. I'll tell you, and you can give her a message. Look, I was coming down on the train with Arthur, but now I'm not. Don't get excited. I'm coming all right. Someone offered to drive me down, and I thought perhaps Miriam wouldn't mind if he came to dinner.'

'I'm sure she wouldn't. Is it someone I know?'

'No, but he's nice. He's on the stage—you've probably

heard of him.' She mentioned a name, which Louise did not recognize.

'I shall enjoy meeting him,' Louise said carefully, stifling the curiosity, which always frightened Eva off like a young deer. She had been wishing for so long that Eva would stop drifting about with those queer, talented young men from the B.B.C., and settle down with a solid man.

'Shall I go and ask Miriam if it's all right?'

'Don't bother. I'm sure it will be,' Eva said briskly, not wanting to give Miriam the chance to object.

Anne would have to stay the night, because it was too far to drive back to her draughty, vegetable-surrounded home. She came without Frank, who could not leave the goats and chickens. Fond though he was of Louise, he was glad of an excuse not to have to go to *Pleasantways*. Arthur treated him well, and Miriam was always very gracious—but too gracious, as if she were a marchioness at the servants' Christmas treat.

'Who the hell is Gordon Disher?' Anne examined the letters on the hall table as she came into the house. She always entered a house without ceremony, as if she had only left it five minutes before. Even if you had not seen her for months, you were lucky if you got a proper greeting from her.

' He's a man I know in London,' Louise said, coming into the hall to kiss her youngest daughter.

'Well, *I* never heard of him,' Anne said, although there was no reason why she should have, since she took little interest in her mother's affairs.

Anne was thick-bodied, ungraceful and slovenly. Before her marriage she had possessed a certain wind-blown appeal. Now that she was stuck in the Bedfordshire mud with a man whom she had married partly to defy her father, and partly because no one else had asked her, any ladylike habits that Louise had managed to teach her were disintegrating. Her hair was cut by the village barber, who did not normally 'do ladies.' She wore it short, to save trouble, and only washed it every three weeks, for the same reason. Her full mouth was coarsened by a slap-dash coating of lipstick. Her skirts were baggy, and her sweaters tight over her large bust, and gone at the ribbing. Her voice was loud and often querulous, except when she talked to the dogs. She chain-smoked away a quarter of Frank's hard-earned money. She was disastrously lazy. She would lie about the house, reading magazines and spilling ash on the floor, while the dirt piled up in the corners, and the dogs climbed on to the beds and chairs, and the milk went sour in the musty larder.

She would seldom bestir herself to help Frank out of doors. Often, after he came in with his soiled hands held carefully, so as not to touch anything until he could get them under the kitchen tap, he had to cook the supper, which he did uncomplainingly, for he had been taught not to raise his voice against a woman.

He had met Anne at a local cinema, whither she had escaped from the tedium of a week-end with her godfather. He had subsequently spent a lot of money on a new suit and trips to London, fearful each time that Anne would not meet him where they had arranged. He had been so proud when she agreed to marry him. In spite of her slapdash ways, she was, as Frank told himself, a lady. Through her he would better himself.

There were times, however, when Anne's slovenliness and disregard for the niceties of life made him wonder whether he would not have done better to have married a girl of his own class, who could sweep a floor and hoe potatoes. But he stifled the thought as soon as it occurred. Frank made many allowances for Anne, and stubbornly continued to love her.

In spite of the despair into which the sight of her youngest daughter often plunged her, Louise loved Anne, because she was her baby. When she was small, she had been endearingly chubby, and was the only one of the girls who would allow Louise to cuddle her for long without wriggling.

She is getting fat, Louise thought, as Anne took off her grubby camel-hair coat, which had looked so smart when Louise had gone with her to buy it at Jaeger's. I wonder if she——? But she knew that Anne did not want a baby. 'I couldn't face the wear and tear,' she had said, laughing at her mother's shocked face.

Frank would have loved a baby. 'O.K.,' Anne said. 'If you'll carry it around for nine months, and then have it for me.' She shocked him, too. Frank did not think that women should talk obstetrically, even to their husbands.

Anne went into the drawing-room and opened all Miriam's cigarette boxes, to see what brands she had. Simon was in there, unusually tidy and subdued, with his best suit on, and his hair beginning to rise stiffly from the plastering water. He was going back to school to-morrow, and although he liked it well enough when he got there, his thoughts to-day were dour.

As it was his last night, he was to be allowed to have dinner in the dining-room. Since Ellen was older than he, she had to be included in the honour, and Judy was howling upstairs with futile resentment.

'Hullo, Aunt Anne,' Simon said unenthusiastically from the window-seat.

'Get up, Si,' said his father from the doorway, 'when a lady comes into the room.'

'It's only an aunt,' Simon muttered. Anne made a face at him and cast herself down on the sofa like a sack of groceries, and asked for beer when Arthur offered her a cocktail. She reminded Arthur of his gay, but rather squalid bachelor days in Chelsea. She was depressingly bohemian.

Eva arrived in a sports car. Louise went to the window to see what her young man was like. He was not so young as Louise expected. A little too old for Eva, she thought. He was about forty; slim, with a mobile, actor's face. As he helped Eva out of the car, he kissed her.

The rest of the family were gathered in the drawing-room. 'This is David, everybody,' Eva said casually, trying to carry off the nervous knowledge that her relations were all alert to see what she had dragged up this time from the suspect swamp of the theatre.

She put her hand on David's arm, and introduced him

protectively, as if he were shy, although his manner was easy and unabashed.

She is too possessive, Miriam thought. She is afraid he'll get away from her. Why is she always like this? She wants too much.

Eva had known David for three weeks. Their affair was only just beginning. Heaven or hell waited in the future before her.

Dinner started well. The family gathering would have looked charming to anyone peeping in through the window. Miriam had cooked an excellent dinner, and Mrs Match pounded in and out, breathing through her mouth, and beaming on those present. Arthur poured the wine attentively, and made a delightful little birthday speech when he toasted Louise. She tried to blink away the tears without having to put her hand to her eyes. Perhaps he did not mind having her in the house after all. The affectionate things he said sounded so spontaneous that she would have never guessed that he had written them down in the bathroom while he was dressing.

David was a success, and soon dispelled the family's fears that he might be 'stagey.' He said the right things to everybody, even to Anne, whose interest was difficult to capture, and he paid just the right amount of attention to the children, without being over avuncular.

Miriam had not placed him next to Eva, and from time to time he looked across the table and gave her a sweet, private smile. She glowed with pleasure in him, and her mother, who saw every glance, glowed with her. He seemed such a nice man, and perhaps twelve years difference was not too much after all. Louise began to view him as a son-in-law. Eva was looking so pretty, in spite of the odd, wispy haircut she had acquired since Louise last saw her. Perhaps because of it. The audacious chopping of her dark-brown hair into ragged petals startlingly suited her pointed, changing face, which could look suddenly gayer than anyone's, or sadder than anyone's.

Anne lolled in her chair, but she had brought a passable dress to wear, and she was not arguing. She told a really funny story about Frank staying up all night in his camouflaged Commando battle-dress to shoot a fox, which made everyone laugh.

Miriam was serene, and for some reason, a little matronly. Perhaps the ardent hopefulness in Eva made her feel old. Simon had not yet cried, which he usually did when he was going back to school, and Ellen, though excessively shy, because she was sitting next to David and she did not know if he was teasing her, had not spilled anything, or blurted out any information that was better unimparted.

It was as successful a family affair as anyone could wish for. Then, without warning, in the way of so many family parties which are embarked on with the best intentions, little quarrels began to pop up like bubbles in hot mud.

An argument started about Communism, and because it was among the family, the argument could not be maintained as an interesting discussion. It had to generate into bickering, with personal remarks instead of general ones brought in to prove a point. At one moment, Louise was afraid that someone was going to say something about the Catholic church. Should she champion it or not? She did not know what was expected of her. The moment passed, but Anne continued to dogmatize on some trivial point. Arthur became more caustically legal, Mrs Match grew anxious and dropped a spoon, and Simon finally burst into tears and said he did not want to go back to school.

He was removed to bed, and Ellen with him. The family, no longer in harmony, straggled out of the dining-room. They sat in tired attitudes and talked about nothing very much, and Miriam whispered to Arthur: 'For God's sake, get the liqueurs and pour everyone a drink.' She was beginning to regret, as she invariably did, the impulse which had prompted her to draw the clan together into an attempt at a Galsworthy gathering. Louise's happy birthday party was degenerating into just another evening.

David was bored. Eva could see that. He talked to Arthur in a corner, but she knew that he was wondering how soon he could take her home. Would this evening alter his opinion of her, which, whatever it might be, was only just developing? She had wanted him to like her family, and to see another side of her—a complete person, with a background; not just the cute little actress, who flitted among the modern furnishings of her London flat.

What did he think of it all? Her mind tried unsuccessfully to jab into his, like a thin needle into leather. She had inherited from her mother this anxiety about what people thought of her. Moreover, this was not people. It was David, with whom she thought she was falling in love.

At the end of the evening, when David was comparing his watch with the clock on the mantelpiece, and Louise was tired, and would have gone to bed if she had not been the guest of honour, Miriam said to Eva: 'Mother is a little uncertain about her plans. She wants to know when she is going to you.' It was unfair of her to say this in front of everyone. She looked foxy as she said it, which showed that she meant to be unfair.

'That's all right,' Louise said quickly. 'I never said——' She felt like the shoe in Hunt the Slipper, which is passed from hand to hand, with everyone wanting to get rid of it as soon as possible.

Eva was embarrassed. She was going to hedge, and then she saw her mother's face. Pity, and disgust at herself pushed even David from her mind.

'Whenever she likes,' she said, quickly affectionate. 'I'm longing to have her. How soon can you come, Mother? Your room's all ready.'

Then she saw David's face, and knew what he was thinking, and wondered in confusion: What is going to happen now?

CHAPTER THREE

EVA'S FLAT in London was like a thousand others; a rabbit warren of small, square rooms, with thin walls that let the sound through. You could also hear noises from the flats on either side, when the tenants dropped saucepan lids, or raised their voices; and the hum of the lift and the clash of its gates was a ceaseless accompaniment to life, often far into the night.

Although London was familiar ground to her, Louise did not have enough to do when she was staying with Eva. She could clean the flat, when Eva was out, but if Eva came in and caught her at it, she would say: 'Do leave it, Mother. I don't want you to work for me.' She said it kindly and meant it kindly, but she was also irritated by the sight of Louise pottering slowly about with a duster and a tin of polish. Eva liked to clean the flat herself; not at conventional times, but suddenly, in the middle of the night, with a frantic whirl of activity and the gramophone playing.

Eva was terrified of normality. She liked to eat at peculiar times. She got up either at dawn or half-way through the morning. She often wore clothes that did not suit the occasion, and dropped a new fashion like a hot brick as soon as everyone else took it up.

Louise fitted in as best she could with Eva's irregular life, keeping herself going with snacks in the kitchen when she had no idea what time dinner would be. Theatre people, she knew, were always unconventional, and she felt almost a part of that thrilling world herself when she was sharing Eva's restless life.

She tried not to get in Eva's way, as she did with all her daughters, conscious always of her heavy debt to them, which she could never repay or evade. She went out when it was fine, but there is not much you can do in London if you have no money to spend. Louise grew to know the museums of Kensington by heart, and the area of the Park near the Round Pond became as familiar to her as her own garden.

Eva was generous, when she thought about it, and if Louise was ever forced to ask her for a small sum, would gladly give her mother more than she asked for. You cannot, however, expect a daughter to give you two and four every time you want to go to the cinema to pass the afternoon.

Eva sometimes took her mother out to a restaurant or the theatre, but she was usually too busy to go out with Louise. Although she had not yet made her way very far on the stage, she had managed to storm the dignified gates of the B.B.C., and her voice was becoming well known to listeners as the ingenue in many radio plays.

Louise had all the humble British admiration for anyone who wrote for the newspapers or was heard on the wireless. She was intensely proud of her daughter, although Eva always insisted that the B.B.C. for her was only a bread-and-butter stopgap until she could get more regular work in the theatre.

'But just think, darling,' Louise said. 'A theatre audience is so small, compared to the thousands of people who hear you on the air. Your voice goes into homes all over the country.'

'As background music to conversation, or the sewing machine.'

'But think of all the sick people,' Louise said sentimentally, 'and the lonely ones, to whom you bring so much pleasure.'

'Oh, Mother,' Eva said, 'don't drool. I'm not in this game for charity."

'You always pretend to be so tough, dear,' Louise said. 'I can't think why. You don't know how many fans you have. Only this morning the grocer told me he heard your play last night, and how wonderful you were.'

Louise loved to talk to the local tradespeople about Eva. If she was invited to the home of one of the very few London friends her life with Dudley had enabled her to make, and it was a night when Eva was broadcasting, she would ask eagerly if the radio could be turned on. She thought that the friends would want to listen, and would be excited to think that the mother of one of the voices was sitting in the room with them. It was annoying when they talked through the play, or turned off the set unthinkingly, even when Eva was speaking.

When she was at home, Louise would sit glued to the radio to listen to the plays, nodding her head when she approved of a point, and drawing in her breath at dramatic moments. When Eva came in, tired, and wanting something mad, like a mustard-pickle sandwich, instead of the nourishing stew her mother had cooked for her, Louise wanted to talk about the play, and ask Eva if she didn't think it was the man's own fault that his wife had left him; or why had the woman shot herself just when everything was beginning to come right?

Louise was surprised when Eva not only did not care to discuss the play, but did not even seem to know much about the plot. She understood this better when Eva took her to see a studio recording. Louise sat cramped in a corner behind the music stands, hardly daring to breathe for fear she should be heard in a thousand homes, and watched in astonished disillusionment the casually-clad actors stroll up to the microphone, read their lines, and fall back in their seats to pick up their knitting or their books until the next cue. When she listened to the wireless, she had always imagined it like a proper stage set, with the actors in costume, and speaking their lines by heart.

'You're lovably naïve, Mother,' Eva told her; but now that she had been in a studio, Louise was naïve no longer, and took pleasure in destroying whatever illusions the grocer and the milkman entertained about the goings-on at Broadcasting House.

In addition to her radio work, Eva was now involved with a lot of highly intellectual talk about a 'difficult' play, which was to be put on by a progressive young producer as soon as he could find the money. The chief character was an amateur prostitute, discovered half-way through the play to have the gift of healing, and the producer wanted Eva for the part. When the author saw Eva, he wanted her too.

'But, my dear,' he told her. 'You *are* Deidre! You are my conception of her come alive. It's too thrilling.'

The two excitable young men, with wild hair and spectacles and prematurely loosened figures, spent a lot of time at Eva's flat, discussing, waving their arms about, listening to her read lines, or reading significant passages themselves in the sort of awe-struck, intoning voice that is usually reserved for a Greek chorus.

Eva was wild to get the part. If the play were ever produced, she knew that it would attract notice, even if it did not run for very long. She would much rather attract notice in an odd play, which would mystify or nauseate many people, than in a drawing-room comedy which would nurse the matinée audiences along for years.

When the two young men were throwing themselves about the flat, Louise would keep out of the way, since she did not know what to say to them, and knew that anything she did manage to say would not be relevant. Many times she wished that she were a rich woman. She would finance the play, although she could hardly understand a word of the scribbled-over copy that Eva had given her to read. But she would willingly put up the money, and it would be a success, all due to Eva, and Louise would have a black moiré dress and a new fur for the first night, and be photographed in the foyer chatting to dazzling people.

When the Greek chorus was in session, and it was too wet or windy to go out, Louise stayed in her room, which was a small cell, with space for not much more than the bed. The window looked on to a brown brick well in the middle of the block of flats. Sitting on the bed, Louise could see the milk bottles on window-sills, and the backs of taps and tins of scouring powder in people's mysterious kitchens.

This May and June with Eva were particularly lonely ones for Louise. Often, coming in and seeing her mother jump up so eagerly from her solitary vigil in the tiny flat, Eva would reproach herself for her neglect. She tried harder than either of her sisters to make Louise happy, but her life at this time was

so full of other, absorbing things. She moved in a state of
nervous exaltation, between her hopes for the play and her
growing passion for David. She was often distracted and
vague when she was with her mother. Louise's presence
disturbed the dream world in which she was passing the
increasingly beautiful summer days.

Louise longed to break through the barrier which kept her
out of those parts of Eva's life which mattered most. There
was no point, however, in Eva discussing the play with her,
since Louise thought it a sordid and unreal concoction and
could not see what all the fuss was about. Nor could Eva be
persuaded to talk about David, whom Louise still thought
charming, though disconcertingly sure of himself.

He came frequently to the flat after the evening performance
of the play in which he was appearing. He had given Louise
a ticket to see the play, and she had admired him in it very
much. He reminded her a little of Gerald du Maurier, since
whose death, Louise would hardly admit that there had been
another actor.

When she told David this, as the most complimentary thing
she could think of, he had said: 'Thanks, Mrs Bickford, but
actually I don't want to remind people of anyone except
myself.' He said it with a pleasant smile, however. He was
always very polite.

If Louise was still up when he came to the flat, sometimes
with traces of his make-up still darkening the edges of his
pepper-coloured hair, he would make agreeable conversation
to her; but when he began to look at Eva, Louise knew that
it was time for her to go to bed and listen to the murmur of
their voices through the flimsy wall.

Sometimes, David left before she fell asleep. Sometimes she
slept without knowing what time he went home, and consoled
herself with the hopeful thought that it was a good thing she
was there in the flat as chaperone.

Louise was to stay with Eva for two months. By the middle
of June, with the warm days coming, her aimless life began to

seem a crime against the benevolence of this London summer.
Everyone else seemed to have something to do, someone to
enjoy it with. Louise was merely killing time, and she felt that
her life was slipping by unused.

The trees in the Park were richly clad with the same dark,
urban green under which Louise had walked as a girl. The May
trees were loaded with marshmallow scent, and the view from
the bridge across the Serpentine, with the traffic sounding miles
away, was a dreaming idyll of willows and lazy boats and still
water that held and gave back whatever light was in the sky.

The Park was beautiful, and Louise had all the day to enjoy
it, and so could not enjoy it as she would have if she were
snatching a stolen hour there from other things that claimed
her. Girls came out in new cotton dresses, but they were in
pairs, or with men. They walked lightly, admiring their skirts,
and thinking that the money had been well spent.

Louise bought a blue dress, because she felt that she would
die if she did not have something new. When she tried it on at
home, she did not like it so much, although Eva, hurrying out
to meet David for tea before his show, gave it a quick, nodding
glance, kissed her mother before the mirror, and told her it
made her look ten years younger.

What if it did? Louise had nowhere to go in it, no purpose
in putting it on, except to pass the hours until it was time to
take it off again and go to bed.

Like many other lonely women in London, Louise was
having to learn the art of killing time cheaply, without pausing
in a vacuum to admit defeat. She knew all about taking a long
time to dress in the mornings, and spinning out the ritual of
retiring at night. She knew about dawdling in teashops over
the kind of light meal that other people were bolting and running from as soon as possible. She knew about the half-price
morning shows at West End cinemas, where women ate their
lunch out of crackling paper bags, and about stopping wherever
a crowd was gathered, to see a wedding, or a political agitator,
or a comic man with a desperate face dancing in the street,
with his hat on the ground for pennies.

Once, she waited nearly two hours at the corner of Exhibition Road to see a foreign royalty drive by. When David came that night, Louise heard him tell Eva that he had been caught in a traffic jam that afternoon on his way to the theatre.

'The police were holding up the traffic for some king or other with no country left to speak of. The incredible thing was that there was quite a crowd of people waiting on the pavement to see the cars go by. Who are these people, one always wonders, with nothing better to do?'

'It's me,' Louise wanted to say. 'People like me.'

But she never told Eva the way she spent her days. When Eva, flying out of the flat without hat or gloves, called to her: 'Have a happy day!' or asked when she came home: 'Did you have a happy day?' Louise always answered Yes, she would, or Yes, she had.

One afternoon, walking among the vacant, pushing crowds in Oxford Street, Louise was so bored with herself that she turned into the shop where Gordon Disher worked, and took the lift to the bed department. She wandered among the rows of beds that offered themselves bleakly to the human body, but there was no sign of the breathless, fat man with the gentle voice. An assistant came up, and Louise asked nervously for Mr Disher, trying to sound like a customer.

While he was being sought, Louise began to wish that she had not succumbed to the impulse that had brought her in off the street. Would he think that she was taking advantage of their brief encounter, which he might not even remember? He had not answered her letter. She would make that the excuse. She would say that she had come to see whether he had received it. Or would that look as if she were reproaching him for not having answered ?

He came towards her, moving among the supine beds assuredly, like an elephant shouldering its way through a familiar jungle. When he saw who it was, he increased his pace, and arrived a little out of breath before Louise, in his neglected dark suit that surely only just scraped by the standards of the store.

Did one shake hands? He solved the problem for her by holding out his hand. 'I'm delighted to see you,' he said, in that soft voice, which could not help sounding intimate. 'I didn't think I would.'

Louise had been going to say something polite, like: I'm afraid my letter to you must have gone astray, but instead, she found herself saying abruptly: 'You didn't answer my letter.'

'No.' He looked down, and dropped his voice into the carpet.

'Why didn't you?' Again, Louise had that queer, exhilarated feeling she had known in Lyons, of being able to talk to him as if she knew him quite well.

'To tell you the truth, after I gave you the book, I thought I shouldn't have. It didn't seem right, and I was sure you'd think that too. So I thought probably you had written the letter because you were kind, and you thought it rude not to.'

'It was rude of you not to answer it,' Louise said instructively, as if she were speaking to a child.

'Perhaps. But I thought that would be imposing further.'

'How silly of you,' Louise said gaily. 'It was true, what I said about the book. I loved it. I'd like to read some more.'

'You would?' His heavy jaw creased in a delighted smile. He looked round automatically to see if the floor manager was aware that they were talking about anything except beds.

There was no one near them, however. The department was as empty as furniture departments invariably are, so that, walking through them, you wonder how the store can afford to keep so much stock. There were only the beds, without character now, but each waiting to become the centre of some-one's existence; the haven for tired limbs and plagued minds, the resting-place for sickness, the battle-ground for love.

'I'm sure I shouldn't keep you talking,' Louise said, seeing the glance. 'Unless, of course, I buy a bed, and I don't really need one. Perhaps we could have tea again some day, and you could bring one of your other books?'

'Oh, yes,' said Mr Disher. 'I will. I'll bring you *Kisses and Corpses*, if you like. I've only got one copy, but I'll give it to you to keep, if you'd accept it. No one has ever taken such an interest in my work before.'

Through her daughters, Louise had met a few writers. Even the ones who could not get their work published had talked of it with some conceit, and taken it for granted that their listeners would be interested. Gordon Disher was the first author she had met—although she felt sure Miriam would not call him an author—who was proud of his writing, yet honestly diffident about it.

I shall ask him to tea, she thought. Next Sunday, when Eva is out. She won't mind. She said she was going to Richmond. I shall ask him to tea and buy a lemon cake and make sandwiches.

When she asked him, he accepted at once, to make up, perhaps, for having been foolishly humble about the letter. He seemed delighted. He leaned his fat hand on a nearby bed and prodded the springs, smiling like a boy offered a treat.

An assistant was approaching with a sheaf of papers 'Till Sunday, then.' Louise held out her hand, and was going to take it back, recollecting that this would not do before another assistant, but Gordon Disher took it and held it softly for a second, his own hand quite enveloping it. Evidently, he had been here long enough to have favourite customers, who came to him through the years for marriage beds, cots, beds for daughters getting married, cots for grandchildren, until they were on handshaking terms with our Mr Disher.

On Sunday, Louise began to get ready for her tea-party almost as soon as she came back from church. She pinned up the short, off-colour hair, which her daughters had made her cut ten years ago, riding over their father's protests like a charge of cavalry. She ironed the blue dress, and trimmed her unvarnished nails. After an early lunch, she started her preparations in the kitchen.

Although she usually longed for company in the flat, she was glad now that she was alone. Eva might have laughed at her for taking so much trouble over Mr Disher. Not that Eva was a snob. She had picked up some people in her time who had disgusted Miriam; but she never took extensive trouble over any guest, yet managed to entertain successfully and with aplomb.

Louise laid everything out on a tray, ate two of the biscuits, and went to her room to change her dress. The weather had broken in a storm that was heavy with far-off thunder. Outside Louise's window, the rain fell vertically, as if someone were emptying a bucket into the well of the flats. What a pity. It would spoil Eva's tennis party, and she had looked so nice going off with David in her white dress. However, Louise supposed that it did not matter so much when you were in love.

* * *

The lift whined, the gates clashed open and shut, the front door of the flat banged, and Eva and David went into the sitting-room and shut the door.

'I'm glad we got away,' Eva said, turning into David's arms, as she always did when they came into an empty room. His hair was wet, and she smoothed it for him, to stop him doing it himself, with that familiar, palming gesture he repeated dozens of times a day.

'I expect they thought us rude as hell,' he said, 'leaving right after lunch; but honestly, those people they had there. And then suggesting bridge——'

'It probably would have been better than tennis on that dreadful court. Did you see it?'

David let her go, and sat down to light a cigarette. 'I can't think why we went, really,' he said, leaning forward with the cigarette between his fingers, watching the smoke.

Eva knew why. She wanted to meet all his friends, and to establish herself with him as a couple, who went everywhere together.

'Did you ever go there with Frances?' She had to say it, although she knew it would annoy him.

'Well, of *course*. You know I've known Jack and Diana for years. What if I did? Evie, I do wish you——'

'How did Frances look in white?' Eva said lightly, deciding to make a joke of it. She stood on tiptoe before the wall mirror, to see as much as she could of the flaring white dress, with which, surprisingly, she had met the conventions of a tennis party.

'Awful,' David said glumly. 'Stop goading me, and let's have some coffee.'

'In a minute.' Eva turned round. 'I do love you,' she said, her face confirming it. The first time she had said that, it had been difficult, and a little frightening. Now she had to keep on saying it, as if it was a grappling iron to hold on to the happiness she had.

'Do you really?' David asked. 'Or is it just that you need a man?'

Someone else had said that. Who was it? Arthur of all people. 'Eva,' he had said, after several drinks, 'you're getting jittery. You need a man.' She had been afraid for a moment that he was going to suggest himself, but he had taken his eyes away from the front of her dress, and lit a cigar. Not Arthur. There would never be anything like that about Arthur. Poor Miriam. That must have made it doubly difficult for her.

'The coffee?' David suggested.

Eva sat down beside him, spreading her skirt and pointing her toe. 'Don't go to see Frances next week,' she said. 'Why must you? It could be done just as well by letter.'

'Oh God, Evie, we've been through all that. Leave me alone about this, will you?'

Eva's eyes filled with tears. She turned away her head, struggling to resurrect her pride. The doorbell rang. There were voices in the hall, one male and murmuring, the other her mother's, carefully hushed, as if there were a child asleep.

'Mother's boy friend,' Eva said flatly. 'I'd forgotten.'

She's been crying, Louise thought, in the middle of her embarrassed explanations to Gordon Disher, as Eva came through the door. Eva's face, however, recovered in an instant. She breathed charming apologies at the bulky man in the

shiny new tie, who stood in her narrow hall, almost touching
the walls on either side.

'Do come in,' she beamed. 'I'm delighted to meet you.
Mother's told me so——'

'Oh, no, it's all right, dear,' Louise said quickly. 'We're
going out. We'll have tea somewhere. The rain's slackening
off, I think.' She hoped that Eva would not feel bad when she
saw the loaded tray in the kitchen, and that she and David
would eat the cake and sandwiches, so that they would not be
wasted. The biscuits would keep. Even in distress, Louise
could not help having these economical thoughts.

When they were out in the street, Mr Disher took a deep
breath, and said: 'The tea places will be so crowded on a
Sunday. Would you consider—please say no, if you don't care
to—having tea at my place? I could show you my other books.'

'I'd like that very much,' Louise said immediately. 'How
do we go? Bus or tube?'

'No, no,' Mr Disher said. '*You* must have a taxi. We'll
find one on the high street.'

The hall porter would have got them a taxi, but Louise did
not like to ask him. He was tall and military, with a stiff leg,
and he always saluted Louise, and called her Madam. She did
not want to be called Madam when she was with Gordon
Disher. As they walked to the corner, she smiled at his
assumption that she was accustomed to travelling in taxis.
He did not know that she often walked quite long distances
to save a bus fare.

When the taxi drew up and pinged its flag outside the tall,
pale house, which was attached to a string of identical houses
with many chimneys along the defeated-looking street, a face
appeared at a lower window, and was gone with the agitation
of the lace curtain.

Various names identified the bells by the door. Mr Disher's
was the top one. He was out of breath by the time they reached
his two rooms, which were under the roof, with sloped ceilings
that made him appear to take up more space than ever.

'Those stairs are a crime,' he said, sinking into a chair

without waiting for Louise to sit down, which showed that he must be distressed. Louise felt quite bad about the lift and porter in Eva's block of flats. She did not want Gordon Disher to think of her as one of the enemy class, the customers, with money to spend. She would like him to understand how poor she was; poorer than he, undoubtedly, since he had a job and could afford a place of his own, with furniture that was comfortable, in a run-over-at-the-heels way.

He made the tea with an electric kettle getting the cups and plates out of a cupboard under the basin in his dark, untidy bedroom, and the milk off the window-sill. When he opened the window, his cat walked in, a great scarred tiger, who accepted milk, and then sat on Louise's lap, purring rustily while she drank her tea.

Mr Disher had panted downstairs and back with a plateful of sugar biscuits. 'Mrs Dill, in the ground floor back, always obliges, God bless her,' he said. It seemed odd that such a fat man did not have such delicacies already on hand to regale himself. He did not eat the biscuits. He ate a piece of bread and butter and some dry crackers, and drank his tea without sugar or milk. He looked after Louise without fussing, and they were both relaxed, as if it were quite usual for her to be there.

'What a nice, cosy room this is,' Louise said, looking round at the restful, sagging furniture, and the typewriter and papers left askew on the dusty table, among the other odds and ends of a man alone who does not have to put things away. 'If it were mine, I should put some chintz curtains up, I think, and have plants on the window-sill. I wish I had a little place of my own like this.'

Mr Disher looked at her with gentle enquiry, and Louise suddenly put down her cup and said: 'I can't afford it, you see. I have hardly any money of my own. I have to live with my daughters.'

'I'm sorry,' he said, as if he understood. Stroking the noisy cat, Louise began without self-consciousness to tell him about herself, spurred on by the relief of having someone to talk to.

Most people would have been bored. She had discovered soon after Dudley's death that to talk of your misfortunes reduced people to stiff-jawed fidgeting. But Gordon Disher listened seriously, breaking his crackers into small pieces, nodding his head and murmuring from time to time, like an old-fashioned family doctor with time to listen to his patient.

Louise found herself telling him what it felt like to live under an obligation, and to lead an aimless life in which you were no use to anybody. She had never said these things to anyone before. She had only said them to herself when she woke in the middle of the night with her defences down.

She would never have been able to say them in Eva's flat. If they had had their tea there, as planned, she knew she would have acted the courteous hostess, making light conversation, pressing Mr Disher to cake, while he sat on the edge of one of Eva's uncomfortable chairs. They would have got nowhere at all, and would probably never have seen each other again.

As it was, sitting under the roof with him, half afraid that whoever had agitated the lace curtain might come up and say: No ladies allowed, Louise felt that she was making a friend. The oddest, but the most comforting friend she had ever made.

'Were you ever married?' she asked him, when she had finished telling him those few things about Dudley which her misplaced loyalty would allow.

'Alas, no.' He sighed. 'I'm what they call a confirmed bachelor, though I've often wished it otherwise.'

'Why?' Louise asked, with the bluntness that often got her into trouble in other places.

'I lived with my mother, you see, until I was really past the age of thinking about such things. She didn't want me to marry.'

That sounded like Dudley, and his futile objections to Anne's marriage. 'How could she stop you?' Louise asked with interest.

'She had reason on her side. I wasn't in the shape for it, aren't now, and never shall be, even if I got the chance.'

'But that's absurd——' Louise had been going to say something diplomatic about plenty of women liking fat men, but was glad she did not, for that was not what he meant.

'A diabetic shouldn't marry,' he said, quite cheerfully. 'At least, my mother didn't think so. She took wonderful care of me—far better, she always said, than any wife could have. I miss her very much now that she's passed on.'

'Of course you do.' Louise thought Mrs Disher sounded something of a monster, but she admired his devotion, and she was only giving half a mind to the conversation now. The other half was skating away along the thin ice of her scant medical knowledge. A diabetic! What a good thing they had not had tea at the flat. It would have been embarrassing about the iced cake and the sandwiches. Or perhaps he would have eaten them out of politeness, and fallen to the floor in a coma, immovable as a beached whale.

'I hope you don't mind my telling you this.' He recalled her attention from her hypothetical worry about how she would have got hold of an ambulance. 'Some people think it's not nice to talk about sickness.'

'That's silly,' Louise said. 'I think it's interesting.' Perhaps interesting was the wrong word. 'I think it's bad luck,' she amended. 'I'm sorry.'

'Please don't be,' he said. 'I wasn't complaining. It's merely an inconvenience, having to regulate one's diet, and that. I'm quite happy, you know. I have my job, and my writing, and a place to live. What more could anyone want?'

'Company?' Louise suggested.

'I'd rather live on my own than with someone who didn't share my ways. There was a girl once . . . before they found out what was wrong with me. She faded out of the picture when I had the long spell in hospital, which was lucky. She was the social, ambitious type. She ended up as a councillor's wife.'

He is happier than me, Louise thought. He is alone and sick, and he has no family to care, and he must be bored with selling beds, but he knows where he stands, and he is free.

When she left him, adamantly refusing a taxi, because she was afraid he would try to pay the driver for her, they did not make any arrangement about meeting again. Like old friends, they knew that they would see each other by and by. It could be months, for Louise was going to Bedfordshire soon, and then to Miriam's; but they would pick up where they left off. Her daughters would probably be surprised at the friendship, but even they, with their variously biased standards, must see how kind he was—kinder than Louise had thought a man could ever be.

'He's so very kind,' she told Eva, who was not really listening. 'I went to his rooms in Fulham. Miriam would think that disgraceful. no doubt, but he's so—I mean, not brilliant, like Arthur, or—well anything much at all—but he's so kind.'

'Why do you keep harping on "kind," Mother?' Eva asked, a little irritably. 'Aren't we kind to you? We try—mean to be.'

'Oh, my darling——' Louise fell over herself not to be misunderstood.

'But I forgot about your tea-party, didn't I? I'm a beast. You were going to have him to tea here—we ate your sandwiches, by the way—and I had to come blundering in and spoil it all. Ask him next week, why don't you? You can have the flat to yourself any day you like.'

'That's not necessary. I don't like to interfere with your plans.'

'Shan't have any, except work. The boys are going into a sort of tentative rehearsal, though they still haven't got a theatre, or enough money, and David will be away for a few days. His play closed yesterday.'

'What a pity. Such a lovely play, I thought, though I didn't care for the girl in it. You could have played the part much better. Is David going on tour ?'

'No. He's going to Windsor to see his wife about some legal thing.'

'His *wife?*' Louise's visions of David as a son-in-law crumbled into horrified dust. 'Eva, I didn't know——'

'They're separated,' Eva said shortly. 'There'll be a divorce soon.'

'Are there any children?'

'One.'

'Oh—*Eva!*'

'Now Mother, don't "Oh, Eva" me. I haven't broken up his home, if that's what you think. His wife is poisonous. We hardly ever talk about her; but I know that she is.'

'But, darling——' Louise fumbled for the right thing to say. She would be a poor mother indeed if she let this pass. 'Going out with a married man . . . one doesn't do that sort of thing.' Then she remembered that Eva was in love with David. She put out her hand, and cried in awkward pity: 'Oh, my poor Eva!'

Her daughter turned away. 'I told you. He's going to get a divorce. Please leave me alone about it, Mother. I'm twenty-seven. I have to go my own way.'

CHAPTER FOUR

'So Eva's going to Italy, I hear,' Anne said. 'With that matinée idol she brought to Miriam's, no doubt.'

'David's going, yes; but only as one of a party.' Louise hoped that what Eva had told her was true.

Anne made a disbelieving sound, and humped up her thick shoulder. 'And what about this new play she's been so excited about?' she asked, on a grumbling note. 'Or did someone else get the part?'

'Of course not,' Louise said. 'They just had to postpone it for a while. I'm glad. Eva needs a holiday.'

'Who doesn't?' Anne heaved herself up to get a cigarette from the cracked china jug on the mantelpiece. 'But they don't get one, it seems, unless they've got a boy friend to take them.'

'Now, Anny,' Frank said mildly. 'You know I'd like nothing better than to take you to the sea, but who would look after things here? I can't trust old Harry. You know you can go away any time you like if you need a break. Auntie Edna would love to have you at Hunstanton. She said so.'

'Oh, Frank!' Anne often spoke without looking at him, tossing remarks like carelessly thrown cricket balls. 'Can you *see* me?'

'I don't know why not.' His patience with her was everlasting. 'Auntie Edna has a very nice place.'

'Not as nice as Portofino with a man.'

'Don't always jeer at what Eva does,' Louise said, looking up from the pillowcase she was darning lumpily. She always found an overflowing mending basket waiting for her when she came to stay with Anne. She struggled through it during her visit, knowing that whatever she left would stay in the basket until she came again. 'You always want to pick holes in everything your sisters do. I can't think why, because when you were little, you used to follow them about like a dog, copying everything they did.'

'When I was little was a long time ago,' Anne said. 'You mustn't harp on the past, Mother, or people will think you're getting senile.'

'Anny!' Frank embarked on the remark which he made so often during Louise's visits. 'You mustn't talk to your mother like that.'

'That's all right,' Louise said. 'That's the way young people are nowadays.'

'I can't even annoy you, can I, Mother? Why don't you care what I say, the way you do with Miriam and Eva?' Anne asked shrewdly.

'Because you're my baby,' Louise said. 'And you're a silly girl. I'm not afraid of you.' She laughed, but there was truth behind her joke. Although Anne made little attempt to make her comfortable, Louise felt more at home in the damp, ugly stone house than she did in Miriam's beautifully run home, or Eva's brightly painted flat. Anne said what she thought, while the other two had more civilized ideas about what can be said to a mother, and Louise minded more about what she thought they were thinking than about what Anne actually said.

Anne's home was uncomfortable, and the life she led in it ungracious and slovenly, but she left her mother alone to do what she liked. Louise did not mind staying there, although she was always glad to get away to a bath with hot water, and a meal without dogs clamouring round the table.

There are many unattractive houses in Bedfordshire, but Frank had picked the most unprepossessing of all to start his market garden. When he took the place, he had been interested only in the land and outbuildings that went with it. He had scarcely looked at the house, and he did not look at it too closely now, for the state in which Anne maintained it offended his innate sense of cleanliness and order. He knew that it was no use asking her to clean or tidy up. She would only say: 'Not now. I'm reading,' or 'I'm going to the movies,' or 'I ran the vacuum last week. Do you want me chained to that damned thing? The place wouldn't get so dirty if you didn't bring all that filthy mud in from outside.' Which was unfair, because Frank was meticulous about wiping his boots and brushing off his trousers.

It was a square, grey house with a slate roof, and a flat, blank look about its front, as if it were an uninteresting hoarding set up beside the rutted road that ran by it. One side had no windows at all, only two different coloured spaces which had been blocked in during the days of the window tax. The back of the house was a jumble of irregular windows that did not all open, with rickety coal-sheds leaning against it among the battered dustbins, as if too exhausted to stand up under their own weight.

Frank had no time to spend on the house. He lavished all his care on his chicken-houses and pigsties and goat-sheds. The outbuildings were whitewashed and in impeccable repair. His vegetables grew in neat rows in the two little fields on which his property was set. He was not interested in flowers, and Anne would not lift a spade, and so the narrow garden at the front and side of the house remained a jungle of waving grass and tangled shrubs, over which Anne's washing-line flapped its unheroic banners of grey and faded laundry in the searching wind.

The wind always seemed to blow in this part of the country, even in summer. The land all round was flat for miles, with few trees, and a vista of sour brussels sprouts and turnips, that did not hide the main railway line, along which the great trains roared disdainfully through Bedfordshire towards the glamour of the North.

Anne hated the house, so did not bother to do anything to improve it. Frank had hung some limp curtains when he lived there as a bachelor, and Anne had left them, as she had left the inadequate masculine furniture and the worn stair-carpet and the patched linoleum in the old-fashioned bathroom, whose geyser gave forth more noise than steam.

She seldom bothered to empty ashtrays or straighten the

rugs when guests came. She did not notice them looking round, if they were in clean clothes, to see if there was any chair that they could sit on without collecting dogs' hairs. She did not have many guests. During the years she had been there, she had made few friends, apart from one or two rather raffish couples from the local Air Force camp, who came and drank beer, and called Frank: 'I say old chap,' in accents that were unconvincing copies of the Battle of Britain pilots who had put R.A.F. talk on the map of the English language.

Frank's friends dropped in from time to time, with heavy feet, to talk about the price of balancer meal or cabbages, but Anne was no more at home with them than Frank was with her Air Force friends, with their crêpe-soled shoes and shrill, sharp-featured wives.

It was a peculiar marriage; unsatisfactory, and yet restfully undemanding; held together by Frank's invulnerable regard for his wife, and Anne's lazy acceptance of any kind of life that came her way.

Having no home of her own, Louise kept her clothes and the few possessions she had not sold in Miriam's storeroom, picking out what she needed for wherever she was going to stay. When she left Eva, she had gone to *Pleasantways* for the night to put away her town clothes and get out all her oldest things to take to Anne's.

'Mother,' Miriam had said, coming in while she was packing, 'you can't possibly wear that linen dress another summer. I remember you buying it ages ago—before I was married, I believe.'

'So I did.' Louise held up the shabby dress. 'My goodness— before the war! Clothes were made differently then. They were made to last.'

'That wasn't,' Miriam said. 'It died quietly some time ago, but no one buried it. Let me buy you another one. We could go into Wincham in the morning before your train goes and get you something—let's see—pink, I think. A lavender pink, or a whitey pink, like a rose. You always look best in those sort of garden colours.' When Louise was only staying for a short visit, Miriam managed to be very affectionate and attentive.

'Thank you, dear,' Louise said, folding the linen dress into her suitcase, 'but I wouldn't dream of it. A new dress to go to Anne's! Whatever for?'

'I see your point,' Miriam said. 'All right, I'll buy you something when you come back here in September.' Her mother hoped that she would remember.

Louise pottered comfortably about Anne's house in bedroom slippers and overalls, cleaning up anything that had not already gone too far for her limited domestic talents to rectify, often cooking the meals, for Anne was glad to stay out of the kitchen, and did not mind when her mother broke things, or burned a saucepan. When the wind was not driving the rain across the flat fields, Louise would go out with a scarf over her head and Anne's large Wellington boots on her feet to see what Frank was about, and to help him with the things she could do, like feeding the chickens, or sorting eggs.

It was July now, and the muddy stretches that connected the various items of Frank's smallholding were caked and cracked, and smelled like rotten river beds. He yearned to pave his yard with concrete, but had not yet had the time or the money to do it.

Louise went out in the old linen dress, with a light chiffon scarf over her intractable hair, because the wind was a hot, sluggish one to-day, and found Frank bent double, thinning out lettuces. He wore stained and shapeless grey flannel trousers, a broad leather belt round his narrow waist, and an open-necked blue shirt that echoed his bright eyes. When he straightened up, Louise saw the golden brown hair curling on his chest, and the muscular arms and firm hands, and thought again what an attractive man he was. Although Dudley had raved and protested, and called his daughter an idiot, Louise had always understood why Anne had married Frank.

'Hullo, Mother.' It had been quite a time before he would

stop calling her Mrs Bickford. 'Come to do some work for me?'

'I wouldn't mind doing whatever it is you're doing,' Louise said. 'It looks good for the figure.' She would like to be slimmer, although since Anne's birth she had been this same stumpy shape, without ever managing to recapture her waistline. It would be nice to be able to get into dresses that were the right length for her, without the sales-girl having to leave the zipper open and call the fitter. She would like to be slimmer for the new dress that Miriam was going to buy her. She would save up and buy a new hat to go with it, and go up to London to see Gordon Disher.

She worked in the field all morning with Frank, and in the afternoon she helped him with the animals. She liked to be with Frank. He did not talk very much, and when he did, it was about something practical. Louise had a child's liking for being given information. She preferred it to being given ideas.

She knew that she was sometimes more of a nuisance than a help to Frank, because she so often had to ask what to do and how to do it; but he never got impatient, or said: 'Here, it'll be quicker if I do it myself.' He instructed her kindly, and Louise began to remember things that she had done on the farm when she was young.

'You're getting to be a real help to me,' Frank said finding her struggling out with buckets to feed the chickens at the right time, without asking. 'You've got quite a way with those chickens, too. Not everybody has it. People think fowls have no sense, but they like to be treated right. Old Harry puts them in a fluster every time he goes near the houses.'

'That's because he's the executioner,' Louise said. Harry's speciality was killing chickens. He did it with a grab, a twist and a grunt, so quickly that the bird was dead before you or the chicken knew it. He seemed to enjoy the slaughter. Chicken-killing time was one of the few occasions when he smiled.

He was a spare, stooped old man, with a toothless skull and a cloth cap that seemed to have grown on to his head. No one knew whether he had any hair. He helped Frank erratically, coming punctually for weeks, and then suddenly staying away for several days, usually when there was the most work to do. When he returned, shuffling sideways into the yard like a bundle of old clothes with nothing inside them, he would raise a gloomy, unshaven face to Frank, and say: 'I've been a bad boy. Don't tell me. I know it.'

When Frank asked him: 'Why don't you be a good old man and stay off the beer?' Harry would say, with a tremulous head: 'I'm going to, boy. It won't happen again. If you don't want to keep me on no more, that's all right. But if you could see your way to letting me stay, I give you my word, it won't happen again.'

'Till the next time.' Frank would laugh and pat him on the shoulder.

'Why don't you throw out that old drunk?' Anne often complained. 'He's never there when you want him. He just takes advantage of you being so soft.'

'I like the old devil, and I couldn't get another man as cheap. He works all right when he is here, and if I didn't employ him, no one else would. People round here are sick of him.'

'There you go.' Anne shrugged her shoulders. 'That's typical.'

Louise liked old Harry. When they were working close together, he talked to her about his dreary childhood, although she could not understand everything he said, and he could seldom hear her answers.

She and Frank and Harry finished the day's jobs in the golden diffusion of the evening sun. Louise was tired. She left the bent old man and the agile young one contemplating the pigs, which they did with pride each night, and went in to see if Anne had done anything about getting tea ready.

Anne was sitting on the torn leather chair in the kitchen, with her bare feet on the rung, painting her fingernails a crude shade of orange.

'I thought I'd come and put the kettle on,' Louise said, thinking how nice it would have been to come in and find the

table laid and the kettle welcoming her with a thin murmur of
steam. She would have liked to sit down, too, and watch
someone else move about the kitchen, making a friendly noise
with cups and saucers, but Anne made no attempt to help.
Her nails were not dry, so she sat and waved them in the air,
while Louise rallied her strength to get things ready before
Frank came in hungry for his tea.

'You're tired, Mother,' Anne said. 'Why do you stay out so
long? It's silly to try and do so much at your age.'

Louise was not offended. Anne's spade-calling remarks
were somehow not insulting.

'There's so much to do,' Louise said. 'And I like to help
Frank. He works so hard.' She tried not to make it sound
like a criticism of Anne's idleness, although it grieved her that
her daughter took no share in the work, and no interest in
the results that Frank achieved.

'You really ought to go out and see the pigs,' Louise said.
'Frank has done wonders with this new feeding. They're
monsters.'

'Brutes,' said Anne, unwinding her legs from the chair, and
getting up with a rumpled skirt to tramp into her shoes. 'They
all look like Charles Laughton, except the one that looks like
Marie Dressler.'

'I'll pick a lettuce and some tomatoes for supper, shall I?'
Louise suggested, looking in the larder to see what was there.
'The lettuces are beauties. Frank certainly has a way with
vegetables. They're growing splendidly.'

'Why shouldn't they?' Anne yawned and looked at her
nails. 'Frank puts them in the ground. They take root. Why
shouldn't they grow?'

'You don't know the half of it, Anny,' Frank said, leaving
his boots at the kitchen door and coming in in his socks.
'You ought to come out with your mother some time and help
do some of the things that make them grow.'

'Don't keep on at me,' Anne said, although he hardly ever
tried to persuade her to help him. 'I'm tired. My legs are
tired.'

Frank looked round from the sink. 'Not ill are you, dear?' he asked with concern.

'If you must know,' Anne said sulkily, 'I'm going to have a baby.'

'Anny!' Frank came towards her with dripping hands, the cold water weaving along the hairs on his sunburned forearms. 'Oh, you clever girl!'

'What's so clever about it?' Anne said. 'I think it's awful.'

'It's just lovely.' Frank held out his arms to her, and Louise, in confusion, slipped out of the room before she could see whether Anne stood still to be embraced, or turned away.

Anne's godfather, Bruce Cory, lived ten miles away in an airless Victorian house besieged by overgrown laurels. It had always been a gloomy place, and was even gloomier since his wife died four years ago and left Bruce in the martial care of a housekeeper who kept the blinds half-way down for fear of the sun on the carpets.

Bruce had been Louise's friend before she married. She sometimes hinted that if circumstances had been different, she might have married him, although the question had actually never occurred to either of them. It had only occurred to Louise in later years, when her affection-starved fancy remembered more poignancy into those dances and tea-parties than had ever existed.

Louise was going to tea with Bruce. Frank was driving her there, since he had to go into Bedford to see about his livestock rations. Louise wished that she had something better to go in than the green knitted suit which was the nicest thing she had brought. She had forgotten about Bruce when she packed to go to Anne's. Not that Bruce would notice what she wore. He accepted her as a contemporary, although she was nearly fifteen years younger, and assumed that she had given up trying to keep pace with the world, as he had. It was still an outing, however, and to Louise an outing meant clothes that were not everyday, and a carefully performed toilet, which left her looking just the same, but feeling different.

Frank was waiting for her when she came down from her room, where she had been arranging herself since lunch. Anne wanted the car to go to the village, which was only half a mile away, but beyond the limits of Anne's legs; so Frank was taking Louise in his little truck, which said: 'F. C. NIXON, MKT GDNR, STONE FARM, HADLEIGH, BEDS.' in home-painted letters on the door.

Louise climbed into the truck and sat down with a surprised jolt on the flat, unyielding seat. Anne had wandered into the garden to see them off, walking well back on her heels and sticking out her front in a way she had assumed since her pregnancy, although it would be a long time before her naturally thick figure altered enough to make this necessary.

'Give old Bruce my love,' she said, without enthusiasm.

Louise leaned out of the glassless window. 'Can I tell him about—you know?'

'If you like. I'm past caring. He won't be interested though.'

'His god-daughter? Of course he will.' Louise was glad to have some news to cheer Bruce's twilight hibernation.

He was not interested, however. He had no children, and anyone of a younger generation was to him mere protoplasm, incapable of leading an existence of any significance.

He sat in his darkened library, with a scarf round his neck, because the thermometer, although high, was lower than yesterday, and grunted appreciatively while the housekeeper creaked in with Rockingham china and the anchovy toast and sponge cake that he loved.

Bruce looked at the clock. 'Right on time,' he nodded. 'When one gets to our age, Louise, one likes meals to be punctual.'

He made Louise feel very old. He had surrendered to the years, and she felt that if she did not appear to have done the same, he would think her skittish.

When he asked her: 'How is life with you, my dear? Are you happy?' she was going to say: 'Perfectly,' before she caught the disbelieving look in his faded eye.

'You know how it is,' she said glad in a way to be able to

grumble to someone who expected nothing else. 'It's not easy, being dependent on one's children.'

Bruce cut the cake and smiled, his beliefs confirmed.

'Don't think they're not good to me,' Louise hastened to say. 'They're wonderful. But however hard they try, it's not like having your own home.'

Bruce munched, and had a little trouble with his teeth. 'You're not happy, are you, my dear?' He did not ask it. He said it.

Louise toyed with the fine old lace tablecloth, which might, she fancied, have been hers, but would surely be ruined by now if it had been. What should she say? Did it matter what she told Bruce? He probably did not care enough about anyone but himself to remember what she said to him over tea. And so she asked, without dissembling: 'What have I done, Bruce? What have I done wrong? There ought to be some reward in life for having lived through the longest part of it.'

Bruce raised the grey feelers of his eyebrows. 'Why should there be? You're a criminal, didn't you know?'

'What do you mean?' Louise frowned. 'I——'

'You, my dear, have committed the crime of growing older. The greatest crime in our society. People shouldn't do it. It doesn't pay.' He wagged his head, and rang the jerky porcelain bell for the housekeeper to bring more hot water.

Louise was depressed when she left Bruce. Was that what it was like to be seventy-five? Would she be like that—a passionless hermit, waiting merely for the tedious ritual of days to end?

'It's dreadful to grow old,' she told Frank, driving off with him in the truck, which he had parked in the tunnel of drive between the laurels.

'Is he very old then?' Frank asked. 'Getting to be a hundred, or something?'

'Heavens, no. He's only seventy-five, but he's given up trying. He's finished, and he makes me think I ought to think about being finished, too.'

'You!' Frank's laugh vied with the gear-box to be heard. 'God bless you, why you've only just started. You'll be marrying again one of these days, and surprise us all, I shouldn't doubt.'

'Don't be silly, Frank.' Louise began to feel better.

'No boy friend?' Frank had fought a successful battle with the Feeding Stuffs Officer, and was feeling jaunty.

'How could I? I never meet anybody.'

'What about old Harry? Now there's a nice, spry young widower for you.' This was the sort of feeble joke that Louise and Frank enjoyed together.

'Poor old Bruce,' she said, shaking off the enervating mists of the stagnated house she had left. 'He's really given up the struggle. To think I might once have married him! But perhaps he wouldn't have got like that if I had, unless, of course, I'd died, like his wife did.'

'Why didn't you marry him?' Frank asked.

'Oh, I don't know.' Louise leaned back on the hard seat and clasped her knee. 'You know how it is when you're young. He was a good deal older than me, but he was very attractive, though you wouldn't think it now. We used to go skating together. It seems as if there were more frosts in those days. And we went to the same dances. But it was just one of those things. . . . Too good to last, perhaps.'

She had once reminisced in this vein to Anne, and Anne had said: 'You mean he never asked you.' But Frank said eagerly: 'Romantic, isn't it—the past? I bet you could tell some tales.'

'Not many, I'm afraid. I was quite gay though, and pretty in a way, I think, though I always had trouble making my hair stay up. Those curling tongs! One could never move without them. But I married so young, you see.'

'I dare say.' Frank avoided the subject of Louise's husband. He never said what he thought about Dudley's insulting hostility. He took refuge in a meaningless: 'Ah, well, life goes on, they say.'

'Slowly,' Louise said. 'I thought, when I was with Anne's godfather, that mine was chugging to its end. But it isn't really. Do you know, Frank, I picked up a man not long ago. In London.'

'Good for you,' Frank said. 'London's the place for that, I hear.'

'In Lyons,' Louise continued, 'and we've become friends.'

'So you have got a boy friend?'

'No, but—well, in a way. Miriam thinks he's dreadful, although she's never seen him. But you know what Miriam is.'

Frank nodded.

'But he's different, you know. You'd think he was quite ordinary, and rather pathetic, if you went to buy a bed from him, but when you get to know him——' Louise was eager to talk about Gordon Disher to someone who would bother to listen, but Frank jammed on the brakes with a jolt that gritted her teeth, and stopped the truck for a girl who was standing by the side of the road with her hand raised, and her skirt blowing against her legs.

The girl went to the window on Frank's side. 'Give a person a ride?' she asked, staring up at him. She was pretty, with chestnut hair hanging over one eye, and an acquired resemblance to some film star whose name Louise could not remember.

Frank got out and the girl climbed nimbly in and sat balanced between the two seats, closer to Frank than to Louise.

'This is Freda Rivett, Mother,' Frank said, in some embarrassment. 'My mother-in-law, Freda.'

'Oh, I've seen you in the village,' the girl said, tossing back the lock of hair, which immediately fell down again, as she meant it to. 'Staying at the Stone Farm with your daughter, aren't you? Well, that's a nice enough place, I dare say. I live in that cottage on the corner, by the memorial.'

'I've seen it,' Louise said, anxious to be friendly. 'It's so pretty, with those roses, and the little porch. Quite the nicest house in the village.'

'Which isn't saying much.' The girl's eyelashes were endless, and curled at the tips. 'What a hole. I'm getting out of it as soon as I can. I've had an offer of a position in town.' She looked at Frank, staring at his profile, while he kept his gaze on the road.

'Have you?' he mumbled. 'I didn't know.'

'Oh, well, you can't know everything that goes on in the village. We don't see you about so much since you got married. Quite a stranger to your old friends. Very nice of you, I'm sure, to give me a lift.' She pitched her voice affectedly and tapped her long red fingernails on her knee, which showed in a nylon curve below her hitched-up skirt.

Then she put her head on one side, smoothed her skirt, and spoke less haughtily. 'I recognized your truck coming half a mile off,' she said, showing her white, uneven teeth in a smile. ' "That's Frank," I said, so I stopped walking.'

Louise's mind was churning. Why did she talk like this to Frank? How did she know the truck so well? Why, when the space on which she sat was so narrow, was there a gap between her and Louise? She must be pressing closely against Frank.

But I trust him, Louise told herself, as she stepped clumsily down from the truck outside the grey house. The girl had said: 'Why don't you drop Mrs What-is-it first, to save taking her out of her way, and then run me home, Frank, if you've time?' and Frank, looking hunted, had mumbled agreement.

Louise went into the house and began to tell Anne about Bruce.

'Where's Frank?' Anne asked. 'Harry says one of the goats has broken its tether, and he can't catch it.'

'He went up to the village for something,' Louise said. 'He'll be back directly.' She would wait to see whether Frank told Anne about picking up the girl with the eyelashes, before she began to get worried.

Before Frank turned the corner into the village, Freda put her hand on his arm and said: 'Drop me here. This'll do. I'll get a bit of air before I go in.'

Frank stopped the truck under an oak tree that bowed over the road, and waited for Freda to get out. If it had been Louise or Anne, he would have jumped out himself and helped them down.

'Well, go on,' he said. 'Aren't you going to get out?'

'Not until you hand me down.' The girl laughed at him. 'I thought you were such a little gentleman these days.'

'All right.' Frank got out, walked round the truck and opened the door. Freda stepped down daintily, keeping her hand in his after she was standing in the road.

Her nails scratched his palm. Frank pulled his hand away. 'Look, Freda,' he said roughly. 'For God's sake, leave a chap alone, can't you? I'm married. Get that into your head.'

The girl leaned against the truck and laughed at him again. 'Oh, pooh,' she said, 'What kind of married is that with that lazy slut you've got? You were daft to take up with her, and you know it. She's no good to you.'

'Shut up, Freda.' Frank clenched his hands to keep them off her body. 'Anne's a good girl. She's the right wife for me. I love her, do you hear? You don't understand that.'

Freda lowered her lashes. 'I understand what it was like with you and me before you met her.' She came closer and put her hand on his shirt. 'And you haven't forgotten either, have you, Frank? What it was like——'

Frank sweated, kissed her roughly, jumped into the truck and drove off, leaving the girl standing smiling in the road.

'You've got lipstick on your face,' Anne said placidly, when Frank came in.

'Damn it—excuse me, Mother.' He wiped his mouth with the back of his hand. 'Look here, Anny, I——'

Louise sat in terror on the edge of her chair, and waited for the storm to break; but Anne kissed Frank lightly on the cheek and said: 'Don't worry, Frankie boy. I shouldn't let you out on your own when that red-headed bitch is around, should I?'

Frank relaxed, and Louise released her grip on the sides of the chair.

'I don't want you to think anything wrong.' Frank wrinkled his forehead.

'I don't. I know you. And I don't care what you did before you met me. God knows I had my moments, too, didn't I, Mother?'

Louise was silent. She did not want to be dragged into this.

'Remember that Italian?' Anne chuckled. 'I wish you'd seen him, Frank. He was hot.'

'I'll bet,' Frank said, without resentment. 'It's the Latin blood, they say.'

'Don't sit down,' Anne said. 'You've got to go out. One of the goats is loose again. Here——' She stopped him on his way to the door. 'You've missed a bit of Rita Hayworth's lipstick.' Anne fished a grubby handkerchief out of her sleeve and wiped his mouth. Frank pursed his lips like a child being cleaned up after a meal.

'Thanks, dear. Well, I'd better go and see about that goat. Come out and help me catch it, Anny?'

'If I must.' They went out arm in arm.

Louise got slowly up from her chair and went automatically to the sink to peel the potatoes for supper. She was relieved and amazed. How extraordinary they were, dealing with the situation like that, but how devastatingly sensible ! They talked as if they were quite sure of each other. For the first time, Louise began to see that there could be something fundamental and lasting about this marriage.

Anne was sulky again by the time she returned with Frank. He had given her the goat to hold while he fixed its bedding, and it had dragged the rope through her hand, chafing the skin. Anne always made a fuss about the smallest physical pain. She put an unnecessary amount of salve on her hand, and grumbled protractedly at Frank. 'Enough,' he said with a grin, 'to make a man want to go out and kiss a girl again.'

'Go, then.' Anne pushed him away when he bent to look at her hand. 'I don't care. Maybe she likes the smell of goats.'

Such a short time ago, it seemed to Louise, that she had watched and understood every new facet of Anne's developing character. But there came a time with all children, when they grew sly, and did not tell you things, and after that it grew harder to understand them and the way they behaved. Louise was puzzled by Anne and Frank, but not worried. They had worked out their rough-and-ready solution to the problem of living together, and did not seem to notice its inadequacies.

Anne was at her worst with Frank when his people came. They lived in the next county, but they did not come very often, for they liked Anne no better than she liked them.

When Frank looked up from a letter and said: 'Mum and Dad want to come Sunday,' Anne said, 'Oh, God!' and banged a plate down on the table so that the toast bounced off it.

'Now, Anny,' Frank said, putting the toast back on the plate. 'You haven't got to be like that. They're your people too, now, you know.'

'Don't rub it in.' Anne sat down heavily. She was wearing a faded cotton wrapper, with the front of her hair in pins and her face still unpowdered, although Frank had been up and working for two hours.

'They only come to get eggs,' she grumbled. 'If you didn't keep chickens, they wouldn't come near us. Hah! What a loss that would be.'

Louise wondered how Frank could bear her to talk like this. He looked hurt, so she ventured to say: 'You mustn't mind what Anne says, Frank. At these times, one is more nervy, especially in the mornings.'

'What's that got to do with it? I didn't want to see Frank's people before I got this way. Stop dragging in my condition, Mother. You're like some old midwife.'

'I know what it is,' Louise said soothingly. 'I've been through it, don't forget. I know it makes you jumpy.'

'You can't know.' Anne was determined to make a grievance of her pregnancy for the whole of its span. 'You can't possibly have felt like this, or you wouldn't have gone on having us. You don't know how ghastly I feel.'

'Indeed, I do.' Embarked on the absorbing topic, Louise forgot that Frank was there, and fidgeting. 'I was sick every morning with Eva for three solid months.'

'Well, I was sick last week,' Anne retaliated. She had stuck her finger down her throat to make Frank feel sorry for her. 'I'm sick all the time.'

'Looks like rain.' Frank cleared his throat. 'Maybe I won't need to water to-day.' The female talk passed over his head, ignoring him.

'When I was carrying Frank's brother,' Mrs Nixon said comfortably, settling back in her chair, 'I hardly got a wink of sleep, for the way he'd kick.'

'There they go.' Frank's father raised his eyes to heaven. 'They're all the same. Give them a baby on the way and they'll talk it to death long before anyone sets eyes on it.'

Frank grinned. 'Let's go out for a bit, Dad, till lunch is ready.' He pretended to be exasperated by the feminine conversation, but actually, he liked to think of the three women in the house talking in that conceited, martyred way about the thing that women were made for, and the centre of them his Anne, who had never before been reduced to talking like a woman.

Frank's father was a wiry little man, with a spiked moustache, which he had copied from the sergeants as soon as he got out of the Army. His mother was a slow, suspicious woman with sad, round eyes, who had grown too big for her husband. When they sat in a bus together, she spread half-way over his side of the seat. She was a woman of few ideas, and those she had were rooted in her as deeply as dandelions. You could argue at her for hours on end, and she would listen to you with bovine eyes and then say: 'You have your way of thinking, and I have mine.'

One of her convictions had always been that Frank would marry a healthy, willing girl, whom she visualized permanently in a print apron, with her hair tied back and a smell of baking about her. When he married Anne, his father had done his best to see it through Frank's eyes, as a step up for him, but his mother thought it was a step down from the kind of woman the Nixons had always married.

Anne felt her resentment and made no effort to disarm it.

To her, a mother-in-law, whoever she was, must always be more of a liability than an acquisition. She often wondered at Frank's friendliness towards Louise, who was, after all, his mother-in-law, and therefore a burden.

She would not lift a finger for Frank's parents. If they chose to come, they must take cold ham, if there was any; if not, Frank must cook them bacon and eggs. This Sunday, Louise had cooked the lunch, and tried to make up for Anne's deficiencies as a hostess by waiting on Frank's parents over-zealously, so that they felt quite uncomfortable, and Mrs Nixon began to wonder whether Anne's mother was trying to take over her home from her, or what.

'If you could spare us a few eggs, Frank——' Mrs Nixon said after lunch, with that false humility that food rationing imposed on its victims, even towards their relations.

'Frank has to send them all to the packing station,' Anne said. 'It's the law.'

'They won't miss a few.' Frank pushed back his chair, anxious to get his parents out of doors where Anne would not follow to make things difficult. 'Let's go out and see what there is, shall we? Mum and Dad, I want you to see the pigs, too. There'll be several more of them before you can turn round. Daisy won't be long now. Come and see her. She's splendid.'

'Yes,' Anne said, 'you must see Daisy before you go.' although the Nixons had no intention of going before they had been given tea.

Anne stayed in the house while everyone else went out. She did not want to look at Daisy, so hugely and happily gravid. It made her feel that she was only one of the farm animals herself, fulfilling her functions to everyone's satisfaction. If only they would not talk about it so much, it would be more bearable. Her mother could not keep off the subject, even when snubbed, and Anne supposed that her interest would increase morbidly as time went on, and extend suffocatingly to the infant itself.

While Frank and his parents admired the mammoth sow and scratched its harsh back with a stick, Louise stood in the background with her hands over her hair and wondered what

Daisy thought about it all, if anything. Did a pig feel afraid, as she had each time, and forgotten immediately afterwards what it was she had feared ? Frank would be up all night, excited as a boy, when Daisy had her litter. Louise would get out of bed at intervals to put the kettle on in case Frank came in, and Anne would snore through the whole night's drama, and complain in the morning that she had not been able to sleep for all the walking about. Louise had been through tarrowing time at Stone Farm, and knew the routine.

Frank's parents left after tea, taking three dozen eggs and a basket of vegetables. There had been no serious arguments, and Frank was beginning to hope that the mellowing process he looked forward to in Anne was already beginning to take effect.

'That's that, then,' Frank said, as the little box of a car drove off with the front seat full of Mrs Nixon and the back seat full of eggs and vegetables. 'A nice family day.' He rumpled Anne's hair, patted Louise on the arm to thank her for the cooking she had done, and went whistling off to run the chopping machine for his evening feeds.

Ten minutes later, he came back ashen-faced, staring at the mangled fingers in the blood-filled cradle of his other hand.

After Frank had been taken to hospital in the doctor's car, Anne went all to pieces. She sat on the floor with one of the dogs, and cried into its neck, while Louise went out alone to shut up the chickens. Fortunately the goats were already in the shed. Louise knew that she would never have been able to get them in. She had seen even Frank being dragged this way and that by the rope of an insanely prancing young Billy.

When Louise got back to the house, Anne's tears had dried to gasping sniffs. She had poured herself out a glass of gin.

'Oh, Anne, you know Frank doesn't like you to drink now,' Louise said. 'I'll make you a cup of tea instead.'

'I need a drink.' Anne swallowed half the gin neat, and shuddered. 'Better. Have one, Mother?'

'I think I will. I must say I feel a bit shaky, too. What a

dreadful thing to happen. I'll never forget seeing Frank come in at that door——'

'Don't talk about it,' Anne said tersely. 'I can't bear it.'

Louise was surprised that Anne was so upset. She never showed Frank any affection when he was there ; but she must really care about him more than anyone guessed.

'You shall go to bed early, dear,' Louise said tenderly, 'and I'll give you some aspirin, so that you can get a good sleep and not worry about Frank.'

'I'm not worrying about him,' Anne said. 'Silly fool, doing a thing like that when he's used the cutter hundreds of times. He'll be all right in a couple of days. The doctor said he would. But that hand! It looked so horrible when he came in. I'd given anything not to have seen it. It's made me feel as if I were turned inside out. He never should have brought it in like that. He might at least have covered it.'

'How can you be so selfish, Anne?' Louise asked wonderingly.

'I'm not. But Frank knows what it does to me to see blood. He might have thought . . . But just coming in and standing there with that stuck expression on his face, and the blood all thick like oil—ugh! Let's have another drink and play the gramophone and think about something else.'

Anne had three drinks, and having recovered from her nausea, demanded supper and went to bed quite cheerfully, with the dogs on Frank's side of the bed. Her mother had seen her more concerned when one of the dogs had a splinter in its paw.

She fetched a cloth and wiped up some blood that she had missed on the tiled floor. Kneeling, she shook her head and said: 'Oh, dear,' out loud, as she did sometimes when she was alone.

Louise rose early, to be dressed and downstairs by the time Harry came at eight o'clock, so that she could tell him what to do.

Frank had been fretting as he was carried off in the car, his hand a swollen lump of bandages, and Louise had reassured him: 'Now, you're not to worry. We'll take care of everything. Harry will be here to-morrow, and we'll see to everything.'

Upset as she was about Frank, she felt a pleasurable sense of responsibility. She was in charge now. She would hold the fort for Frank.

By half-past eight, Harry had not appeared. Louise put on a pair of Anne's old shoes and went out to start feeding the animals. They were making an impatient clamour, and the sow was rubbing herself against the gate of the sty so forcefully that Louise was afraid she might break out.

She mixed the chickens' food, and staggered through the dew with buckets that were too heavy for her, fearing that the food was wrong and that the chickens were grumbling at her as if she were an incompetent waitress who had got her orders mixed.

The two nanny goats were weaving about among their dirty bedding. Louise remembered that Frank always milked them before breakfast. What now? She looked at her small hands and then at the bleating goats, of whom she was afraid. She never went into their shed unless Frank was with her.

If Harry did not come, she would have to get someone from the village to help. She went back to the house and called up the stairs to Anne. The bed creaked, and Anne answered something half awake and unintelligible. Louise longed for a cup of coffee, but the goats could not wait. Which would be quicker—to run up to the village herself, or to get Anne out of bed to drive the car there?

The bed did not creak any more. Anne had gone back to sleep. It was beginning to rain. Louise would have to walk to the village and get Dick Bennett or someone to come and help. If the men were all at work, she would find some woman who could do it. There must be someone in the village who knew how to milk a goat.

She tied her scarf over her head, and was going out of the back door, when she saw Harry amble into the yard, looking more bent than ever, as if somebody had pushed him over and he could not straighten up.

Louise ran to him, her heart full of gratitude to the derelict old man, because he had come to help her, and everything would be all right now. She did not know whether to chide him for being late ; but when she came close to him, she realized that chiding would be pointless, for Harry was not sober. He was not drunk, but Louise knew him well enough to see that he had not breakfasted off tea.

Louise told him what had happened, and asked him if he could manage the work.

'Why not?' he answered, aggrieved. 'Young Frank ain't the only one who knows how to care for a few fowl, and such.'

'Please milk the goats first,' Louise said, trying to order instead of beg, because she wanted Harry to understand that she was in charge. 'It's long past their time.'

'All right, all right,' Harry grumbled. 'One thing at a time, gal. One thing at a time. I got to light me pipe first.' He sat down on a bale of straw and went through a fumbling ritual of cramming his pipe with dark, straggly tobacco, and striking several matches before the smoke belched out, while the goats trampled and bleated, and a small, pointed beard was lodged plaintively over the edge of the half door.

Harry grumbled to himself and munched his jaws all morning, and Louise did not expect to see him return after lunch. He came back, however, with beer on his breath, and worked slower and slower as the shadows lengthened, with frequent maddening pauses to consider such details as a loose pin on a barrow wheel, which were unimportant when there were so many other things to attend to.

Louise had not realized how slow he was when Frank was there doing most of the work. By the end of the afternoon, there were still dozens of things to be done, and the lock on the feed-house door was not mended yet, although Harry had been on his way to do it every time Louise passed him.

Anne had stayed in the house all day, reading Gordon Disher's *Kisses and Corpses*, which Louise had lent her. Louise asked her if she would come out and help, but Anne said: 'Why should I? It's no concern of mine, and I don't see why you're running round in small circles about it, either. Harry's there, isn't he? It's not my worry.'

'But it's Frank's living,' Louise protested. 'And you are married to him, after all.'

'That's his worry.' Anne went back to the book. 'This is tripe, Mother,' she said without looking up. 'Do you really know the man who wrote it? One never imagines anyone actually sitting down and writing this kind of bilge.'

'I think it's very good. It takes a lot of skill. I'm sure I wouldn't have any idea how to go about it, and I don't suppose you would, either.'

'I wouldn't try,' Anne said. 'I haven't sunk quite that low yet.'

Louise went out and swished angrily with a stick at the nettles outside the kitchen door as she went by them. Harry was shambling about in the goat-shed with his head lowered, looking like one of the inmates. 'Please hurry,' Louise urged, 'or we'll never get done before it's time for you to go, and we don't want Frank to come back and find things all gone to pieces, do we?'

She hoped to appeal to whatever pride in his work was buried in the desiccated coils of his brain; but he stopped what he was doing, as he always did when addressed, and said: 'It's all very well for him. He lays in bed there at the hospital and leaves me to do all the work. Don't nag me, gal.' He moved slower and slower, like a clock running down. At five-thirty to the second, he pulled his watch out of his sagging waistcoat, leaned the hay-fork against the water-barrel, and made a bee-line for the gate, without a word to Louise.

Louise had worked with desperate incompetence all day in a drizzle of rain, and after supper she was exhausted. It was a proud exhaustion, however. Frank would surely be pleased with her. Although she had made many mistakes, and it was a pity there were quite so many eggs in that basket she had dropped, she had not let Frank down. If she could only keep it up until he came back, she would have accomplished something really useful for once in her life.

She telephoned to the hospital, surprised that Anne had not yet done so.

'They say he's fine,' she told her daughter. 'The woman I talked to was very nice and helpful. Not a bit like someone in a London hospital. She said that the hand's been stitched, but he'll probably be out in a few days.'

'He'd better be,' Anne said, 'or he'll find his mother-in-law in the hospital with him. You've really pooped yourself, Mother.'

'I have, haven't I?' said Louise with pleasure.

'Good of you,' Anne said shortly. Louise was glad of her unwonted praise, although it would have been more help if Anne had stirred herself to do some of the work.

Anne yawned. 'I'm tired,' she said, although she had done nothing all day. 'Let's go to bed.'

Even the hard, iron bed in Anne's uncomfortable spare room seemed like paradise to Louise. Dragging herself up the stairs towards it, she stopped, remembering that she had not locked the chicken-houses. Frank was always most particular about that, for there had been chicken thieves in the neighbourhood. How dreadful if he were to come back from hospital and find his precious poultry gone, through Louise's negligence!

She put on Frank's jacket, which was hanging behind the kitchen door, and went out with a torch. The rain had drifted away, blown before a rising wind, and the moon was scudding in and out of the clouds like a racing yacht. As Louise picked her way along the path to the yard, she heard the restless tossing of the trees, like tired people looking forward to a sleepless night.

She did not like to be out on her own after dark, especially in the country, where there were more unexplained noises than in town. There was a strange noise in the pigsties, but it was probably only poor Daisy trying to settle her overburdened bulk. On her way back from the chicken-houses, walking in the middle of the yard in case marauders should be lurking in the shadow of the sheds, Louise heard the noise again. One of the pigs was grunting and bumping about against the walls.

She stopped dead. Not that, she thought, transfixed in a wave of moonlight, with the torch held before her like a bludgeon. Not that, please, her tired mind begged. That would be too much.

She began to walk on, but hesitated and turned back. She listened over the gate of the run outside Daisy's little house, and knew that something was wrong. Picking her way over the wallowed mud, she crossed the run, bent to open the low door, and shone her torch into the sty. There was no doubt about it. Daisy was in labour.

'You would be!' Louise said wildly, and ran back to the house to tell Anne. Anne would be no help, but Louise had to tell someone. She could not bear this crisis on her own.

'So what?' Anne said, slumped against the pillows with a melting bar of chocolate staining the sheets. 'Pigs have babies every day. Let her get on with it.'

'But there's something you have to do for them, and I don't know what it is.'

'If I were a pig,' Anne said indolently, 'all I'd want anyone to do would be to leave me alone to get on with the revolting business by myself.'

'No, no.' Louise wrung her hands. 'You have to help them in some way. You know Frank always stays up with the pigs when they have babies.'

'More fool him.' Anne kicked her foot to move the weight of a dog. 'He's daft about those beastly sows.'

'But he has to. I seem to remember he once told me why, but I can't think what it was. Oh, please, Anne, put on a coat there's a love, and come and look at Daisy.'

'What good would I be?' Anne slid farther under the bedclothes. 'I'm not a midwife.'

'Neither am I. But if you'd just come and look——' Louise turned away forlornly.

'What are you going to do?' Anne asked with the comfortable interest of one who is going to stay in bed while someone else is up and busy.

'I don't know what to do. I'd better fetch Harry, I think.' Louise thought that Anne would at least offer to come with her to Harry's cottage, but all Anne said was: 'Take one of the dogs if you're going down the road. Take Boxer. He's the fiercest.'

Louise felt safer without the booming, slobbering dog, who was always charging against her like an American footballer, intent on knocking her down. She took him downstairs, however, and as soon as they were outside, he bounded off into the darkness, barking frantically, and was seen no more that night.

Feeling very small, Louise was blown down the road by the wind to where Harry's cottage stood lopsidedly on the edge of the wood. The trees were in torment now, hurling themselves this way and that with a noise like the sea. There was a light in Harry's window. Thank goodness, he was still up. Harry would help her. He would know what to do. Thank God for Harry, Louise thought; but when she knocked with her fist on the bare door, and Harry opened it, lurching in the doorway against the fumy background of his slovenly kitchen, she saw that he was quite drunk. He gibbered at her. He did not even understand what she said.

Louise turned and ran, retching at the memory of the old man's breath as he swayed towards her. She struggled back against the wind, pushed open the heavy yard gate, and went in dread to the pig sty. One baby pig had been born. It lay dead on the bloody straw where Daisy's weight had flattened it.

'Oh, poor Daisy!' Louise cried out in distress. 'I'm sorry. I'm so sorry——'

The sow had her eyes closed and was making a noise like fifty sows. Louise wanted to leave her, yet had to stay. Kneeling in the doorway with her skirt in the mire and Frank's jacket hunched up round her ears, Louise watched helplessly as one by one the pigs were born and crushed to death by the lubberly weight of their barbaric mother.

Louise crept back to the house, the strength drained out of

D

her mind and body. There was something she should have done. She did not know what it was. Frank would have known, but he was not there, and she had failed him. She had lost Daisy's litter, and she did not know how she was going to face his disappointment.

Early the next morning, Dick Bennett knocked at the door on his way to work to enquire about Frank. Louise dragged herself out of bed, feeling as if she had not slept, and came down in her dressing-gown to tell Dick about the horrors of the night.

'She should have been in the farrowing pen,' he said. 'It's made so that the piglets fall through it, you see, so the sow can't roll on them.'

'I didn't know——'

'Why should you? You did your best, I'm sure. It wasn't proper that you should be there at all. No place for a lady. I wish you'd have fetched me. It was no use thinking of old Harry. I don't know why Frank keeps on with him. Poor old Frank. That's a lot of money gone down the drain for him. Poor old Frank.'

He bicycled away shaking his head, and left Louise feeling worse than ever.

Harry did not come that morning. Louise had not expected that he would. Feeling her age, she forced herself to the yard to do what she could for the clamouring livestock. The goats were rattling their small, hard hoofs against the door. They would have to be milked. Someone had to do it, and Louise had been through such a bad time already that she thought despairingly that it might as well be her.

Walking like a condemned man, she fetched a bucket and slowly lifted the latch of the shed. She had not milked a goat since she was a child. She remembered nothing about it except that it was difficult.

She chirped to the goats placatingly as she went gingerly inside. They watched her movements with unfocused eyes. 'Nice girls,' Louise said foolishly. Perhaps they would stand

still when they realized that she was going to help them. She
put a collar on one of them and tied it to the wall. It strained
back with straddled legs and bulging eyes, trying to choke
itself, but at least it was standing still. When Louise knelt in
the straw and touched it with trembling hands, it began to
thresh insanely about the narrow stall, kicked over the bucket
and knocked Louise on to her back.

'You fool!' Louise screamed. She scrambled up and ran
out of the shed, sobbing with fright and with rage at the stupid
animal's ingratitude.

Anne was in the kitchen, surprisingly up and dressed.

'Anne.' Louise stood before her defeatedly. 'I'm finished.
I can't go on any longer.' Her tears started again.

Anne stared at her. 'What on earth's the matter, Mother?'

'It's the goats. The goats have to be milked. Harry's not
'here, and I—I don't know how to do it.'

Is that all? Well, my goodness, I know how to do *that*.'

'You do?' Louise stopped a sob in mid-breath.

'Of course. I learned at that farm camp you used to send me
to; don't you remember? I don't do it when Frank's here,
because he thinks I don't do it right. He's so damned particular so I let him get on with it. Come on, Mother. Mop your
eyes with the dish towel. Don't let's be silly. I'll milk the
blasted goats till their insides drop out, if they're not
careful.'

'God bless you,' Louise said fervently. She had never loved
Anne so well. While Anne was milking the goats, with shouts
and curses, Louise drove Daisy into an empty sty. Turning
away her head, she took the dead piglets out one by one on a
shovel and buried them in a shallow grave behind the manure
heap. Looking round guiltily in case Anne should see her, she
said a *Hail Mary* over the pigs before she left them, and tried
to comfort herself with the thought that now at least they
would never squeal under the slaughterer's knife.

Anne helped Louise all that day. She worked carelessly,
with many oaths, and almost seemed to enjoy herself.

Louise told her: 'I could never have managed without you. It's sweet of you to help.'

'Why shouldn't I?' Anne was impossible to praise or thank. 'It's my property, isn't it? Even though Frank paid for it. With all his worldly goods he me endowed, and my God, what hellish goods they are!' She tugged at a hundredweight sack of meal which the corn merchant had dumped in the yard when they were not looking.

'You shouldn't do that, dear. You'll strain yourself.' Louise fluttered round, pushing at the sack with futile hands. 'Leave the thing where it is.'

'Can't. It may rain to-night. Damn that man. He'd have taken it inside if Frank had been here.'

'We'll put a mackintosh over it, or something. Do leave it, Anne. You'll hurt the baby.'

'So what? Don't *talk* to me, Mother. No one can talk when they're lifting things.'

'What you doin'?' Harry had come into the yard, and stood behind them, swaying and blinking his eyes. He did not look like himself. His face had fallen away to nothing; his lips were sucked in, and a patchy beard grizzled his bony chin.

'What you doin', I say?' he demanded.

'Playing the piano,' Anne grunted. 'Can't you see?'

'Help us with this sack,' Louise said in her most command-ing voice, which came out higher than she intended. 'It's too heavy for Mrs Nixon'

Harry leered at her. 'I ain't taking orders from no woman.'

'Well, then, get on and do some work, and we won't have to tell you. There's too much for us to do. To-morrow's the poultry man's day and the chickens have got to be killed and trussed. Harry, you must help us.' Louise's commands changed to pleading.

'Must, must, must. Who's musting me?' Harry wagged his head idiotically.

'Go away,' Anne said. 'You're drunk.'

Harry stood for a while and watched her drag the sack over the sill of the shed door, and then seeing that he was going to get no more attention, wandered off, muttering and moving his hands jerkily from the wrists.

'You shouldn't have sent him away,' Louise said. 'We need him.'

'Not in that state. Drunken old sod. We can get on better without him. I'll take a stiff drink to-morrow and then murder some chickens.

'I thought you couldn't stand the sight of blood.'

'I can't, but chicken's blood is different. Thinner. And the brutes look better dead. I'll do it. Don't panic, Mother. I'm not such a fool as you think.'

Louise was amazed at the change that had come over Anne. She seemed suddenly to have embraced the cause of looking after Frank's interests. It was delightful working together like this, tiring themselves out in the hot, steamy sun that had followed the storm. Anne was monosyllabic and disparaging, but Louise felt very close to her, and wished that it could always be like this. Perhaps now that Anne had overcome her stubborn apathy, she would go on helping Frank. They would work together as a team, running the place as a model farm. Anne might even have her name added to Frank's on the side of the truck: 'F. C. AND A. NIXON, MKT GDNRS, STONE FARM, etc.'

Standing back to wait while a bucket filled under the tap, Louise was lost in a charming dream of the future. Anne would be so much happier now, and she could go on working, if she was careful, almost until the baby was due. Country women did it. Perhaps Anne would become a real country woman, as nature had intended when she gave her that physique. How pleased Frank would be when he came back and found Anne working for him in one of his blue shirts with the sleeves rolled up. He would adore her.

Frank came back unexpectedly the next day. The hospital had been telephoning all morning to ask Anne to come and fetch him, but since they could not get an answer and they wanted his bed, they had sent him home in a hospital car.

Finding no one in the house, Frank came to the yard with

his hand in a sling, and found Anne contemplating a tin bath full of dead chickens.

'She killed them all,' Louise said, bursting with the news of Anne's heroism. 'Isn't she wonderful? She's been working like a black while you've been away. She's been absolutely grand.'

An amazed grin spread over Frank's candid face. He went towards Anne to embrace her, but she said: 'Don't touch me in that suit. I'm filthy.'

He kissed her just the same. 'You're a wonderful girl,' he said. 'I'm proud of you.'

'You don't have to be. It's a good thing to get some of these damned birds out of the way, if you ask me.'

'These will have to be trussed before Barker's man comes,' Frank said, automatically becoming efficient. 'Where's Harry, anyway?'

'Drunk, of course. You might have known he'd be no use.'

Frank picked up a chicken and put it on the table. 'I shan't be able to do much with this hand for a while.' He frowned impatiently at his bandaged fingers. 'Anny, do you think you could possibly—if I show you how——?'

Anne had intended to attempt the plucking and trussing, but now she threw the chicken back into the bath, where it landed with a wet flop among its fellows.

'For God's sake, Frank,' she said, in her old, surly tone, ' I've been working myself to death ever since you went and mashed yourself up. I'm not doing any more. I'm tired and I want food. You'll have to get one of your village pals to help you.' She wiped her hands on a sack and walked out of the shed. She went back to the house and took off her shoes, and for the remainder of Louise's visit, she did not go near the yard again, except to ask Frank for money when she wanted to go into Bedford.

'It was you that did most of the work, wasn't it, Mother?' Frank asked when Louise brought out a mug of tea to him, since Anne would not wait for hers until he came in.

'No, honestly, Anne did work hard, after the first day. I

can't think why she suddenly did it, but even more, I can't think why she suddenly stopped as soon as you came home.'

'Anne's a funny girl,' Frank said thoughtfully.

Louise nodded silently, not wanting to criticize his wife, even though it was her daughter.

'You were wonderful, Mother,' Frank said, shaking himself out of his thoughts, and smiling at Louise over the mug. 'I can't thank you enough for helping me out.'

'I enjoyed it. I don't often get a chance to be useful. I just wish I could have done more. We had to leave a lot of things.' She looked at the ground for a moment, biting her lip, and then looked up and said urgently: 'Frank, there's something I've got to tell you. It's not very nice. You won't like it.'

'Spill it.' He balanced the mug on the top of the fence. 'I can take anything after that hospital.'

'You know I promised you everything would be all right? Well, it isn't. I did something wrong. Come with me. I want to show you something.'

Frank followed her to the humped earth behind the manure heap. 'What's this?' he asked. 'Been doing some digging? What are you going to grow here—pumpkins?'

'Don't joke, please,' Louise said miserably. 'Frank, it's—it's Daisy's babies.'

*   *   *

'Anny,' Frank said, when they were undressing in their bedroom, 'how about asking your mother to stay on a bit longer than she planned ? I know she was supposed to go at the end of the week, but I'm a bit of a cripple now. I need all the help I can get.' He held his damaged hand awkwardly in front of him. He was trying to undress with one hand, not liking to ask Anne to help him.

'I shouldn't have thought Mother was much help.' Anne pulled a cotton nightdress over her head and tied the sash too loosely, so that she looked bulkier than ever.

'She is, though. You'd be surprised. Look what she did while I was away.'

'I suppose I didn't do a thing?'

'Of course, dear, I know you did the most of it, but still——

'Still what?' Anne was brushing her teeth in the china basin, making grotesque faces.

'Well, she feels so bad about the pigs. I thought if she could think I needed her here, it would make her feel a bit better about it, see, and not think it's the end of the world; though, of course, it was a bit of a blow, I must say. But she couldn't know. I hate to see her—well, you know how she is—so sort of sorry and humble.'

He tried to make Anne understand, but could get no response. She climbed into bed with a creaking of the springs. 'It's all arranged for her to go at the end of the week,' she said indifferently. 'You'll have to get someone else to help you if Harry doesn't sober up. Miriam's expecting Mother, and she won't like it if things are changed. She's probably got her dainty little vases of flowers already in the spare room.'

Frank got into bed, holding up his pyjama trousers, because he could not tie the string. 'I never knew Miriam was all that keen to have your mother,' he said.

'Don't be bitter.' Anne picked up a magazine. 'It doesn't become you. Now go to sleep and let me read. Mother's going on Friday. I've already looked up her trains and written to Miriam.'

CHAPTER FIVE

THE little vases of flowers were there in Louise's bedroom at *Pleasantways*, but not so tastefully arranged as usual. Ellen had done them. Instead of picking flowers from the garden, she had gone into the lane and gathered what had looked like a beautiful fistful of wild flowers and grasses, until she got them home.

She sneaked into the pantry, so that no one could laugh at what she had in her hand, and took down two of the little china jugs that Miriam collected for the colourful miniature bouquets she liked to dispose about the house.

'Your flowers are always so charming,' Miriam's friends told her. 'So individual. One gets tired of the eternal gladioli and roses. What little loves these cyclamens are—are they cyclamen ? But posies take a lot of trouble. I wish I had the time.'

Ellen stabbed the wilting flowers into the jugs, and mimicked to herself the things they said, nodding her head and mouthing with stretched smiles, ending each recital with: 'I wish I had the time.' This was what people said when they were envious of something that another person could do better.

No wonder they were envious of her mother. No one could arrange flowers as she could. Ellen like to stand back on her heels and watch her mother's fingers, deft and delicate among the blossoms that always seemed to stay fresh for her. Sometimes Miriam asked her to help, but Ellen's fingers were so clumsy that Miriam grew impatient and sent her away, or at best told her that she could stay and watch if she stopped scraping her feet in that maddening way.

Ellen knew that she often annoyed her mother, although she could not think why. That she annoyed her father was no cause of worry to her, since he was obviously a man destined

101

to be annoyed by children. Simon and Judy seemed to have
discovered how to avert this destiny as far as they were concerned, but Ellen did not bother about it. A lot of people's
fathers were like that. Gone all day and missing everything,
and coming home at night to tell everybody what they should
have done. Faraway figures who only half belonged during
the week, and lords of the manor at week-ends, who made the
house a different place. Jolly and noisy with you one minute,
and then suddenly rounding on you irritably, as if you gave
them a headache.

Ellen had long ago given up trying to please her father. She
was too busy trying to please her mother, whose bounty she
craved. She sometimes thought that she might have to give
that up, too, since the results were not worth her efforts, and
Miriam rarely noticed that there had been any effort at all.

When you are an annoying child, and a plain one, whose
smile reveals not sweetly comic gaps, but protruding tomb-
stones with a gold band on them, grown-ups are apt to forget
that you are not like that on purpose, and to give you no
credit for trying to be otherwise.

With her grandmother, it was different. Poor old Granny,
Ellen thought, with affection, not pity. She always wants to
think the best of you. She always says: 'You didn't mean to
do it, I'm sure,' even when I did mean to do something, like
going out in my night-dress when I had flu, and trying to catch
pneumonia. Even though these flowers do look awful—she
stood back and looked discouragedly at the sadly drooping
stems—she'll tell me how pretty they are, and I shall be
pleased, although I know they're not.

She began to nod her head and smirk again. 'Why, Miriam!'
she said out loud. 'How attractive! That's *so* original, putting
dandelions in with dead vetch. I just wish I had the time to
play about with flowers like that!'

'What on earth are you doing?' Miriam came into the
pantry, moving smoothly on the long, cool legs that seemed to
insulate her against the day's heat. 'Talking to yourself?
That's a bad sign, they say.'

'It means you're going mad, doesn't it?' Ellen asked.

Her mother nodded, reaching glasses off a shelf.

'Well, I wasn't,' Ellen said. 'I was reciting poetry, as a matter of fact.'

'Rupert Brooke?' Miriam had given her the collected poems at Easter, and Ellen knew many of the sonnets by heart.

'Yes. *Is it the hour?*' Ellen asked eagerly. '*We leave this resting-place made fair by one another for a while. Now, for a God-speed, one last mad embrace; the long road then, unlit——*'

'Why don't you learn the less morbid ones, like: *White plates and cups, clean-gleaming*? What have you got in these jugs, darling?'

'Because the dying ones seem more like poetry. These are some flowers for Granny's room. You said I could do them.'

'So I did. But I told you you could pick them from the garden.'

'I know, but Granny likes wild flowers, you see. We study them. It's botany; though not pulling them to pieces with tweezers, like we do at school.'

'Yes, of course. Well, they look very nice,' Miriam said. It did not sound nearly as convincing as Ellen knew it would when her grandmother said it.

'How nice the flowers look!' Louise exclaimed, when Ellen went with her to her room. 'You did them, didn't you? Our kind of flowers. There's a foxglove.'

'They don't look quite as fresh as they did when I picked them,' Ellen admitted. 'But do you really like them?'

'Immensely. They're charming.' It would have been difficult to determine who was trying harder to please the other. Louise was trying to show her appreciation for the trouble the child had taken, and Ellen, though ashamed of the flowers, was trying to hide her knowledge that Louise was pretending to like them.

'How was it at Aunt Anne's?' Ellen asked, opening Louise's

dressing-case and laying out the dilapidated tortoiseshell brushes that had been Louise's wedding present from her mother.

'I enjoyed it. I worked all the time. Uncle Frank had an accident to his hand, and I had to run the farm all on my own for a few days.' Louise always thought of it as a farm, although Miriam told her that it was only a smallholding.

Louise knew that Ellen was aware of some of the facts of life, for she had told her herself, since no one else appeared to have done so. She retailed, therefore, the tragic history of Daisy's parturition.

When they went downstairs, Sidney and Alice Cobb were there with cocktails in their hands. Ignoring them, for they were almost as frequent as the milkman, Ellen boiled over with the news.

'Did you *hear* about the pigs, Mummy? Didn't Granny tell you in the car? I'd have thought she would have.'

'What? What?' clamoured Simon. 'What about the pigs?'

'Ellen, dear, not now.' Louise put out a hand, but Ellen, trampling her feet and swallowing her words, had already embarked on the story.

The Cobbs were delighted, and filed it away in their gregarious minds for retelling. Miriam said, with an amused laugh: 'Mother, really. Is that the sort of thing you go in for at Anne's?'

'It happens all the time,' Ellen assured her. 'You've no idea what it is with pigs.'

Arthur pulled down his lip, as he had been doing all day in court with a witness he was trying to discredit. 'That's enough, Ellen. Your grandmother has been to Bedfordshire. That is enough, without dwelling on the sordid details.'

'She buried them, didn't she?' Simon asked Ellen. The originator of the story was forgotten now. It was Ellen's story.

'Yes. She carried them on a spade, the poor massacred corpses,' Ellen gasped, drunk with the attention she was getting.

'It was a holocaust. The blood ran like wine.' The Cobbs were, as they afterwards said, in fits.

'Well, let's forget it, there's good kids,' Arthur said, avoiding the heavy father role, which he only played when no one was there, and putting on the jocose parent. 'A little less necrology, and a little more going to put away the bicycles which sprawl in the drive and hazard all-comers. Mother—martini for you? Welcome back. We've missed you.'

'It's nice to be back,' Louise said, nodding politely over the delicately stemmed glass. It felt strange to be wearing her good silk dress again and not to be worrying about cooking the supper. Strange, and—a deprivation? Or was it a relief?

It was hard to switch your manners so quickly from one household to another. Only last night, she had been padding about the kitchen in her slippers and the torn apron which she and Anne shared indiscriminately; and now here she was in her pearls and silk dress, sitting in a comfortable chair with a cocktail, while Arthur suavely dismissed the things which yesterday had been the centre of life.

Miriam had not forgotten about the new dress. She promised to take her mother to London to choose it, but with the holidays drawing to a close, there were so many children's functions that had been postponed earlier because of rain, that she could not find a free day.

There were horse shows, and Pony Club competitions, and fêtes, and sports and pageants. Someone was always getting up something in and around Monk's Ditchling. The women were indefatigable organizers. Committee meetings and refreshment tents and loudspeakers in trees were the breath of life to them, although they pretended that they only did it because: 'One must do something for the village.'

The village people, who had been here long before the Londoners came with their passion for uncovering bricked-up fireplaces, took little part in these revels. Their children were encouraged to join in by the democratic ladies of the committee, but most of the village children preferred to stand on the sidelines and jeer. Occasionally a farmer's son trotted hopefully into the ring on a fat, hairy pony with a rusty bit, and was mortified to find that his beloved steed hardly looked like a pony at all compared with the expensive, well-bred animals that were cantering smoothly round, or giving a hysterical ride to some iron-fisted child whose parents thought that it must be able to ride if only they spent enough money.

Miriam managed to avoid having any function on her property, since there were plenty of people only too willing to offer a lawn or a meadow; but she attended most things with Simon and Judy, and with Ellen when she could be persuaded to go. It was *de rigueur* for mothers to accompany their children, and gossip idly with their friends, or call shrill admonitions to their heedless young. It was also necessary, to protect your child's interests, for the mothers waged such a subtle partisan warfare in the background that a child who came alone was liable to get left out of things, and to find himself going home without a prize.

'I don't see when I'll be able to get to town,' Miriam told Louise. 'Why don't you go up by train one day and get a dress on my account somewhere?'

'I couldn't do that. I wouldn't know what to spend. I don't want you to spend your money on me, anyway.'

'Oh, Mother, don't be so diffident. A present's a present. Don't quibble about accepting it.'

That's all very well for you, Louise thought. You've never had to take things from people, except as your right, as a daughter or a wife. Wait till you're a widow and Ellen offers to buy you a dress, and you want to say yes, but would love to be able to say no.

But of course, that could not happen to Miriam. Arthur would never be so careless as to die without making adequate provision.

Miriam finally had to tell her mother how much she could spend, which was a little embarrassing, and forced her to name a higher price than she would probably have paid if she had gone herself. Louise agreed to make the trip. She consulted her engagement book, which recorded only the Cobb's garden party and tea with the doctor's wife, and told Miriam: 'I think I'll go to town next Saturday, if you're sure you won't need me here.'

'You're not a servant, Mother. You know you're welcome to come and go as you like. We're going to a horse show on Saturday, but why choose a day like that which will only give you the morning to shop? Even if you took an early train, you wouldn't have much time to look round.'

'It won't take me long. I know what I like,' Louise said, although she could never make up her mind when buying clothes, and invariably wanted to take the garment back and change it the next day.

'I'll go on Saturday,' she said firmly. 'If you can't take me to the station, I'll get a taxi.' She had her reasons for choosing this day, but she was not telling Miriam.

'Mummy,' Ellen asked on Friday night. 'Can I got to London with Granny to-morrow? It will save me having to go to the horse show.'

'Which would be no loss,' Simon put in from the floor, where he was reading a comic paper, his nose touching the garish print. 'You're always such a pest, wanting to go home all the time, and last time you ate all the sausage rolls while Judy and I were riding.'

'You can't talk to me like that,' Ellen said half-heartedly. 'I'm older than you.'

'I'm a boy. That makes it even. And being older doesn't seem to give you any more sense.'

'Children, please!' Miriam sighed. 'It's so boring. I don't see why you shouldn't go to London, Ellen; but does Granny want to take you?'

That had not occurred to Ellen. She looked so dismayed that Louise, who had been wondering how she could find a kind excuse not to take her, had to say: 'Of course I want her. That will make it more fun.'

There went her *tête-à-tête* lunch ; but perhaps Mr Disher

would understand. Louise could not imagine him not being nice about children.

'Can we go to the cinema, Granny?' Ellen came over to stand before Louise and finger her skirt. 'There's a film about Lassie on. I saw it in the paper.'

'We'll see how we get on,' Louise said, putting her hand over the child's thin, grubby fingers. 'We'll have to see.'

Miriam had begged her mother to buy a dress that was gay and unpractical; but Louise chose a safe black wool that would see her through the winter and could be worn in the evenings at Sybil's hotel, where she was scheduled to go in October.

'Where are we going now?' Ellen asked, as her grandmother took her into another store and went towards the lift.

'To see a friend of mine.' Louise pulled Ellen's hat forward gently as they ascended, and tucked back a perverse strand of hair.

'Is it the fat man who sells beds?' Ellen asked, loudly enough for the lift-girl to turn round and raise her eyebrows, which were drawn in a slanting line that bore no relation to the natural growth. 'How exciting. Why didn't you tell me?'

'Never mind now.' Louise fussed, pushing Ellen out through the crowd of people who were trying to get into the lift, for it was nearly closing-time. She had not told Ellen, because she did not want Miriam to know. Absurd though her secrecy seemed to her—almost as though it were a clandestine rendezvous—it saved a lot of talk.

'Oh—beds!' Ellen cried, as they went through the archway to the sea of legs and mattresses. 'Millions of beds!' She was a stubbornly unsophisticated child, in spite of her 'sensible' upbringing. Simon or Judy would have walked composedly through the department, talking in the hushed voices that Miriam had taught them to use in shops; but Ellen went prancing away in the outgrown skirt that left a long gap of skinny legs above her trodden-in socks, and began to sit on one bed after another, trying the springs. She was not unruly.

It was just that she was expected to be so careful and grown-up at home that when she got away, she sometimes reverted to excessive juvenalia.

Louise saw Mr Disher navigating slowly round the corner of a mound of mattresses, and left Ellen to go to him.

He was carrying a pillow ceremoniously in front of him, as if it had a crown on it. When he saw Louise, he clutched it to his stomach and beamed. 'Hul*lo* there!' he said, with a boyish greeting of unaffected pleasure. 'You're late,' he added softly, his eyes saddening at the recent memory of how he had watched the clock and worried.

'Better late than never,' Louise vouchsafed, and wished that she had not, because it might sound as if there had been a question of her not coming at all.

'So they say, but I was afraid you wouldn't come before I had to leave the department. We can go now. It's just on time.' He had not yet seen Ellen, who was stretched out on a double four-poster, with her arms crossed over her chest.

Louise told him about the child and apologized. 'Perhaps you and I could have lunch some other day,' she said. 'I'll be coming up before I go to the Isle of Wight. Ellen and I will go off now and get a snack somewhere. I'm so sorry to upset our plans.'

'But you haven't,' he said. 'I'm glad to have the little girl too.'

'Oh, no. I wouldn't dream of letting you. I'm just so sorry that it happened like this to-day, but you know how it is with families. It couldn't be helped.'

'I'm glad to have her, I said,' he repeated, so firmly that Louise stopped apologizing and explaining. She called to Ellen, who ceased to be a dead crusader, swung her legs over the edge of the bed with a display of baggy knicker, and came towards them, hitching at her skirt.

Mr Disher was even fatter than she had imagined from her grandmother's description. She stared at him as he shook her hand. He did not ask how old she was, which was all most grown-ups could think of to say. He enquired after her health, and how she found the beds.

'Very comfortable, thank you,' Ellen said, allowing herself to smile, which she would not do until she felt it was safe to show a new person the ugly gold band on her teeth. 'I think I'll buy one with the knobs that unscrew and the blue mattress.'

'I'll have it shipped for you, madam.' Ellen looked at Louise, uncertain whether he was laughing at her, or sharing her game. Louise smiled at her and nodded.

Why! Ellen suddenly thought, I believe Granny's quite pretty. Can you be pretty when you're so old? She usually looks so worried, but now her face has a sort of dropped-down and smoothed-out look, like shaking out a wet hand-kerchief.

'We must go,' Mr Disher said, 'or we'll be locked in here for the week-end.   You ladies go out the front way, and I'll meet you outside.'

'Where are we going?' Louise asked.

'I was going to take you to a little place I go to sometimes in Soho,' he said, as he guided them to the stairs, for the lifts had stopped. 'But I think perhaps it would be better if we went somewhere like the Trocadero.   That will be more fun for Ellen.   She'll see more people.'

'He's nice,' Ellen said, tugging at her grandmother to walk faster down the stairs.

'I told you he was,' Louise said smugly.

'The Troc!' Ellen marvelled. 'Just wait till I tell that Simon. We've only been there once, when Uncle Bill took us, and Mummy won't let him take us out again, because he let us drink his beer. It was my fault for telling her about it. Simon beat me up; but I always forget what to tell and what not to. And you never know with Mummy. Sometimes she laughs, and sometimes she's cross about the same thing she laughed about before.'

While they were waiting for a table, Louise took Ellen into the ladies' cloakroom and told her that she must not comment on what Mr Disher ate, because he was on a diet.

'For his figure?' Ellen asked. 'It doesn't seem to have done him much good. Aunt Anne's the one who ought to diet. She looks awfully fat in that picture you took.'

'Hush, dear.' Ellen had inherited Miriam's clear, carrying voice. 'She's going to have a baby. Oh dear—I wasn't supposed to tell you that. She doesn't want people to know about it yet.'

'Well, I won't tell a soul. I just hope she doesn't roll on it like Daisy did with hers.' The cloakroom attendant looked up from her knitting, startled, and Louise lost the courage to put a shilling into the pin tray and take out sixpence. She dropped in the shilling, and led Ellen away.

Louise did not have to worry about Gordon Disher's diet, for he explained politely to Ellen why he must be careful of what he ate.

'It's all due to the pancreas, they say. That's a thing that lays under your stomach like a fish under a stone.' He cleared his throat, looked at Louise and added, 'If you'll excuse my mentioning it.'

Ellen would have liked to hear more. Her mother did not trouble to give scientific explanations. She was usually too busy to answer a question with more than: 'Because that's the way nature made it,' or 'You wouldn't understand if I told you.' Her father, who liked to give information, would answer a question if he was sure it was not frivolous, but he quickly grew impatient if you did not understand at once, or said something irrelevant.

They had a cheerful lunch, and Louise was glad after all that she had brought Ellen. It solved the problem of what she and Gordon Disher were going to talk about. Ever since the lunch had been arranged, she had been wondering whether they would be able to pick up again the same easy note of their conversation at tea in Fulham, or whether they would be shy of each other after three months.

You could not be shy with Mr. Disher, however. He was too uncritical. He had a way of listening benevolently, with a half smile, that made you feel that your silliest remark had some point to it. He had no small talk to keep them apart, and no special manner for children to embarrass Ellen. He did not try to press on her rich things she did not want and then laugh at her appetite when she was forced to accept them. He let her study the menu for as long as she liked.

'Liver and bacon with fried potatoes!' Ellen said. 'I'd love to have that—if I may, please.' She glanced at her grandmother to make sure that Louise noticed her manners. 'Oh—but it costs four and nine. I'd better not.'

'Money no object,' Mr Disher said, and ordered it.

'Can I take my plate out?' Ellen whispered to Louise when the food came.

'You're not supposed to, are you?' Louise whispered back. 'Well then, perhaps, as this is a treat.' Ellen took out the wet gold band and Louise wrapped it quickly in a handkerchief and hid it in her bag. Mr Disher was very discreet and pretended not to see or hear.

In the cloakroom after lunch, Ellen said to Louise: 'He must be awfully rich.'

'I don't think so, dear.' Louise looked in the mirror and was disappointed with her hat. She had bought it that morning to go with the new dress, and she realized the truth of Miriam's statement that no one over fifty should ever try to buy anything in a bargain basement.

'But look what we ate!' Ellen reminded her. 'And he didn't look at any of the prices on the menu, and when the bill came, he didn't add it up, like Daddy does. Why don't you marry him, Granny?'

'Don't be silly.' Louise saw the reflection of her startled face, and changed it to a laugh, 'People don't get married at my age.'

'They do. Miss Porter in the village did. She married that old man at the smithy who'd been waiting for his wife to die so he could marry Miss Porter. His childhood sweetheart, Mrs Match said. Marry him, Granny. I read in Mrs Match's magazine that a woman can always get a man to propose if she wants him. I could wear that pink party dress for bridesmaid, and you could be rich and have a house of your own, and not have to live in people's spare rooms all the time.'

'Here's my comb,' Louise said. 'Take off your hat and try to do something about your hair.'

'Where are we going? Will he take us to the cinema?'

'We'll see.'

Ellen was disappointed when her grandmother agreed to Mr Disher's suggestion that they should go to the Saturday market in the Portobello Road; but when she got there, she realized that it had been a good idea.

All down the narrow, shabby street that leads decaying Bayswater into the morass of North Kensington, there were stalls loaded with delightful junk. Behind the stalls, dark little shops spilled their debris out on to the pavement: stacks of pictures, broken furniture, old gramophone records, piles of rags and buttons, a complete set of rusted armour, and enough dusty glass and china and silver to have come from the back of all the pantry cupboards in the land.

A slow-moving crowd milled along the stalls and down the middle of the road, which was littered with paper and broken crates and trodden refuse from the vegetable stalls. A rough passage awaited any car that foolishly tried to come through, for the street belonged to the people on Saturdays, and they held their ground like a flock of sheep in a narrow lane, so that the car had to crawl at their pace, with small boys slapping at its sides and clinging like parasites behind.

Some of the people looked poor, as if they lived in the street or its dingy neighbourhood, but the people who were peering and poking most intently at the stalls were quite well dressed, and there were several Americans, who talked in monosyllables in the forlorn hope of concealing their vulnerable nationality. Ellen watched one of them with an English girl. He would make her ask the price of pieces of silver, while he stood back among the crowd, with his hand over his jaw, like a spy in a film. The girl would report to him, and he would tell her out of the side of his mouth to go back and offer less.

'Ten bob!' said the man behind the stall, keeping his eye on the American. 'But it's Jacobean, dear. That's less than I gave for it.'

At the antique stalls, people were trying to bargain craftily, telling each other: 'It's like in the East. They don't expect you to pay what they ask at first.' The stallholders handled them with cynical indulgence, pandering to the belief that they did not know the value of the things they offered, so that a customer who bought something for three or four times what it had cost should think it a triumphant bargain.

Out of nowhere sprang a stunted man in crazy clothes, who went straight into an unintelligible song, to the accompaniment of a banjo with one string missing. The crowd stopped to watch amiably, but moved away when he threw his scarecrow hat on the ground for coins. The man began a jerky dance, his face working up and down with his knees.

'Come along, Ellen,' Louise said. Mr Disher dropped three pennies into the hat, and they moved off. Ellen lingered, and watched them pottering from stall to stall, an oddly matched pair, like an elephant and a sparrow. The stunted man gave a yell, scooped up his hat and put it on his head with the pennies still in it, and disappeared as abruptly as he had come.

Biting her nails, Ellen turned to look at the pictures that were stacked against the front of a shop, in whose low doorway a woman in a stretched green sweater sat and knitted herself another loose garment on big needles.

'Take a look, my young lady. That's right,' she said, as Ellen crouched to examine the darkened, frameless oils where cattle browsed under a stormy sky, and ships sat rigidly with all sails blowing on a corrugated sea. Old brown photographs of wedding couples and fuzzy-haired women grouped outside villas were piled on a rickety table among framed postcard scenes of Wales that had let the damp in patchily through the back. Everything smelled of old, shut-up houses and forgotten people. Who would want such things, except the people to whom they had once belonged? It would have been better to burn them than to let an auctioneer consign them in a job lot to end their days in the Portobello Road, brought out without hope on Saturday mornings and taken in again without disappointment in the evening, to turn their faces to the wall in

the bomb-gutted cavern of the shop. To a child, the pictures
were pleasant but meaningless. Ellen's mind wandered as she
turned them over, getting a faraway sensation from them,
without noticing the details.

Suddenly she saw it, the picture of her heart. She took it in
her hands and adored it, knowing that life would be quite
different if she could have this on the wall of her room to look
at every day.

It was a cleanly coloured print of a horse, accoutred for
battle in the first war, and lying in a tragic heap with its neck
stretched in the mud, and one great knee drawn up towards its
chest. In the sky, shells were bursting like fireworks, and beside
the horse knelt a soldier in tattered khaki, with the ravaged
face of a hero. There was a lot of realistic blood, both on the
man and the horse. The text beneath the picture was: 'Good-
bye Old Friend.'

A lump rose in Ellen's throat, as she knew it would rise
every time she looked at the picture. She had to have it.

'That, dear?' The woman looked briefly up from her
knitting. 'Five bob, that one, and worth a lot more.'

'But I've only got half a crown,' Ellen said, not believing
that such a thing as money could come between her and her
treasure.

'Sorry duck,' said the woman laconically, losing what little
interest she had shown.

Ellen put down the picture and lingered, running her finger
along the splintery edge of the table. Granny never had any
money to spare, and yet she always gave if she thought you
needed it. Would it be unfair to ask her for the loan of half a
crown?

A man in a dirty beret brought a cup of tea for the woman in
the doorway.

'What she want?' He jerked his head at Ellen.

The woman told him, cradling the cup of tea automatically,
although the day was warm.

'Oh, let her have it, Doris,' the man said. 'Poor kid. Thank
God she likes the bloody thing.'

'You've got a bargain there,' the woman said sternly, dropping the half crown into the baggy pocket of her sweater.

'Oh, I know!' Ellen held the picture flat against her chest. 'Thank you very much. It was most kind of you.' The woman jerked up her head, surprised that anyone should speak to her like that.

Ellen ran, threading her way through the crowd to find her grandmother.

'Look, Granny, look what I bought!' Ellen tugged at Louise's skirt. 'It's to hang over my bed. Look, the frame isn't broken, or anything. It's even got the string on.'

'It's beautiful, darling, but it's very sad,' Louise said mournfully, knowing that Ellen had chosen it for its sadness.

'Oh, it's all right, Granny. Don't be upset. It isn't the horse that's dying. It's the man.'

Louise had bought a little lustre jug for Miriam's flowers. Beneath the faded rim was a picture of a drooping, willowy woman, rather like Miriam, saying good-bye to a red-cheeked man in tight trousers. It was called 'The Sailor's Farewell,' and had a verse in old-fashioned script.

> *Sweet, oh Sweet is that Sensation,*
> *Where two hearts in union meet;*
> *But the pain of Separation,*
> *Mingles Bitter with the Sweet.*

'Do you think Mummy will like it? This is rather sad, too, don't you think?' Louise said, but Ellen could not pretend that she thought it was. She was interested only in her picture, and wished that they could go now and catch the train, so that she could rush up to her room and shut the door and prop the picture on the chest-of-drawers and brood over it. If they did not go soon, Judy, who shared her room, would be in bed by the time they reached home, which would spoil everything.

She wished that Mr Disher would hurry. He was buying something at a stall farther up the road, counting money carefully into the blackened palm of a sharp-faced man, who chewed rapidly on a matchstick.

'What have you bought?' Louise asked, as she and Ellen came up behind him.   Mr Disher started and turned round, his broad cheeks reddening under the shapeless grey hat.

'Oh, nothing much. Just a present for someone.' He took the newspaper-wrapped parcel and hurried it into his jacket pocket, which was big and baggy, as if he had been poaching rabbits.

'Can I interest the wife in something?' the sharp-faced man said, removing the match to study its chewed end. 'There's a nice Victorian pin-cushion here.   Or what about that little silver mirror for your daughter? Dainty, isn't it?'

'Yes—dainty,' Louise said in a fluster, not daring to look at Mr Disher.   'But not to-day. Not just now, thank you. We've a train to catch. Come along, Ellen. We'll have to go.'

She had to look at Mr Disher now, to tell him that it was time to leave for the station, and when she looked, she saw that he was not annoyed or embarrassed, but was smiling, and holding Ellen by the hand. Louise unscrewed her face and smiled back at him, and the three of them walked up the street together, just like a family, just as the man with the match had thought.

They were too early at the station.   Louise hoped that Gordon Disher would not stay to see them off, and spoil the pleasant friendliness of their day with one of the nervous, repetitious conversations that take place on station platforms. He said that he would go to the bookstall to buy her an evening paper.

'Can I come, too?' Ellen asked, rising on her toes to look up at him. 'I want to see if they've got any of your books. Lester Drage!' She chanted it with awe. 'That's a much prettier name than Gordon Disher.'

'The publisher thinks so, anyway,' he said, as they went off together.

Louise hoped that if they found one of his books he would have the sense not to let Ellen open it on the staccato phrases of passion and horror that he so surprisingly was able to perpetrate. She sat down on a grimy bench next to a defeated woman with a strapped suitcase, who was whining back at her two whining children. Louise wanted to tell her not to let them wander in the path of the man who was driving the little motor with the string of trucks, but she had nearly started a street fight once by interfering with a mother whose child was hanging head downwards out of its pram.

'Hullo, Mother!' Louise turned and saw Eva, in a slick linen suit and tiny white hat standing beside her. 'Miriam called me yesterday about the Cobb's garden party, and told me what train you were catching, so I thought I'd come and say hullo. I knew you'd be here half an hour too early.'

'And I am. How nice of you, darling, and how brown you are.' She had not seen Eva since she came back from Italy. She got up, because Eva did not want to sit on the bench in her light suit, and the defeated woman ostentatiously hauled her suitcase on to the seat, as if she had been waiting for Louise to go.

'Oh, it's fading now. You should have seen me. I was mahogany. Where's Ellen? How are you, Mother? Was it hell at Anne's? Let's go and have some tea. You've got hours yet.' She sounded for some reason a little nervous and jerky.

'You look tired,' Louise said, seeing the unusual shadows in her face.

'No, I don't. Mother, don't always——' Eva bit her lip, and then said quickly: 'I'm not sleeping very well as a matter of fact. But it'll pass. You know I get spells like that. But it's not overwork this time. Things are a bit slack all round. The boys are still messing around rewriting the third act of the play. I've been trying to get into some rotten thing that's being done at Oxford, but I'll be just as pleased if I don't.'

'How—how's David?' Louise asked hesitatingly. She had to ask it.

'Oh, he's fine. Sent you his regards, as a matter of fact. He likes you.'

'I like him, too,' Louise said, 'but——'

'He's going to do a film.' Eva hurried on, before Louise could say more. 'He says there's a chance he might be able to get me into it, too. Don't look so nervous, Mother. Denham isn't Hollywood.'

'I'm not nervous.' It was difficult to talk when they had to keep stepping back and forward to avoid being struck by baggage as the hurrying crowd flowed round them. 'I hope you get the part, dear,' Louise lied.

When she heard that David was going to be in a film, she had been pleased, because that would keep him busy and away from Eva for long hours; but if they were going to be in it together, things would be worse than ever. They would be together all day, as well as . . .

What was Eva doing? Louise did not know. Whatever it was, she was powerless to stop it. She could only say her *Hail Mary*, and ask the Virgin Mother to send her daughter down some caution.

'If you are still worrying about me and David,' Eva said, 'don't. Things will come out all right. You'll see. You won't have to be shocked.'

'Nothing you did could ever shock me,' Louise said.

'I believe that's true,' Eva said slowly. 'It could only distress you.' She looked at her mother for a moment with serious affection, and then they were abruptly parted by a heavy man with a bag of golf clubs and a sharp-cornered suitcase, who thrust his way feverishly between them, pursuing the five-fifteen as if it were the Holy Grail.

When they came together again, Eva was once more bright and inconsequential. When Gordon Disher found them and was introduced, Eva said: 'But of course I know you. You're the man I was so rude to. About the tea-party.' She laughed unnaturally, and began to chatter to him in a brittle, flippant way that reduced him to silence.

She is tired, Louise thought. So restless. Not really as gay as she's pretending to be. 'We'll have to hurry if we're going to have tea,' she said, looking at her watch.

'Mother always panics about trains,' Eva told Mr Disher. 'Come and have a cup of tea with us. Please do. Let me make up for the tea you didn't have before.' Whatever she thought about his being at the station with her mother, and Louise could not help wondering what she thought, she did not show it. Mr Disher backed away a step from her bright charm.

'I'll have to be getting along,' he said. 'Thanks all the same.' He raised his hat, which had left a dent round his silky grey hair. 'I'll say good-bye then, Mrs Bickford. Good-bye, Ellen. I enjoyed it so much.'

With Eva watching, it was a flat, unsatisfactory good-bye that was said between them, without the real gratitude that Louise would have liked to convey. As she walked to the tea-room behind the other two, who were looking at Ellen's picture, Louise felt a touch on her arm. She turned and saw Mr Disher, breathing heavily, as if he had run to catch her.

He took the newspaper parcel out of his pocket, and thrust it into her hand. 'This is for you,' he said almost in a whisper. 'I couldn't resist it. Please don't be offended.'

Louise unwrapped the parcel and found a Victorian cut-glass scent bottle, with a round silver cap. On the cap, in facsimile of someone's handwriting, was engraved the name 'Louise.'

Mr Disher watched her nervously. She looked up at him in surprise. 'But it's lovely,' she said, stroking the smooth, round cap. 'I can't thank you enough.'

'I felt I had to get it for you. The coincidence of the name seemed too much. Do you really like it?'

'It's the nicest present I ever had,' Louise said, and heard him give a little sigh of relief. She had always disliked her old-fashioned name, but now she was glad of it, because it had brought her the scent bottle, and him the pleasure of finding such a fitting gift for her in the Portobello Road.

The gardener met Louise and Ellen at the station, mutely aggrieved, because he had been all day at the horse show and wanted to go home to supper.

Miriam was in the kitchen, feeding the younger children. 'Come straight in here, Ellen,' she called. 'Your egg's cooked.'

Ellen pretended not to hear, and ran upstairs to hide her picture in a drawer. She did not want anyone to see it until it was hung in its glory on the wall. Louise also went to her room. She did not want her prize to be bandied about either, although sooner or later, Miriam would have to know that they had been with Gordon Disher, because Ellen would tell her.

When Ellen came down, Judy, in dressing-gown and slippers, screamed at her: 'What do you think, Elly! Simon was fourth in musical chairs. He was fourth, I tell you! He would have been third, only one of those beastly pros knocked him off the chair, and so he didn't get a prize. Wasn't it a swiz?'

'I got a rosette, though,' Simon said smugly, and pointed to the door, where his bridle hung among the aprons, decorated with purple ribbon.

'Jolly good.' Ellen slid into her chair, thinking of her picture, and how she would hang it after supper before Judy went to bed. She could not feel any enthusiasm for Simon's triumph at the horse show, so remote from the delights of her day. She was irritated by Judy's boasting prattle about the show. She did not want to hear about Michael Fitt's new bay pony, which had been third at the White City, nor how they kept putting up the jumps for Mrs Slazenger, but she never touched a thing.

'We had a super time,' Judy said, her blue eyes misted with fatigue. '*You* wouldn't have liked it though. You miss all the best things.'

'Well, listen to this then.' Ellen waited for silence. '*I* went to the Troc!'

Simon put down his knife and fork. 'To the Troc! Lucky swine. Have you been with Uncle Bill?' he asked suspiciously, and glanced at his mother to see if she heard.

'Of course not. Uncle Bill's in Spain. Even a fool like you knows that. We went with Granny's friend, Mr Disher, but his *nom de plume* is Lester Drage.'

'Was he common?' Simon asked. There had been some talk in the family about Gordon Disher, and the children had not missed a thing.

'Don't be such a snob, Simon,' Louise said tartly, coming into the room. 'I never heard of a child talking like that.'

'Well, you hear now,' Simon said rudely. He was tired, too. Louise did not like to reprimand him with Miriam in the room. She wished that Miriam would do it herself.

Miriam dried her hands and tipped hand lotion into them. 'I didn't know you were going to see your car salesman friend, Mother.'

'Beds.' interrupted Ellen laconically.

'I thought you were going to the cinema. Why didn't you tell me?'

'You mean, you wouldn't have let Ellen come,' Louise said wearily, sitting down on a chair by the wall. How nice it would be to come home to a peaceful welcome, instead of to the cross-examinations that invariably greeted anyone who had been away from the house or a few hours.

'If you want to know ' she said, feeling like having a quarrel with someone, and wishing that the children were not here so that she could have it, 'I didn't tell you because I knew you'd scoff.'

'I? Scoff?' Miriam raised her symmetrical russet eyebrows. 'How ridiculous. Why should I scoff? I think it's delightful that you've made a new friend. Why don't you ask him down here some time?'

'Oh, no. That wouldn't do. I mean, I don't think he'd like it really.'

'You mean we'd bore him.'

'Of course not. Don't try and misunderstand me. I mean he's a bit shy.'

'Oh, Granny, he's not!' Ellen, like the other children, had been following the conversation closely. 'He wasn't a bit shy with us at lunch. Even when I took my plate out, he didn't mind. Oh, Lord'—she clapped a hand to her mouth—'I shouldn't have said that.'

'Where is it now?' Miriam removed the hand and looked at Ellen's teeth.

'In my bag,' Louise said. 'It' hurts her, Miriam.'

'You know she has to wear it. How do you think I'm going to like taking about a daughter with protruding teeth when she grows up? Mother, I wish you wouldn't always give in to the children. It makes it so difficult for me.'

The quarrelling impulse had died in Louise. Seeing how small and downcast she looked, Ellen changed the subject. 'Mummy, can I have the hammer to hang a picture up in my room after supper? I bought it in London with that half crown you gave me.'

'I gave you that to buy a book with,' Miriam said. 'Now why on earth go and buy a picture? Where did you get it, anyway?'

'In the Portobello Road market. Mr Disher took us there.'

'What an extraordinary way to spend the afternoon,' Miriam said distantly.

'It wasn't,' Louise said. 'It was wonderful. They had some lovely things. I bought you this little lustre jug.' Perhaps this was not the right time to offer it, with Miriam on edge; but she could not sit holding it in her lap any longer. 'I thought the woman on it looked rather like you.'

Miriam took the jug, and thanked her graciously, knowing that it must have cost more than her mother could afford.

'*The Sailor's Farewell.* It is a little like me, too.' But the man with the chubby cheeks and the boyish stance was nothing like Colin; and she had not drooped like that when she said good-bye to him before he joined his ship and sailed out of her life. She had stood by the window with her head up, and pretended to believe, as he did, that it was all for the best.

She read the verse on the little jug. Why had she been thinking of Colin all day to-day? And now this . . . *the pain of separation, mingles Bitter with the Sweet.* Bittersweet. That had been one of Colin's words when he was being synthetically romantic, as he was that last evening, when Miriam had waited to cry until he had shut the front door and run too briskly down the steps.

'Mummy, can't you hear me?' Ellen was standing behind her. 'I'm asking you, can I have the hammer to hang my picture?'

Miriam shook away the dead and useless past. 'You know

you're not allowed to knock nails in those walls,' she said impatiently. 'They crumble. Don't keep on about it, Ellen. I've said no.'

After supper, Ellen went to her room to look at the picture, but Judy was sent up to bed almost at once, and Ellen quickly pushed the picture back into the drawer. She went to bed herself when Judy was asleep, and waited in the dark until the house was still before she took the picture out again. She must have dozed off while she was waiting. The atmosphere of the house felt as if it was very late and the grown-ups had all gone to bed.

She took the picture into bed with her, and shone her torch on it, travelling the beam over each tragic detail. How sad it was! It wasn't really the man who was dying, but Granny must be protected from too intense a grief. Ellen's eyes grew pleasurably moist. She turned on the light the better to indulge her emotions.

Judy sat up suddenly, her red-gold hair in a rumpled cloud above her flushed face. 'What are you doing, Elly? What's the matter? Is there a fire?'

Judy was a child who suffered from night terrors, which was why she shared a room with Ellen. She had delusions that she smelled burning, and that there was a cellar full of spikes on to which her bed would drop through the floor, although she knew that there was nothing below the room but the familiar kitchen; and Ellen was constantly having to crawl under her bed to look for bombs or snakes.

'It's nothing,' Ellen said. 'Go to sleep.'

'I want to see. Let me see.' Judy ran barefoot across the floor in her flowered nightdress, and jumped on top of Ellen's legs. Resignedly Ellen turned the picture towards her. Judy took a long look, and then abruptly threw back her head and screamed.

She continued to scream uncontrollably, while Ellen tried to muffle her with a pillow. In no time at all, the room was full of grown-ups, all fully dressed to Ellen's surprise, for what seemed to her like the still watches of the night was only ten o'clock.

Simon arrived, too, holding up his pyjamas, and Judy, catching her breath for a moment to see what kind of an audience she had, continued to scream and sob more hysterically than ever.

It was all Ellen's fault. That was agreed, and although Louise was on Ellen's side, she could not make her voice heard, because Arthur was shouting against the noise that Judy was making. Shouting when he was angry was the one fault he had not been able to exorcise when he was cultivating the controlled, mature manner, lightened by dry wit, which his profession demanded of its ambitious young men. He was occasionally guilty of shouting in court, when a witness was obtuse. He always recollected himself quickly and dropped his voice back to the acid purr of cross-examination, hoping that people would merely think: That young Chadwick is a firebrand.

The distressing commotion in the bedroom was ended by Arthur taking the picture away and saying that he would burn it. Ellen began to cry then, and Simon said: 'Oh, for heaven's sake ! ' and shuffled back to bed.

Miriam picked up Judy, now quietened and hiccuping. 'You can come and lie in my bed for a bit while I undress.'

'I want to stay in your bed all night!' Judy wailed.

'Perhaps you shall, my pet, as you've had such a fright. It's a shame.' Miriam, usually so hard to deceive, and so sharp where Ellen was concerned, was vulnerable about Judy, and Judy knew it.

'No, Mother,' she said, as Louise lingered. 'Don't stay and pet Ellen. She's not a baby. Certainly old enough to know better than to frighten little Judy like that. You go to sleep now, Ellen, and we'll say no more about it. You should have been asleep long ago.'

Ellen lay awake, and heard her mother moving about in the room next door. It sounded as if it would be comforting in that room. Judy was singing softly to herself in her mother's

E

bed. Presently her father came up, and Ellen heard his voice and her mother's, with Judy's chirp interrupting now and again. Discussing her, no doubt.

She heard the click of the light switch and someone getting into bed. Her father yawned, and there was silence. Ellen got out of bed, opened her door stealthily and pattered down the corridor to the door at the end, where the moonlight lay in squares on the carpet. Slipping into the room like a ghost, she crept into her grandmother's bed, and finished her crying unchided until she fell asleep.

Eva came down for the day to go to the Cobb's garden party. She could not think why she had accepted the invitation, except that she had an arresting red dress, and it would give her an opportunity to see Miriam and her mother, without making a meaningless visit. She liked to see Miriam occasionally, although they often quarrelled. Miriam was a stable element in a precarious world. She was one of the few people Eva knew who seemed to have come to terms with what life had dealt her, without wishing it were different. Eva did not like Miriam's conventional way of life, but that did not prevent her from thinking sometimes how soothing it must be to be able to accept conventionality and abandon the search for Arcadia.

She liked to see her mother, too, and knew that she should see her more often. There never seemed to be enough time. The days spun round Eva in a whirl of scattered events, all shot through like taffeta with the bright, nervous colours of love.

As she stepped from the train at the little station, grey with the threat of rain, Eva sniffed the soft air and felt that London and her restlessness were a hundred miles away instead of twenty. For a moment she wished that she lived in the country. Life was much easier to handle. It did not go so fast, and you knew where people were. They could not slip away from you in the crowd.

Miriam was waiting for her in the black family car, which signalled Arthur's respectable prosperity from every one of its smugly rounded highlights. As they drove, the sisters gossiped idly about family matters and people they both knew.

Miriam said: 'By the way, I met Susan Pierce the other day.'

'That hag. I never could see why you were friends with her.'

'I'm not, really. She's just one of the people one knows, and asks to parties. She's been to Portofino—but you know that, of course. She was staying in your hotel, wasn't she?'

'Yes.' Eva spoke casually. She had known this would come sooner or later. 'I only saw her once though. We left the day after she arrived.'

'She told me. She said you were with an attractive man. Quite the lover, Susan said. You know the way she says things in that high, surprised voice. David, I suppose. But I thought Mother said you were in a party.'

'We were,' Eva said defiantly.

'Don't get excited. I don't care if you weren't. Go ahead and make a fool of yourself, if you want to. I suppose you traipsed round Portofino holding hands and being starry-eyed over bottles of Chianti in romantic little cafés. Lovely for you, my dear,' Miriam said briskly, 'and I'm sure you don't care about people like Susan Pierce. But don't tell Mother that David is married.'

'How do you know he is?'

'He married a rich girl, didn't he? Her father makes biscuits, or something, and she was the Number One Deb. of God knows when. Arthur remembered seeing the wedding pictures in the papers. Arthur remembers things like that.'

'Well, they're separated,' Eva said. 'She's a bitch. Perhaps Arthur knows that, too, since he's so well informed. Mother knows about it, anyway. I told her.'

'That was silly. What's the point of upsetting her?'

'She'll have to know sooner or later, when their divorce goes through. We're going to be married.'

'Indeed, indeed.' Miriam nodded her head. 'Well, congratulations, my dear.'

'Why are you so crabby about it?'

'I'm not. I'm delighted. Why are you so touchy?'

Who wouldn't be touchy? Eva thought. Who wouldn't be, when they were in love with a man, like a hopeless disease, and they did not even know where he was to-day while they were out of town?

She did not even know when she would next see him. She wasted hours waiting in the flat for the doorbell or the telephone, hating the hum of the lift, because it did not stop at her floor; watching the telephone until she was sick with its silence.

Suddenly, he would call, or he would be there, and everything would be rapturous, and he would only laugh, if she asked: 'Where have you been? Why do you leave me?'

'I always come back to my love,' he said. 'Why worry?'

'No one but us,' the Cobbs said gaily, 'no one but us would have a garden party at the end of September. But you know us—we're crazy!'

All morning, the sky had been clouded with damp, heavy grey. You could almost fancy that you felt the drops of rain, although none were yet falling. Women who had bought new dresses for the party regretfully decided to wear raincoats. Women who had not bought new dresses were glad that they had not.

'Poor Sidney and Alice,' everyone said. 'What bad luck, when everything is arranged, and their garden is so lovely.' Their sympathy was not unmixed with secret pleasure that something had at last gone wrong for the Cobbs, who had too much money, and showed it.

At lunch-time, the skies cleared, and the blurred clouds contracted into healthier white masses. Women changed their minds about the raincoats, and said: 'Isn't that just Sidney and Alice's luck! It's going to be fine after all.'

Louise, however, cherishing her new hat, although she still did not like it any better, took her umbrella when she started off in the car with Miriam and Arthur and Eva. The children waved them off from the lych-gate, looking a little forlorn.

They thought that they should be going, too, but no children had been invited, since the Cobbs had none of their own, and their garden was the sort that did not take kindly to running small boys.

The garden party was quite an extravagant affair. A small band played thinly by the terrace steps. Hired waitresses stood behind white-clothed tables on the lawn, dispensing tea and coffee and Fortnum and Mason refreshments, and clutching at their caps when a breeze arose. On the terrace, there was a long bar, stocked with more whisky and gin than anyone else was able to get hold of in 1951, and presided over by two genuine barmen from the club, with white jackets and oiled hair.

'It puts me in mind of our church fête,' the vicar said, drinking claret cup and surveying the pleasant English scene benignly. 'All you need is a hoop-la stall.' He had caught Alice for a moment, but she was gone immediately, with a nod and a smile and a pat on his arm, which she fancied would compensate for not going to church.

Alice was shrilly in her element as a hostess. She skittered about in a fantastic hat, making holes in the damp grass with her high heels, tearing people apart who were happily talking, and introducing them to people they did not want to meet. Sidney stayed on the terrace most of the time with a glass in his hand, his broad, foolish face gradually deepening to a shade of red that clashed with the vast clove carnation he wore in the buttonhole of his aggressive suit.

Miriam moved with self-possession among the crowd, whose chatter sounded thin on the wide lawns, talking to the many people she knew, and appraising those who had come from London for this event, which Alice and Sidney considered was the biggest of the year.

Eva, as she had expected, attracted some attention in her red dress, which was cut a little lower and a little tighter than was normally seen in Monk's Ditchling.

'Miriam Chadwick's sister. She's an actress, you know,' women said, as if that excused them from looking a little dingy by comparison. A personable young man called Harvey Upjohn, from Sidney's London office, had made a bee-line for Eva as soon as she appeared, and was following her about with conversation that was more daring than his usual cautious line; but he was not getting anywhere with her. Eva was playing at being enigmatic, her small, nervous face shadowed under a huge wheel of a hat. This seemed to encourage Harvey Upjohn. He plied her with drinks, coffee, ice cream, cigarettes, and was even so bold as to offer to show her the greenhouses. Eva was not trying to encourage him. She was merely bored, and mysterious silences or dead-end answers seemed the easiest way out.

Apart from wanting to see Miriam and Louise, she had come to the party because she wanted to try herself out on her own. It was so long since she had been anywhere without David, for their mutual friends always asked them together now, and if Eva received a separate invitation, she took David along if she could, or else did not go.

She wanted to see whether she could enjoy herself without him. It was her last fling at independence, and she was disgusted with herself when she found that she could not. She, who had always treasured her freedom, who had given up so many men at the slightest hint of possessiveness from them, was now hopelessly dependent on a man who preferred her not to be, and hated her to cling.

But the party would have been all right if David were there. He would have been delighted with her dress, and the looks it drew. They would have drunk together, and sat under a yew tree and watched the people, and laughed about them, and made up stories about what Sidney and Alice talked about on the rare occasions when they were alone together.

Waiting on the terrace for Harvey Upjohn to fight his way back through the crowd round the bar, Eva looked unseeingly out over the teeming lawn. Where was David now? He had said he might be at the studio, but she did not think they had even started rehearsing yet. Perhaps when the sky had cleared at lunch-time, he had called her up, wanting to go out in the car, and found her not there. Where would he go instead? He had so many friends. He might go round to Clarissa's, and she would make him drink. Eva wished that she had never embarked on this unrewarding expedition. She should not have left town. David might ring this evening, wanting to take her to dinner. He would not remember that she had told him she was coming down here. He seldom remembered things that she told him about her plans.

'Eureka!' cried Harvey Upjohn, approaching with a tall drink in his hand. 'I finally made it. Tom Collins. That was what you wanted, wasn't it?'

'I did say gin and lime, but this will do.' She had asked for a Tom Collins, but since she was having a difficult time, she did not see why she should not make it difficult for Harvey Upjohn, too.

Louise had lost sight of her family soon after they arrived. She knew some of the guests, having met them during her visits to Miriam, but they all seemed to be talking, so she went to one of the refreshment tables and fed herself, trying to look nonchalant about it, so that the waitresses should think she was alone from choice.

Then she thought that it might look greedy if she stayed there too long, so she walked busily about as if she had a destination, admiring all the flowerbeds several times over.

'Vile colour, those chrysanthemums.' Mrs Glover, the doctor's wife, square and unashamedly dowdy, stood beside her with legs apart. 'No one but the Cobbs would grow monstrosities like that.'

'Hush, Mary,' Louise said. 'You mustn't talk like that about your hosts.'

'Haven't seen either of 'em since I came,' grumbled Mrs Glover, who came from Yorkshire, and wished that her husband had not bought this sophisticated practice. 'I've had a good tea, but Alice is too demented to give me so much as a hullo. She's after big fish to-day. There's a cabinet minister coming, so she's been telling everyone for weeks, but no one has had a smell of him yet. Well, I'm off, if I can ever get my car out from among the Bentleys. I have to get back and give George his tea.'

'Isn't the doctor here?'

'He's supposed to be on a case, but actually he refused to come. He says that women always start talking to him about their slipped discs.'

'Come and have a drink, Mother.' Arthur, sent by Miriam, rescued Louise from oblivion and took her up to the terrace. Louise was grateful. With a man at her side, she walked through the crowd with more confidence, and was greeted by several people who had not been sure who she was until they saw her with her son-in-law.

When Arthur had brought her a drink, he was drawn into a male conversation. Louise saw Miriam going into the house, which was so artificially 'period' that even the ivy looked synthetic. Eva was sitting in a corner, pouting at a good-looking young man, who seemed attentive. Louise was glad about that. Eva should have good-looking young single men thrown at her until she woke up to the fact that it was possible to be attracted by a man who was not married. Optimistically, she viewed the back of Harvey Upjohn's neck, and wondered how it would look above a morning coat, standing beside Eva, as she had once wondered about David, before she learned the disturbing truth.

Eva saw her, and beckoned, but Louise turned away, pretending not to see. She did not want to disturb what might be a promising encounter. She looked out to the garden, with its over-groomed sweep of lawns and flowerbeds and rhododendrons and self-conscious little pools. The women's dresses made a pleasant shifting of colour on the rich, green grass, which two gardeners had slaved over all summer, and would break their hearts over to-morrow.

As she watched, the voices from below seemed imperceptibly to be growing clearer. You could hear individual remarks, where before there had only been a blur of talk. The sky had darkened and all the leaves were motionless.

'I had wanted so desperately to go to Majorca,' Louise

heard a woman say into the still air, and then suddenly, it came—big, warm drops of rain, that became a downpour in an instant, and sent the decorous garden party scurrying hither and thither as if a stone were dropped into an ant's nest.

With the rain came the wind. The waitresses fought with tablecloths that blew like spinnakers, clutching at their caps, and calling out distractedly, like peewits flying before a storm. Two of them ran crabwise through the rain, bearing the vast tea urn between them. The barmen, their oiled hair streaked over their foreheads, were rushing bottles and glasses into the kitchen like madmen, hating to get wet, cursing Sidney for not having set up his bar between four walls, which was good enough for most people.

A few of the guests ran straight round the house and out through the front garden and were never seen again. Others crowded through the french windows into the Cobb's panelled drawing-room, were pushed into the hall by more guests pressing in from the garden, and were forced out of the front door on the other side like champagne corks, running for their cars over the glistening gravel.

'Don't go, everybody! Don't go!' Sidney and Alice shouted. 'It's only a shower!' But the rain poured solidly down on the abandoned trestle-tables and the overturned chairs of the routed bandsmen.

'Don't go! Don't go!' Alice shrilled. 'We'll all go into the barn. There's loads of room. Bring the drinks in there, somebody!' But the party could not be salvaged. The rats were deserting the ship. One by one they took their leave and dashed into the rain with coats and newspapers over their heads, and in one case, Sidney's umbrella.

Alice and Sidney were left with the wreckage of their party, holding on to a couple who had weakly promised to stay and play bridge.

Eva found Miriam in the hall. 'I'm going back to London with this Upjohn creature,' she said. 'He's got a car.'

'I thought you were going to stay for dinner and take a late train.'

'I was, but I hope you don't mind. This will save me that boring train journey. I think I'd be silly not to take the chance of driving back.'

Poor Harvey Upjohn, so gleeful at the thought of having Eva in his car for twenty miles, and confident that he could persuade her to have dinner with him, might have felt as ill-used as indeed he was, if he had known that she was convinced now that David would come round this evening, and was thinking only of getting back to the flat, to be there waiting for him.

Arthur drove home carelessly, with Miriam nagging at him to go more slowly round the corners. They both felt as if they had been to a wedding, regretting that they had drunk in the middle of the afternoon.

'Why anyone,' Arthur yawned, 'is insane enough to have a garden party in this climate, beats me.'

'Alice and Sidney once went to Buckingham Palace,' Miriam said. 'They've never got over it.'

'I thought it was very nice,' Louise put in from the back seat. When she did not enjoy a party, she always thought that there was something wrong with her, not the party.

'Oh, it was, it was.' Miriam took off her glasses and bent her slender neck to lean her red head against the seat. 'Poor old Alice. I must ring her up to-night and tell her how much we enjoyed it.'

'Good God,' Arthur said, as they turned in under the dark, sodden thatch of the gate and saw a car in the drive. 'The last straw. Visitors. Who on earth is that?'

'I don't recognize the car.' Miriam peered short-sightedly through the streaming windscreen.

'I'm going in by the kitchen,' Arthur said. 'I can't take any more sociability. You and Mother cope with whoever it is, and get rid of them. I'm going up to change.' He had only got his suit slightly wet, running to fetch the car for Miriam and Louise, but he was very careful about his clothes and always put them straight on to hangers when he came in out of the rain.

Ellen met them at the door, looking important. 'There's someone to see you,' she said, looking at her grandmother.

'Who is it?' Miriam asked.

'I don't know. She hasn't come to see you. She wants to see Granny. She's in the drawing-room. I made her some tea.' Ellen looked hopefully for praise. 'She's been here quite a long time. She's awfully nice. She's been playing Old Maid with me.'

Louise took off her hat and coat, and stood her umbrella to drip on the doormat. 'Whoever can it be?' she asked herself.

'Why not go in and find out?' Miriam said, jerking her head towards the drawing-room door. 'One of your London friends, probably. I'll go and give the kids their tea. You won't want me.'

'Oh, but Miriam——' Louise did not know any women with cars who would come to see her. She did not feel like coping with a stranger alone. It might be someone wanting to sell her something.

'And do take that umbrella off the mat, Mother,' Miriam said, starting off towards the kitchen. 'It looks so bourgeois. There's a perfectly good stand.'

Louise patted down her hair and went into the drawing-room. The woman sitting on the sofa stood up and came towards her with a smile. She was tall and dark, with smooth, black hair parted like wings on either side of an olive-skinned, narrow face that might have been Italian. She was not beautiful, but she was arresting. Her shoes were perfect, and her clothes looked as if she had been standing up in them all day.

'Mrs Bickford?' she said. 'How do you do. I am Mrs Graham—Frances Graham.' She looked to see whether the name conveyed anything to Louise.

'How do you do?' Louise said nervously. 'I'm sorry you had to wait.' She sat down, looking to see whether there was a case of samples anywhere in the room, although the stranger did not look as though she were forced to sell lace or Swedish pottery for a living.

'It's quite all right,' Mrs Graham said, sitting opposite her. 'Your grand-daughter has been entertaining me most beautifully, with tea and cards.' She smiled beyond Louise, who turned and saw that Ellen had followed her into the room and was standing on one leg in the middle of the carpet.

Mrs Graham considered for a moment, and then said: 'I don't want to interfere with your tea-time, Ellen. I'm sure I've kept you too long already.'

'Oh, it's all right,' Ellen said. 'Mummy hasn't got it ready yet.'

'Run along, darling,' Louise said, taking Mrs Graham's hint. 'I'll see you in a little while.'

When Ellen had gone, Mrs Graham settled back in her chair and said gently: 'You don't know who I am, do you?'

'Well I—you must forgive me. Should I?'

'I am David Graham's wife.'

For a moment, Louise was puzzled, and then she remembered David's surname. She felt as if the inside of her head and body had dropped right out of her, leaving her cold and empty and dead.

'I'm afraid I've given you a shock,' Mrs Graham said. 'I'm sorry.'

Louise realized how silly she must look, sitting there staring with her mouth open. She shut it and murmured something meaningless, struggling to comprehend the situation.

Why was this woman here? What did she want with her? Had Eva run away with David? But Eva had been down here all day. Had she found out something—found a letter, perhaps, or seen them together? Was she going to threaten, to make a scene, to storm? She looked too serene for that. Was she going to warn Louise that she would name Eva as co-respondent ? Dark scandal washed about in Louise's mind. She saw the courtroom, the prying lawyers, the filthy allegations, the dirt creeping over Eva's foolish, hopeful love. She did not think she would be able to bear it.

'I've upset you.' Mrs Graham leaned forward. 'Forgive me. Perhaps I should not have come, but I felt I had to. I think you are the only person who can help.'

'I? What can I do?' Louise cried helplessly, not knowing yet what she was being asked to do. Had Mrs Graham come to plead with her—was that it ? Would she go down on her shapely knees, like a woman in a play, and beg Louise with tears to help her get her husband back? She did not look hysterical enough for that. Moreover, she did not look, Louise decided, beginning to think more sensibly, like a woman who would lose a husband unless she did not want him.

'I don't know how much you know about—things,' Mrs Graham said, 'but David told me that he'd met you at your daughter's flat, and so I imagine that you guessed something of what was going on. We'll have to talk frankly about this, I'm afraid,' she said, as Louise drew back and kept silent. 'I hope you won't mind. I shan't stay very long. I don't suppose you're enjoying this any more than I am.'

She offered Louise a cigarette. Louise took it, and smoked in short, quick puffs, hoping to draw in a lot of nicotine to steady her nerves.

'David doesn't know I'm here, of course,' Mrs Graham went on, 'although it was he who told me, in passing, that you were staying with your eldest daughter.' She smiled, and Louise was struck by the illogical thought that she knew what it felt like not to have a home of your own.

'It must be nice to have such a devoted family. I understand that Eva is very good to you, too.'

'Oh, yes, she is. Very good,' Louise said abstractedly. Her mind was still struggling with the startling fact that David continued to see his wife, although they were supposed to be separated, and that he had told her about Eva. How much had he told her? It was all so confused. Eva had described David's wife as—what was it?—poisonous; and yet here she was, very polite and charming, sitting in Miriam's wing-backed chair with a face like a Florentine Madonna.

'Tell me why you've come,' Louise said abruptly. Whatever it was, she must know it. She could not endure these tangled thoughts any longer.

'Thank you,' Mrs Graham said. 'I will.' She recrossed her

elegant legs. 'I've come to help your daughter.' She smiled. 'That must make you more confused than ever. No doubt you expect me to come here as a wronged wife, fighting Eva with tooth and claw. But I don't have to fight, you see. I've won already. In fact, there's never been any conflict at all.'

Louise took a deep breath. 'Can I say what I like?' she asked.

'I wish you would. We must be honest. I shan't be offended at anything. You're the one who should be offended, if anyone has to be.'

'I shan't, though,' Louise said candidly. 'I like you. That's what's so queer. You see, the way I understood it, you and your husband were separated because you didn't get along, and were going to get a divorce anyway, even before he met Eva. Am I talking out of turn? My family always says I do.'

'Families always jump on each other,' Mrs Graham said. 'I like you, too. I never thought you would be as nice to me as this. To be quite frank, I was terrified that you'd show me to the door as soon as you knew who I was.'

'You didn't look terrified,' Louise said, and they both laughed.

'It's the way my face is made. It doesn't show what goes on behind it.'

'In any case,' Louise said, 'why should I show you the door? You haven't done anything to hurt me, or Eva. It's Eva who has hurt you. I feel so dreadful about it. My girls were quite strictly brought up. I expect I was too soft with them, but my husband was—well, rather exacting. I never thought that one of them would get into anything like this. I've tried to reason with Eva, but I can never tell any of my children anything.'

'What mother can?' Frances Graham said. 'But you're wrong. Eva hasn't hurt me, although she thinks she has, poor little thing.'

'Do you know what Eva thinks?' Louise said. 'She thinks your husband is going to marry her.'

'I was afraid of that,' Mrs Graham sighed. 'That's why I came to you. I knew it would be no good going to your daughter, because she wouldn't listen to me. I wouldn't either, in the same position. She wouldn't believe anything I told her about David. She's in love with him, isn't she?'

'I'm afraid so. She's changed. She's quite different. Oh—she's been what she called "in love" before, but it never lasted more than a few weeks. This time she—she seems to have lost something of herself. I don't quite know how to explain it. I've never seen her like this.'

'Poor kid.' Mrs Graham looked sad.

'How can you feel sorry for her? I do, of course, but I'm her mother; but I feel ashamed, too.'

'It isn't really her fault. It's David's. David, all the way through. I know him so well, and it's all happened before. We've been through it all before.' She spoke wearily, leaning her head back against the chair, and closing her dark-lidded eyes for a moment.

'David has had other girls, you see. Always "the most gorgeous girl in the world. The greatest thing since penicillin." You know the way he talks. Oh, yes, he tells me about them. Sitting before me with his head in his hands, trying to look boyish, although he's too old for that; casting himself on my mercy, and telling me he doesn't know what to do, and that he can't help himself, and I must help him. Why, my son, at fourteen, has more stamina than David.'

'Has he told you everything about Eva?' Louise clasped her hands, for they were trembling.

'Some things. I'm his sort of father confessor. He runs to me when he's in trouble, knowing that I won't bother to excite myself about it. I sometimes wonder why I don't, but I like to preserve the peace, even in such a decrepit marriage as ours.'

'You're not separated then?'

'Not really, although we don't see each other too often. I have a little house at Windsor. It backs on to the park, and I love it. David has his flat in town, but he comes down for week-ends occasionally, or when he feels the need of a little sanity. I think he feels that I'm good for him. And then, of course,' she added thoughtfully, 'I do have some money.'

'You sound as if you don't like him very much,' Louise said. 'Oh, forgive me. Perhaps I shouldn't have said that.'

'Don't worry. Nothing that anyone said to me about David could offend me. because I've said it all to myself a hundred times. I don't like him, if liking means respect and friendship and confidence. But I'm fond of him, you know, in a disillusioned way. I can't help it. He's rather sweet, even when he's silly. And then, of course, I remember what we had together once. Even David can't kill that. I like to think of it sometimes, though I doubt whether he ever does.'

'I think he's been awful to you,' Louise said vehemently. 'I can't think why you put up with it.' She remembered one of her friends saying that to her once about Dudley, and she had answered: 'What else is there to do?'

What could you do with a husband, except put up with him? Oh—but Eva! Her mind flew to Eva. So pleased with herself in her dashing red dress. So quick and elusive and stubbornly blind to everything except her own desires.

'Please tell me.' She had to ask it. 'Isn't it true—about the divorce?'

Frances Graham shook her head. 'I don't know what David's been saying, but it isn't true. No doubt he believes it when he's with Eva. He gets carried away, you know, and I understand that she's very fascinating. But that doesn't excuse his cruelty, because he doesn't mean it. We've had this talk about divorce before, but he's always dropped it, without my having to argue.

'He really needs me, you see. And I need him, because of our son. I'd stick to David whatever he did, to keep Terry out of that kind of disaster. If it wasn't for Terry, I might fool him one day by turning him loose on to one of his lady loves, and then where would he be?'

'The—the money, you mean?' Louise asked.

'How do you think he can afford these cars and holidays and night clubs and all the expensive suits he loves to buy? He's a good enough actor, but there aren't enough of his kind of parts to keep him in the way he likes to live. All this sounds very sordid, I know, and it is sordid. It's hateful and humiliating. It sounds as if I were hiring David to be a father to my child, but it isn't like that at all. I let him have the money because I'm sorry for him. I can afford it. I don't need much for myself, and he likes to spend.'

'It sounds as if your life must be so unhappy,' Louise said slowly, 'and yet you look contented.'

'I am. Contented enough to go on with. I have a lot of friends, and my father is good to me, and I like my home, and Windsor's nice, if you keep out of the medical set, and the Guards set, and the Palace set. I fret at times—who doesn't?— but you have to take what you get, and I've got David, with all his failings. I've got used to it. It doesn't matter too much now as far as I am concerned, but it's just when it touches someone like your Eva that it all becomes such a mess.'

Mrs Graham stood up and picked up her gloves and bag. 'I think I'd better go now,' she said. 'I hope I haven't stayed too long. I think I've said everything there is to say. You've been wonderful, to listen to me like this, and to understand.'

'But I don't know that I do understand.' Louise felt the frown knotting her brows. 'What happens now?'

'That's up to you. I just have to wait around to hold David's hand and comfort him when his little affair is over. Forgive me. It's dreadful to talk about it like that when it's your daughter. But, since it is your daughter, my dear,' she said, taking Louise's hand and looking at her with great compassion, 'you have to try and stop her running head first into tragedy.'

'What do you want me to do?' Louise asked in a small voice.

Frances Graham pressed her hand. 'I want you to try and make Eva understand that David will never marry her,' she said. 'It will break her heart, I know, but the sooner it's broken, the sooner it will mend. She's young and pretty. She'll find another man—a much better one than my husband.' They walked to the door together. 'I'd like to think I could meet her some day. She sounds a darling.'

'She is.' Louise was afraid that she was going to cry. 'How can I possibly say this to her?'

'You must. It will probably be one of the hardest things you've ever done in your life; but you must.'

'I'll try,' Louise said wretchedly. 'I'll have to try.'

'Don't come to the door,' Frances Graham said. 'I'll find my own way out.' She bent suddenly and kissed Louise. She smelled expensively fragrant. 'Come and see me one day, won't you? We could talk about nice things.'

'Well, who was it?' Miriam came into the drawing-room after she heard the front door close and the car drive away. 'I didn't come in, because you sounded so earnest through the door.'

Louise turned away to hide her face, fighting to collect herself. 'You weren't listening, were you?' She caught her breath. Whatever happened, Miriam was not going to know about this. That was the least she could do for Eva.

'Of course not. I never heard a word. Why? Was she black-mailing you? We'll have to get Arthur to prosecute, and you'll be Mrs X, in a black veil. Who was it, anyway?'

'Oh—nobody,' Louise said. 'Someone gave her my name. She was trying to sell me some lace.'

'She's got a damned good-looking car to do it in.'

'It's the firm's car,' Louise improvised. 'It's very expensive lace.'

'Well, thanks for not setting her on to me. I wonder why on earth she came to you?'

'I suppose she thought I was the right person,' Louise said bleakly. 'I wish she hadn't.'

That evening, Louise said as casually as she could: 'By the way, Miriam, I think I'll have to go to London to-morrow, if someone wouldn't mind taking me to the station.'

'But you've only just been there. What's the matter—too dull for you here?'

'Of course not, dear. Don't always take me up. It's just that I have some things to attend to. I have to see the bank man-ager. Something about my money.' She had rehearsed this.

'Can I help?' Arthur asked in his dutiful son-in-law voice. 'I'm always glad to advise, you know, if there's any difficulty.'

'I know you are. You've always been very kind. I don't know what I would have done without you when Dudley died,' Louise said, hoping to divert attention from her project.

'Oh, that.' Arthur made a face. 'That's best forgotten.'

'Why is it, Daddy?' asked Ellen, who was there in her dressing-gown. Why is it best forgotten? I don't think we should forget poor Grandpa.'

'Don't be smug,' Arthur said, 'and take off that pious face.'

Ellen turned to her grandmother. 'Can I come to London with you ? '

'Not this time, darling. You wouldn't enjoy it. I'll take you another day.'

'I know what it is,' Miriam said, 'She's off to see that boy friend of hers, who gave her the romantic present.'

Louise had been unable to resist showing Miriam the scent bottle, but had wished since that she had not.

'Aha!' said Arthur, heavily jocose. He and Miriam were feeling better since they had had a drink or two to counteract the effect of Sidney's black-market whisky. 'An assignation. Mother, you're deep.'

'Well, why can't I come,' Ellen insisted, 'if you're going to see Mr Disher—*alias* Lester Drage? He and I are friends.'

'Don't keep on,' her mother said. 'It's time you went to bed. Kiss Granny good night. It may be the last time you can do that. She may be going to elope.'

Louise did not enjoy this kind of teasing, and they were making it more difficult for her to ask for the loan of her train fare, which she was going to be forced to do. However, if they thought that she was going to see Gordon Disher, that would at least stop their curiosity and keep them off the track of the truth, which she was determined they should never know.

Louise did not sleep well that night. She lay awake and tried over and over in her mind the things that could be said to Eva.

They all sounded stupid, or over-dramatic, or unkind. She began to despair. She was not equipped for this. People had been telling her what to do for so long, and now she had to stand on her own and try to influence a wilful girl, to whom she had not given orders since she was a child.

If Dudley were alive, he would have said: 'You'll make a mess of this. Let me handle it.' He would have attacked Eva in a blustering and puritanical way that made no allowances for her being in love. He would have been outraged long before this, however, at her association with a married man. You could say one thing for Dudley; he had been faithful to Louise. She had sometimes wondered why, since he seemed so dissatisfied with her; but Dudley's excesses had followed other channels. He liked to look at women's legs and whistle, and could exchange story for story with other men, but it did not mean anything. He had been the kind of man who likes to talk as if he were a mass of sex, but never does anything about it.

Eva opened the door of the flat, looking radiant in a bright yellow housecoat, with her hair done in a new way.

'How nice to see you.' She kissed her mother. 'I was so pleased when you called and said you'd come in while you were in town. I hardly got a chance to talk to you yesterday, with all the sociability. What brings you up, anyway?'

'I had to see the bank manager,' Louise said, her resolution to plunge straight into her mission daunted by Eva's affectionate welcome. She could hardly bear to look at her daughter, thinking how cruel it was going to be to blot out the smile and the sparkle.

'What's the matter?' Eva said. 'Your eyes look tired. Take off your coat and come on in. I've got some lunch for you.'

'I don't think I want any really.'

'You haven't had it, have you? Well then, of course you do. Come into the kitchen, because I'm starving, and the soup's hot. We'll have it right away.'

During lunch, Louise kept looking for an opportunity to

broach the subject that was tormenting her; but it was impossible, with Eva chattering gaily about the Cobb's garden party, and telling Louise what Harvey Upjohn had said on the way home, and how he had suddenly turned the car into a side road, and stopped hopefully in a gateway.

'Oh, the devil was in him,' Eva said. 'He was on fire with claret cup. But anyway, after I finally managed to get him to take me home, without side-tracking into some dreadful little club he belongs to in a mews, David called and said he'd got theatre tickets. We saw that new American musical, which is heavenly, and had supper and danced afterwards.'

Now, thought Louise, now is the time perhaps; but she could not start saying the things that she had come to say over scrambled eggs and spinach; and Eva was so gay, saying: 'He brought me orchids—those brown ones I love—and I wore that white dress, and put my hair up like this. It was one of those good evenings—you know—when everything goes right, and you get a taxi the minute you want one, and the head-waiter has a steak hidden somewhere, and the band plays all your tunes. David's such fun to go out with. You do like him, don't you, Mother? I do want you to.'

To tell her now would be like slapping down a child who had come running up with laughter for a kiss. Eva had lost the strained, abstracted look she had worn yesterday. She seemed very young and confident. What had David been saying to her? Louise cursed him in her heart. She would have preferred to find Eva in tears.

They took their coffee into the sitting-room. Eva roamed about, swishing the yellow housecoat, looking out of the window and humming, turning on the radio and turning it off with a grimace. She seemed too blithe to be able to keep still.

Louise put down her cup. 'Eva,' she said resolut. 'come and sit down. I have something to tell you.'

'Just a sec.' The telephone was ringing, Eva talked for several minutes to someone called Norma, who had a grievance.

'Poor old Norma,' Eva said, as she hung up. 'She should never be in radio. She takes it too seriously. Whatever part they give her, she's always disappointed because she didn't get some other one. This time it's my part she wants, for Saturday night. Damned sauce. She couldn't play an adolescent if she lived to be a hundred.'

'Do stop wandering about Eva, and come and sit down. I want to talk to you.'

'Talk away.' Eva sat down with a bump, raising her heels in the air and letting them drop. Louise opened her mouth to speak.

'My goodness, you haven't got any sugar.' Eva jumped up again.

By the time she had fetched the sugar, sat down and jumped up once more for cigarettes and finally settled on the sofa with her shoes off and her feet tucked under her, Louise's mouth was dry, and the tactful opening phrase she had rehearsed stuck in her throat.

'Well, what were you going to tell me?' Eva said, picking up a nail file. 'I'm all agog.'

'Eva,' Louise said abruptly. 'Stop being so bright. Keep quiet and listen to me. I'm going to tell you something that you aren't going to like.'

'Tell all,' Eva said, shaping her short nails undismayed. 'I can stand anything to-day. I feel very well, in spite of the champagne.'

'I saw David's wife yesterday,' Louise said. The words hung undispersed in the silence that followed them.

'Bad luck,' Eva said after a moment, her face not showing anything. 'That can't have been much fun for you.'

'It wasn't. Oh—not that she wasn't nice. She was. But what she came to tell me wasn't nice.'

'You mean she actually came down to Miriam's to see you?' Eva put down the file and uncurled her legs. 'What frightful nerve. What was she doing? Playing the wronged wife and begging you to persuade your erring daughter to lay off her husband? My God, these women ! What will they think of next?' She got up and began to walk about the room again without her shoes.

'Eva, please listen. You're making it very difficult for me. If you'd just stop talking, and let me——'

'Let you what, Mother? That woman has upset you. I think it's vile of her, to come and bother you like that. She's not playing the game by the rules.'

'No, no. It's not like that at all. It's you who are not sticking to the rules. You're not playing fair, either with her, or with yourself.'

'Oh, for God's sake!' Eva jerked her shoulders. 'Let's stop talking like the captain of a hockey team. So Frances Graham went to see you. I suppose she towed the poor little orphan child along, crying for its Daddy. What do you expect me to do? Burst into tears?'

'Eva. Mrs Graham came out of kindness.' Louise dropped her words slowly, as if she were instructing a child.

Eva snorted, started to say something, and then kept silent, standing with her hand behind her back and her small, bare feet planted, watching her mother.

'You'll hate what I'm going to say,' Louise said nervously, finding it even harder to talk when Eva was listening silently than when she had been disruptive.

'You've said that before,' Eva said patiently. 'Go on, Mother.'

'She came because she wanted to help you. No—don't keep snorting and tossing your head like that. She was genuine. She honestly came out of kindness. She thinks—and you've given us all that impression—that you think that David is going to divorce her and marry you.'

'Well, he is,' Eva said defiantly. 'I don't suppose you approve of that, but I'm glad that father wouldn't let me and the others be brought up as Catholics.'

'Oh, Eva, don't say that. I'd always hoped——'

'Hoped what? That I'd throw in my lot with you and the Pope one day? How could I now? Look what a mess I'd be in. I can see why you don't like it, but you'll get over it. Other people have married divorced men and not been struck down by the Angel Gabriel.'

'But David will never marry you, darling. He has no intention of leaving his wife. She came to ask me to tell you that, because she knew you wouldn't listen to her.'

'Well, I won't listen to you either.' Eva began to pad about the room again. 'I think it's horrid of you, Mother, to take her side against mine. She comes down to see you, in that disgustingly chic car—oh, yes, I've seen it. I sneaked down to Windsor once, and took a look at her house. Dinky isn't the word. She comes crawling to you, all sweet and mealy-mouthed, and winds you round her little finger so that you believe all the lies she tells you. Wants to help me, indeed! So kind. Kind, my foot? Don't you see that this is only a despairing effort to get David back? She'll pull every trick she knows to try and keep him, although I don't think she wants him. But she doesn't want anyone else to have him. That's the kind she is.'

Louise shook her head. 'You must try and understand. I know it's dreadfully hard, and when one is in love, one can't see straight. I'm only trying to save you from being desperately unhappy.'

'Thanks,' Eva said shortly. 'I can look after my own happiness.'

'How can I make you see?' Louise beat her fists gently on her knees. 'It sounds so unkind, to criticize David to you, but there are so many things you don't know about him. Frances Graham knows him. She's been married to him for fifteen years. He's talked about leaving her before, apparently, but he's never done it. He needs her, in some way that probably neither you nor I can quite understand. And she will never divorce him because of the child.'

'Bitchier and bitchier. Anything else dear Mrs G. told you about David that I don't know?'

'There are—things. But I don't want to tell you unless I have to.'

'All right. Now I'll tell you something.' Eva stopped walking and stood before her mother, with her head up. 'Last night, we talked about our marriage, nearly all the time. He'll get free of that woman if he has to fight her every inch of the way. He loves me, Mother. Don't you understand? He loves me?'

'But you don't know what he's like!' Louise cried in distress. 'I didn't want to tell you this, but he's had other women—lots of them, and no doubt he's told some of them the same things he tells you. Eva, this is just another affair with him. Don't let him break your heart. He isn't worth it.'

'Be quiet, Mother.' Eva was growing angry. 'Don't talk about things you don't understand. What if he has had other women? What man of his age hasn't?—except that pompous husband of Miriam's, and I wouldn't put it past him, at that. What if David hasn't been a good little boy and kept his nose to his rich wife's heels. I don't blame him with a woman like that.'

'But she's nice, I tell you. She's awfully nice. I wish you could meet her, and then perhaps you might see.'

'I'd rather die. Let's stop this, Mother. It isn't getting us anywhere. I don't want to talk about it any more. There's no sense in your agonizing over me. I'm all right, do you hear? I just want to be left alone to run my own life without the family butting in all the time. I suppose Arthur and Miriam are in on this, too.'

'Of course not. They had no idea who Mrs Graham was and I wouldn't dream of telling them. Don't be angry, Eva. I know how I must have upset you, and I know I've been clumsy, and said things all wrong. I hope you'll forgive me. I didn't want to come.'

'Why did you, then?'

'I had to. Wouldn't you, if you had a daughter? Please think it over, darling, even if you're too upset to see straight now.'

'I'm not upset, because I don't believe you,' Eva said, a little shakily. She went to stand by the window, lifting the curtain and looking down at the street far below.

'You must believe me. I'll have to tell you one more thing. It's hateful, but it's true. One of the reasons why David will never leave his wife is because of her money. She gives him

money. When he buys you champagne and orchids, and takes
you out to these grand places, it's her money he's spending.'

'That's a lie!' Eva whipped round. 'How dare you talk
about David like that?' Her voice was thick with angry tears.
'Please go, Mother. I'm sorry, but I can't stand any more.
I'll ring down to the porter and tell him to get you a taxi.'

Louise stood up, exhausted in her defeat. 'Don't bother,'
she said. 'I'll get a bus to the station. I've plenty of time.'
She went into the hall and put on her coat.   Eva did not move
from the window.   Louise came to the door of the room.
Eva was standing with her back to her, looking out again.

'Good-bye,' Louise said tentatively. 'I hope you can be
happy, darling.'

Eva turned round just as the flat door closed. She stretched
out a hand as she heard the clash of the gates and the lift's
descending hum.

'Oh, Mother——' she whispered, and buried her face in the
curtain. 'Oh, Mother, please help me!'

The soldierly porter saluted Louise as she came out of the
lift. 'Taxi, madam?'

Louise shook her head without speaking, and walked quickly
out into the street. For a moment she stood on the pavement
in the shadow of the cliff of flats, uncertain where she was,
forgetting where she had to go; then she walked away, seeing
her feet move of their own accord, in, out, in, out, in front of
her, like independent animals.

At the corner, she turned to look upwards, hoping that Eva
might be waving and calling to her to come back; but she could
not tell which was Eva's window. They all looked the same;
some open, some closed, but nobody looking out of any of
them.

She would have to go to the station and wait there among
the other cheerless women in the tea-room until it was time
for her train. She crossed the road and walked up the High
Street, past the bus stop and on past the next one, walking,

walking, with her misery clinging to her like a shadow. The wind was blowing in her face. There was always a wind blowing, it seemed, at the critical moments of her life. There had been a high wind on the night the pigs were born, and two days after Dudley died, when Arthur came round to the house with his black hat and his brief-case, and overturned the stone of her ignorance to reveal the rotting ruin underneath.

She could see them now, going out to lunch, which Arthur insisted she must have, walking up the street to find a taxi. The telephone had been cut off that morning, because the bill was unpaid. They had walked into a callous wind, Louise striving against it mechanically, just as she was doing now, walking without hope into a blank future.

At that time, less than two years ago, Louise's numbing fears had been all for herself, because she did not know what was going to become of her. Now, as she walked past the posters for concerts and boxing matches outside the Albert Hall, her fear was for Eva. She did not know what was going to become of Eva, and whatever happened now would be her fault.

She had said all the wrong things. She had made a mess of it, just as Dudley would have expected. Anyone else would have known what to say to make Eva listen and believe. She had merely said the things that infuriated Eva into a blinder obstinacy. She had failed her daughter, and failed Frances Graham, who had thought that a mother, of all people, would be the one to put things right.

'Failure!' teased the wind, lifting her hat and tweaking out a strand of hair. 'Failure!' it mocked, rushing chill about her skirts. Louise felt an overwhelming desire to sit down and lay her head on somebody's shoulder. If she ran back to Eva now, and threw herself into her arms, couldn't they weep together, and make everything all right? But if Eva did not melt, Louise would only be making a hysterical scene; and Eva had probably gone out by now, running to David to tell him what had happened.

If only there were someone she could talk to. Even Dudley would have been better than nothing, although he would have said that she had made a fool of herself. There was no one in whom she could confide, unless . . .

She had come to another bus stop. A bus for Oxford Street was waiting there. Would it be betraying Eva? He was outside the family, and he was so discreet. Wise, too. He might be able to help her, and she was sure that he would not be shocked.

Louise climbed quickly on to the bus, just as the conductor rang the bell. 'Come along, lady,' he said sourly, grasping her arm. 'Don't leave everything till the last minute.'

'Please don't push me,' Louise said with dignity. She was usually charming to bus conductors, but to be grumbled at now was more than she could stand.

In the bus, she took out her mirror to tidy her hair and see what her face looked like. It looked terrible, lined and sallow and old. He would understand, when he knew what she had been through, but would Miriam notice any difference in her?

'You look a bit under the weather, Mother,' she would say. 'What's the matter? Your boy friend jilted you?' and Louise would have to pretend to laugh and join in the joke. It was going to be difficult to get through these last few days with Miriam, to behave as if she had no worries, and was just a placid widow, with three nice daughters who never gave her any trouble.

She had not considered that Gordon Disher might not be free to talk to her. It was discouraging when she saw him among the beds, attentively engaged with a discontented woman in a red coat and a Robin Hood hat. Louise saw him bow slightly, which he had to do from the shoulders, since he could not do it from the waist, excusing himself to come over and speak to her.

'Hullo,' he said, with the gentle delight he always displayed at seeing her. 'This is a nice surprise. Come to take me out to tea? I'll be free in a few moments.'

'I don't think I'll have time for tea,' Louise said nervously. 'I have to catch a train. I just wanted to talk to you for a moment if it wouldn't matter.'

'You don't look yourself,' he said. 'Is something wrong?'

Louise nodded, and saw his eyes grow concerned. 'I'll just have to finish with this customer,' he said, 'if you can wait a minute or two. I'll get you a chair.'

Louise sat down and watched him dealing deferentially with the woman in the Robin Hood hat. She went from bed to bed, examining the price tags, punching the mattresses with a face of incurable dissatisfaction, while Mr Disher stood by her, answering her sharp questions patiently, and occasionally throwing an apologetic glance towards Louise.

Would the woman never make up her mind? Now she wanted to look at sofa beds and see how they worked. Mr Disher bent with difficulty to pull levers and push buttons. When the sofa became a bed, the woman lay stiffly down on it in her red coat, refusing to take his word that it was full length.

Louise looked at her watch. She would not have long now to talk to him, and get away in time to catch her train. Now the woman wanted to see the bed turned back into a sofa. It stuck, and she shrugged her shoulders and walked away, pointing to a cluster of divans in a far corner.

'What can I do?' Gordon Disher's face said. Louise looked at her watch again. Five minutes more and she would have to go. Perhaps it would be just as well. Perhaps she never should have come. Why drag him into this? It was no concern of his. There was no reason why he should be interested.

The words that had thronged into her mind as she came here on the bus had left her. She did not know how she would begin to tell him, and she would never be able to gabble through the story in the short time that was left. They would not even be able to sit down. He was not allowed to sit down on duty. The department manager was visible through the window of his little office-shack. They would have to stand among the beds trying to look as if they were talking about the merchandise.

Gordon Disher had his back to her, bending to read a price label. Louise got up and walked quickly through the archway to the lifts. The lift was crowded, and she had to push her way in, but she had never felt so alone in her life.

She thought that Gordon Disher would write to her to ask what had been the matter, and to apologize for not being free. She went down early for several days, to take the letter before Miriam could see it and ask questions; but he did not write.

There was to be a pony show, the last one of the holidays, and Simon, who had progressed favourably, was to be allowed to enter for the jumping event. His pony did not jump very well. It was an unsuitable, nervous animal, with a thin neck and bulging eyes, which Arthur, taking no advice, had bought without trial from a leather-faced dealer.

When the dealer's son rode it, it had jumped well and won some prizes, and Arthur thought that it would carry his son to glory. However, when Simon began to ride it, in his heavy-handed and unsympathetic way, it did not fly over the jumps like a bird, but either swerved sideways at the last minute, or stuck in its toes and threw Simon under, into or over the fence.

This had happened the first time that Simon rode it in a show. 'I knew that pony would be too much for that boy,' nodded the other parents among themselves. Arthur had forbidden Simon to jump any more, and had gone back to the dealer to complain.

'Nothing wrong with the pony,' the dealer said. 'Only wants riding. My Sidney's jumped four foot on him time and time again. Don't blame me, sir, if your boy can't ride.'

This had piqued Arthur into keeping the pony, determined that Simon should not be outdone by the rat-faced Sidney, who rode with his knees to his chin and a multitude of shrill exhortations.

Simon had been somewhat relieved to be forbidden to jump, but he was ashamed, too, and felt compelled to pester his father to allow him to perform at this last show.

Miriam said no, but Arthur finally said yes, and so Miriam

shrugged her shoulders and said: 'All right. The ponies are your department, but don't blame me if the child breaks his neck.' Miriam quite often gave in to Arthur, to avoid the wear and tear of an argument; but she seldom yielded without a parting shot.

Jumps were put up in the meadow behind the stables, and thither Simon repaired with lumps of sugar and the attendant gardener to practise for the forthcoming show. Arthur himself would stride out with his switch to coach his son when the gardener was not there. Although William never said a word, Arthur did not care for the way he clicked his teeth and shook his head each time he replaced the jumps after the pony had skidded into them.

On the evening before the show, when William had gone home, Arthur announced as soon as he returned from London that he would see Simon once more over the jumps and give him some final tips.

'Not now, Daddy,' Judy protested. 'Misty's all cleaned up for to-morrow. William won't like it if he gets his legs dirty.'

'Then William can earn his keep for once and clean him again to-morrow,' Arthur said. 'Unless, of course, you expect me to clean him.'

'Oh, Daddy!' Judy and Simon laughed at the joke. Arthur never did any manual work, either in the stables, the garden, or the house. He was popularly supposed to be too busy to concern himself with such things.

Simon did not want to go out and jump again. He had been riding all afternoon, and the pony had been cross. It would be even more cross at being taken out at this time.

'The light's not very good, Daddy,' he said hopefully, 'and you know he's got that funny eye. Do you think he'll see the jumps all right?'

'I'm not asking him to look at them. I'm asking him to jump them. Why do we always have to have an argument about everything?' Arthur was a little tired, and would have liked to sit down before dinner, but he had made up his mind in the train that it was his duty to give Simon a final polish, and was determined to go through with it, although the light was indeed failing into dusk.

'Go and get Misty ready,' he ordered, 'and I'll meet you in the field in five minutes. Miriam, you come too, dear. I want you to see how Simon's got on. Mother, why don't you come and see the show?' The effort of going out would be more worth while if he had an audience.

Louise hesitated. 'I'll have to change my shoes.' She did not particularly want to go. It made her nervous to see the children jump, and she had been more nervous of everything these last few days. The disastrous scene with Eva had left her feeling as if she had been on a long journey, or had been very ill. She dropped more things than usual, and lacked even the confidence to poach eggs for Miriam, because her hands shook and she split the yolks. She found it hard to concentrate, and did not always hear when she was spoken to. Miriam said that she ought to go to an ear specialist before she went to the Isle of Wight.

'I'll get your shoes, Granny,' Ellen said. 'Let's go and watch. I'll come if you will.'

'Well, keep your mouth shut if you do,' Arthur said. 'You can put up the jumps, but for God's sake, keep out of the way.'

'Of course, Daddy,' Ellen said meekly, and made a face at him behind his back.

'Ellen,' said her mother, who missed nothing. 'I've a good mind to put you to bed.'

'What for?' Arthur asked. 'What has she done now?'

'Oh, nothing,' Miriam said wearily. 'Come on, let's go out if we're going, and get it over.'

Miriam and Louise stayed by the gate of the meadow, at a safe distance from the activity. It was a typical late September evening, damp and subdued. The grass was already wet, and grey with the slight mist that was rising to meet the falling dusk. The hedges were dark with blackberries, and some of the trees were showing patches of russet and gold. Under the oak in the corner, Judy's little pony grazed unconcernedly.

Simon's pony rushed about with its nose in the air, dropping its head suddenly as it approached a jump, to peer at the small obstacle, then switch away outside it, plunging on to the next jump to repeat the same unnerving performance.

'Don't let him keep running out!' Arthur shouted, striding about like a ringmaster in the middle of the field in a pair of truncated Wellington boots to keep his ankles dry. 'What the devil are you doing, Simon? Keep his head straight.'

'I can't, Daddy.' With difficulty, Simon pulled the pony to a stop. 'I don't think he wants to jump to-night. He can't see,' he panted, looking at his father helplessly.

'It's not what he wants. It's what you want. You'll never ride him if you don't remember that. Little devil!' Arthur jerked the pony's rein unkindly. 'Now get on and behave yourself.' He sent it off with a smart slap on the neck. His voice and the flat sound on the pony's wet neck carried clearly to where Louise and Miriam were leaning against the gate.

'Oh, dear,' Miriam sighed. 'I do wish he wouldn't be so violent. No good will come of it.'

'It's safe, isn't it?' Louise asked anxiously.

'Oh Lord, yes, but Arthur's so drastic. I always feel that things would go much better if he didn't make such a noise.' She hooked her arms behind the top bar of the gate and leaned backwards, chewing on a spur of grass.

'Try it again!' Arthur was shouting. 'Take him round as if you meant it. Not so *fast!* Pull him up—pull him up, My God, you'll—Good boy! Fine!' Simon was over the first fence like a rocket, and was pounding on to the next, his small face pale in the twilight. Arthur was running across the field with his arms outstretched to stop the pony swerving out from the fence.

Startled, the pony shied at him, stopped dead, then suddenly leaped straight up into the air and landed on the other side of the fence with its legs as stiff as iron bars. Simon rolled gently to the ground, and the pony walked away, putting down its head to eat grass.

Ellen, who had been dodging about the field like a nervous leprechaun, ran up in gasping distress to bend over Simon.

F

There was a lot more shouting then: 'Get hold of that pony before he treads on his reins! Get out of the way, Ellen. Simon, get up! Don't be a baby—you're not hurt. Catch hold of that pony and get back on him!'

Simon got up, rubbing his back, and went resignedly to catch the pony. He hesitated, glancing round at his father.

'Mount, I said! Get on him and make him do it properly!' Arthur squelched fiercely over the grass in his ankle boots and took hold of his son to hoist him into the saddle.

'Oh, Daddy, please—please!' Ellen ran up behind him, and grasped his coat. 'Don't make him. He's nervous. Can't you see he's nervous?' Although there were times when she hated Simon, there were times like this when she felt passionately protective.

Arthur pushed her roughly aside, and sent Simon off with a swish of his stick under the pony's tail that made it jump forward before Simon was settled in the saddle.

'Daddy!' Ellen screamed. 'He hasn't got his foot in the stirrup! Oh, stop him, stop him! Throwing up her hands, she ran wildly across the pony's path as it galloped for the jump. The pony swerved, and Simon was on the ground again, this time in tears, while the pony, sickened of the whole thing, cantered off with flying reins and stirrups to join its companion.

Louise, who had held her breath for a moment that seemed like eternity, felt her heart beat again with a sob, and started forward. 'Simon's hurt!'

Miriam pulled her back. 'No he's not. He's just frightened. I can tell by the way he's crying. Don't go to him. You'll only make Arthur worse.'

Except for shouting at Simon to get up and stop being a baby, Arthur was ignoring him to give the whole of his wrath to Ellen. The child could not speak. She hung her head and slunk away through the gathering darkness, making for a hole in the hedge where she could crawl through and run back to the house to hide.

Louise's heart ached for the thin little girl, dragging her feet through the grass, with one shoulder drooping and her hand up to her mouth. She turned to Miriam. 'I'm going to her,' she said defiantly, for she expected Miriam to tell her not to. 'It's too bad of Arthur. She was only trying to help. Why is Arthur always so hard on her?'

Miriam looked at her without expression. 'Because she's not his child,' she said. 'Oh, God! Simon *is* hurt. He's——' She ran away from Louise across the field, to where Simon had staggered to his feet, his sobbing changed to short screams as he looked at the arm which dangled awkwardly beside him.

CHAPTER SIX

Louise began to feel better as soon as she got into the train at Waterloo. She had not particularly enjoyed her last winter in the Isle of Wight, although her daughters had all told her how nice it must be at Sybil's hotel, to stifle whatever guilt they felt at being glad to get rid of her so conveniently.

This time, however, Louise was glad to get away. She was tired out. Her family had defeated her. There were too many troubles, too much to worry about. Like a sick person who staggers about with a fever until he finally collapses gratefully into bed, Louise had given up. She could not stand any more.

First Eva, who had not written or telephoned, nor come to the station to say good-bye. Then Miriam's unbearable revelation, which Louise must keep locked in her heart, battering vainly to get out and be explained, for Miriam, she knew, would never refer to it again.

Simon's broken arm, and the rushing back and forth to the hospital, and all the useless argument about whose fault it was, and everywhere in Louise's thoughts, Ellen—trying to keep out of the way, crying because she was not allowed to go and see Simon, bearing, it seemed to Louise each time she looked at her, a load of secret calamity on her bony shoulders.

Why had Miriam told Arthur? Was it even true? Who could it possibly . . . that gay young man with the slanting eyes, who used to be Arthur's friend—what was his name—Donald —Colin someone? Suppose that Miriam, in such an odd moment of indiscretion as had seized her standing by the gate in the meadow, were to tell Ellen at some time? What would happen then? The questions chased themselves round and round in Louise's brain until she was exhausted, and could think no more.

And then there was Anne. Louise had gone to the Stone Farm for the day to say good-bye to Anne, and had found her in bed, pasty-faced, and in a furious temper. She had had a slight hæmorrhage. Frank was beside himself with worry.

'It was her own fault,' he told Louise, too upset to make any more excuses for his wife, who, he knew, would take care not to become pregnant again if she lost this baby. 'She won't do as she's told. She won't look after herself. I had to go North for a sale, and while I'm gone, she goes off to a party at the airfield, and drinks whisky and that, and stays up nearly all night. She was taken bad the next day. I found her when I got home. She hadn't even called the doctor.'

'But the baby's all right?'

'Touching wood. But the doctor says she's got to be more careful now, and you know what she's like. Tell her to do one thing; she does another. You must talk to her, Mother. She won't listen to me.'

I can't, Louise had thought, dragging herself upstairs to do feeble battle with Anne. I can't cope any more. What was wrong with this family all of a sudden? She had wanted everything to go so well for the girls. She had wanted the futile thing she had made of her marriage with Dudley to be justified at least by the emergence of three happy lives.

What had she done wrong that they should grow up into trouble? If it was her fault, there was nothing she could do to remedy it. Her daughters did not need her. They were intent on spoiling their lives in their own way.

The train slipped through the squalor of Vauxhall and on towards the meek suburbs. Louise took off her hat and watched London fall behind, glad to get away, hoping to find some peace; but knowing that as soon as she was settled in with Sybil at the hotel, she would wish that she were back among her family again.

A pale October sun was touching the tops of the miniature waves in the Solent. It was cold on the deck of the paddle steamer, but the cabin was stuffy and smelled of oil. Louise sat in the breeze with a scarf wound round her head and her second coat over her knees, and felt as though she were going abroad.

People who travel to and fro between Portsmouth and the island every day probably pay no more attention to the boat trip than if it were a bus ride. To Louise, it was always exciting to chug out of the busy harbour, feeling proud about the warships, past the amusement park at Southsea with its skeleton switchback, and out among the little boats to cross the stretch of water, where the abandoned section of Mulberry Harbour stuck out of the sea like a memorial to the lost men of D-Day.

The island ahead looked enchantingly green. It was like a foreign country, so far away in the haze, and then all at once so close, with Ryde church appearing and the pier suddenly taking shape out of the background, and people beginning to collect suitcases, while the man stood by the rail to throw the rope for the gangway.

When she stepped on to the pier, the very air smelled different. The Portsmouth air smelled of oil and ropes and the mud in which small boys waded for worms. The air of Ryde still smelled of holidays, although the amusement buildings on the pier were closed now, the ice-cream stalls shuttered, and the paint and placards faded and weather-worn at the end of the summer season.

The little train that took her down the pier was only half full, with people who were soberly dressed, instead of degagé in shorts and open shirts. The season was over. The island was itself again, and the residents came out and looked round thankfully, like birds after rain.

Sybil was waiting at the end of the pier in the green station wagon that said: 'Driffield Court Hotel. Mr and Mrs G. V. Vernon, props.'

'You look ghastly,' she said, handling Louise's bags into the car with ease, since she was too impatient to find a porter. Sybil was a short, square, blonde woman, with muscles of iron, and legs like gateposts.

'I expect I got blown about on the boat,' Louise said. She was used to Sybil's bluntness. 'And I am a bit tired.'

'Too much family,' Sybil announced, zooming up the steep main street as if she were a Roman charioteer intent on mowing down the rabble. 'How are all your girls, Lou?' Sybil was the only person who called Louise that. It was a relic of school days.

'Oh, they're fine.'

'That all?' asked Sybil, who liked her conversation stimulating. 'I should have thought all kinds of things must have happened since I last saw you. Your letters never tell me a thing, except about the weather, and cosy little bits about the children.'

'Well—Simon broke his arm,' Louise said, playing safe, for Sybil was the last person to tell your troubles to unless you wanted half the population of the Isle of Wight to know them. 'He fell off his pony. He's all right though. They only kept him in the hospital a few days, and he's had to go back to school, much to his disappointment. But tell me about you. What sort of a season was it? You grumble at my letters, but you never write at all.'

'Too busy. We've been up to the eyes all summer. Oh, my dear, we've had such funny people! God knows where they come from—but thank God they do come, or we shouldn't be in business. One couple weren't married—I mean, not that some of the others weren't, too; you can always tell—but with this pair, the girl's parents turned up in the middle of the night. They'd chased her all the way from Scotland, of all things, and they made a terrible scene, waking everybody up, and boo-hooing, and talking to me as if I were a brothel-keeper. George went for the police. He hates to be woken up, but the quaint old couple nipped off, taking their daughter with them.'

'What about the man?'

'Oh, he stayed on and had a damned good holiday. Took up with a chesty girl in a sweater.'

Sybil chattered exaggeratedly all the way to the hotel, which was a few miles outside the town along the coast. Louise sat back and relaxed. Sybil talked so much and so fast that she hardly noticed whether anyone was listening. As long as she could talk, all was well with her world. She had talked her way through two husbands and was half-way through her third. George Vernon, like her first and second husbands, had started out as a normally communicative man, but had retreated into monosyllables before the battering-ram of Sybil's voice.

Sybil was a tonic. Everyone said so. She was one of the features of the hotel, which was small, expensive, badly run, and just too far from the sea. It had acquired a reputation, however. People who had stayed there recommended it to their friends, as if to dispel their own doubts as to whether their money would not have been better spent at a hotel where you received the comforts for which you paid. Many of the guests returned year after year, because Sybil had the knack of making them feel that they were privileged friends, who were only presented with staggering bills as a trifling afterthought.

'Old Sybil's a character,' they said, even new guests finding that they could use her Christian name after the first few days, when they had ceased trying to complain that their room had not been cleaned or that lunch was late, realizing that it got them nowhere, except into the bar for a drink on the house.

People brought their friends over for a drink from all round the island, to show them Sybil and enjoy her company. The trade in the bar keeps a hotel going, Sybil knew, and felt justified in spending a large part of her time there, ready to drink with all-comers.

Driffield Court, ivy-clad, and with additions of different periods stuck on in surprising places, had been a private house until George and Sybil Vernon bought it and converted it into a hotel. They had not made many alterations. It still had more the air of a house than a hotel, which was part of its charm, although inconvenient for the staff. They grumbled incessantly about the inadequate kitchen and pantries, and teas served in three small lounges instead of one large one, and breakfast trays to be carried up narrow, crooked staircases. They seldom stayed for more than one season, or even for the whole of one season. Sybil's life, when not at the bar, was beset by the problem of trying to find staff. She charmed them into coming, and bawled at them insultingly when they left. If they stayed, she upset them by interfering with their work, or changing their routine on a sudden whim. They quarrelled with her and among themselves. There was always some complicated vendetta going on behind the scenes, and once there had been an Italian with a knife, who had chased a kitchen porter through the dining-room while the guests were having lunch. The guests had enjoyed it. It was just one of those things that went with staying at Sybil's.

No one thought of it as 'staying at George's.' George was a background figure, poker-faced and unsociable. He would greet guests unsmilingly if he met them about the house, and would carry their bags upstairs without a word if all the male staff had left at the same time; but for the most part, he stayed in the private sitting-room behind the baize door, or in the office, brooding over the ledgers, counting the cash, and locking up the safe when Sybil had left it open.

The only member of the staff who remained from year to year was an elderly woman, who had been Sybil's maid a long time ago. She had retired to Shanklin, and when she read in the paper about the opening of Driffield Court, she had arrived on Sybil's back doorstep, wearing her apron underneath her coat, determined to work for her.

She was small and spare, whittled down by the years, but bright-eyed and sharp-tongued, taking neither orders nor impertinence from anybody, and treating the inconstant staff with disdain, which was one of the reasons for their inconstancy. Her name was Mary Ann Bunt, but she was known as 'Goldie,' although neither she nor Sybil could remember why. Her hair had never been yellow. It had been snow white ever since Sybil had known her, due to a shock in early youth, at which Goldie liked to hint darkly, but could never reveal, since she had long ago forgotten what it was.

'Old Goldie' was as much a feature of the hotel as 'Old

Sybil.' All the guests knew her name, and although she left mops and dustpans in their rooms and mixed up their laundry if she did not like them, they over-tipped her when they left, and sent her Christmas cards.

Sometimes she got on Sybil's nerves, because you could never tell her anything she did not know. She could hardly ever be persuaded to take a day off, because she felt, with some justification, that the hotel would go to pieces without her. Goldie could turn her knotted, blue-veined hand to anything, wherever staff was short. She cleaned, she cooked, she ironed and mended, she waited in the dining-room in creaking shoes, and cut the thin bread and butter for teas. She had even served behind the bar in a crisis, when the barman had flung away from the hotel in a fit of temperament just before a bank holiday week-end. Goldie had tied a white apron over the skimpy, faded print she loved to wear, and muttered up and down among the glasses and bottles, giving scrupulous measure, washing the glasses noisily in a pan of filthy water, and raising a face of quelling indignation above the bar if anyone offered to buy her a drink.

She was waiting at the hotel entrance when the station wagon drew up. She carried one of Louise's bags up the steps, pushing away Sybil's hand when she tried to restrain her.

'Goldie, you old fool,' Sybil said. 'That's much too heavy for a feeble old creature like you.'

'You're not so young yourself,' Goldie retorted. 'Did you get the scones? Forgot. I knew you would. Now I'll have to bake, as if I hadn't got enough to do.'

'Oh, shut up grumbling,' Sybil said. That was the way they talked to each other. The guests said it was as good as a music hall.

Louise greeted Goldie affectionately, and the old woman unleashed a grim, unpractised smile for her. She had been good to Louise when she was here last year, bringing her extra comforts, like early-morning tea and an electric fire, for which Louise would never have asked, since she was paying so little. Sybil was generous in letting her stay so cheaply, and she had impulsive fits of unloading dresses and scarves on to Louise and giving her liqueurs after dinner, but at week-ends when the hotel filled up, she would often forget all about her, and Louise would go about feeling like a charity patient, trying to keep out of the way, appearing only at meals, and hastening over her food at her little table in the draughty corner.

Goldie took her up to her room. 'See, I got you one of the better ones,' she said, opening the door of one of the front rooms on the first floor. '*She* said you should have the one you were in last year, but I didn't see why you should have that poky hole when this one was free.'

She turned back the counterpane and clicked her teeth. 'Slut,' she said. 'That new girl doesn't know how to make beds. She won't last long once I get after her.'

'That's all right,' Louise said. 'I'll make my bed every day, like I did last year. Thank you for getting me this room. It's nice.' She went to the window and looked out across the front lawn, past the putting green and tennis courts to where the little closely-hedged fields jostled each other down to the sea. 'Who else is staying here this winter?' she asked.

'The regulars? Well, there's old Mrs Maddox with the kidneys. She's been here all summer, too, worse luck. I can't think why she stays, because my lady treats her very casual. Then there's the Colonel. You remember him from last year. Dear old gentleman, he gives no trouble. There's a funny sort of woman come yesterday. Says she's a writer and wants peace and quiet. Hah! She's come to the wrong shop, I'd say.' Goldie looked round the room, tweaked at a towel, straightened an ashtray, and flicked on the light to see if there was a bulb in it.

'She's got a mess of papers, though. I looked at one that was in her typing machine. Couldn't make head nor tail of it. Well, I'll leave you. You'll meet the rest of the menagerie by and by. Tea will be on in an hour or so, if I'm lucky with my scones.'

Louise wandered about the room, examining its contents, trying to become at home in the strange, lonely world of a hotel room. Sybil's hotel was less lonely than most, however. How lucky I am, Louise thought determinedly, not to have to live in one of those dismal 'residentials,' where they farm out most widows. That might have happened to me. People have been kind.

She had started to unpack, but she left her bag open on the bed and sat down at the ink-stained antique table, which was beautiful, but groggy, to begin the chain of letters to her daughters, with which she would try to keep herself occupied through the long winter.

Miriam wrote back regularly; neat, amusing letters, which made Louise think that *Pleasantways* was a jollier place to live in than she found it to be when she was actually there. Anne wrote seldom, and without grammar or spelling. Eva had written quite often last year; affectionate, choppy letters, which gave the impression that she was living at great speed. Louise wondered whether she would write at all this year. Perhaps she would not; but Louise would go on writing to her as if nothing had happened between them.

She tore up the letter which she had started to Miriam, and took another piece of Sybil's grandiloquent notepaper.

'*Darling Ellen, here I am, and everything is just the same as last year, including Goldie. I like it, except that I wish you were here too,*' she wrote, and meant it. She wanted to be with Ellen now more than ever. She wanted to take her away from her invidious position and make up to her with love for the wrong that had been done to her.

When she judged that it was time for tea, Louise went down to the lounge. Although the place was so familiar to her, she felt as self-conscious as most solitary women when they enter the public rooms of a hotel. They may, like Louise, have been unhappy with their husbands, but when they find themselves without them, they realize what support a husband gives in public, however unsatisfactory he may be in private.

Having got over her own entrance, greeted the Colonel, and been introduced by him—for Sybil was not there—to the other tea-drinking residents, Louise took the table farthest from the fire, which was all that was left, and watched the diffident entry of a woman who must be the writer, although she did not look it. What did a female writer look like? The ones Louise had met at Miriam's were either smart, enamelled journalists, or intellectuals, with uneven skirts and big, questioning, unpowdered noses.

The woman who stood in the doorway was about forty, neatly dressed in clothes that would never be noticed, modestly made-up, and with a tight, nervous smile that trembled round the room, looking for somewhere to sit.

Mrs Maddox glared at her, pushing her long, bristly eyebrows together. She was a great, swarthy old woman, with a coarse skin and two moles on her chin from which long, black hairs waved like feelers. The Colonel, small and sandy and harmless, was having trouble with one of the many Driffield Court teapots that leaked. The pale young man, who was the son of one of Sybil's friends, recuperating from pneumonia, did not look up from his book. Miss Dott and Mrs Arbuthnot, who ran a successful dress shop in Ryde and lived here all the year round because they could not be bothered with housework, passed each other scones and jam and did not stop talking.

The newcomer rested her taut smile on Louise. 'Come and sit over here,' Louise said. 'There's room for two at this table. We'll get the girl to bring you a tray. What's your name, dear?' she asked, as the waitress came into the room and surprisingly answered her imperious finger.

'Ellen,' the girl said, pouting a mouth that was swollen with glistening fuchsia lipstick.

'What a coincidence!' Louise said. 'I have a grand-daughter called Ellen. I am Mrs Bickford. I stay here in the winter, you know.' She believed in getting on friendly terms with the staff as soon as possible, even though they usually left before she could make friends with them, and she had to start all over again with their successors.

The waitress looked blank. What is that to me, her pudding

face said, whether you are Mrs Bickford, or whether you have a grand-daughter called Ellen?

'Will you bring us one more tea, please?' Louise asked.

Ellen looked round the room, nodding her head as she counted: 'Six teas,' she said. 'They told me there would be but the six teas.'

'It's my fault,' said the woman sitting with Louise. 'I said I'd have it in my room, but then I changed my mind. Is that wrong of me?' she asked Louise when the waitress had left them with a grudging: 'O.K.' 'I meant to work till dinner-time, but then I got stuck, so I thought I'd come down and see a bit of life. But this is such a funny place. In some ways, you can do what you like, but then in others, you can't. Oh, dear—I shouldn't say that to you. You must be Mrs Vernon's friend.'

'Yes,' said Louise, 'but I know what you mean.'

'Well—hullo, everybody!' Sybil exploded into the room, scattering good cheer like shrapnel. She slapped the pale young man on the back, which made him cough, and patted the top of the Colonel's head. 'Tea-time already? My God, I'd no idea it was so late. I've been fighting with a man who wants me to entertain the ironmongers' convention, or some ghastly thing. Have you met everybody, Lou? That's fine. You've made friends with Miss Garnham, I see. She's a real live author, you know. She writes books,' she added explanatorily. 'Isn't that an honour? Fancy us having a famous author in this vulgar old joint.'

Miss Garnham was embarrassed. 'I'm afraid I'm not famous,' she murmured. 'Not many people read my books.'

'Oh, nonsense,' Sybil cried. 'No modesty here. Why, you're actually writing a book now, under my very roof.' Being semi-literate, she had as astonished a regard for anyone who wrote as if they could do double back somersaults, or play the piano with their feet.

'Isn't that something?' she asked, picking up Louise's teacup and taking a sip. 'No, thanks. No more. Tea's not my drink. What's the book about, dear?' she asked Miss Garnham. She was bored with the subject now, but felt that she had to do something to liven up the quiet party in the lounge.

'It's a biography,' Miss Garnham said unwillingly, looking at her hands.

'How too thrilling. What about?'

'Well, you wouldn't have heard of him, I'm afraid. He was a social reformer in the last century. Not many people know of him.'

'Why write about him then?' Sybil gave her a husky laugh, which ended in a fit of coughing. 'Never mind me, dear.' She patted Miss Garnham's shoulder. 'I'm just fooling. You'll get used to me. Good old Sybil, they call me. Nobody minds. Louise will tell you. Has anyone seen George?'

Miss Dott looked up. 'I saw him going off in the car as we came back.'

'The bastard,' Sybil said. 'The electric stove has shorted again and he's the only one who can deal with it. Oh, well. Cold dinner, folks. I'll open some claret for everyone, and pass it off that way.'

'How long are you staying?' Louise asked Miss Garnham when Sybil had gone out.

'I don't know. I had meant to stay here and finish my book, but I don't know that I—— It isn't quite what I expected. Do you live here all winter?' she asked unbelievingly.

'Yes,' Louise said. 'I have to. I've nowhere else to go.' There she went again, blurting out the wrong things. How unkind that sounded to Sybil's generosity. 'No, I don't mean that,' she amended hastily. 'I could stay with one of my daughters, but I like to come here and be with Sybil.'

'I see.' Miss Garnham nodded thoughtfully. 'That girl's never brought my tea,' she said. 'How long does one wait before one abandons hope and goes back to one's room to eat chocolate?'

After dinner, Miss Garnham put on her fiercest pair of spectacles, set her small, pale mouth, and told Sybil that she would have to leave.

Sybil would not hear of it. People often stayed on for longer than they had intended, but nobody left before their time was up, unless for some good reason, like death or disaster. Miss Garnham's reason was not good enough for Sybil, although she had several reasons.

The first was that her after-dinner working time had been shortened, because the meal was over an hour late. When George came home, he had insisted on fixing the stove and having a hot dinner cooked on it, instead of the cold food that the staff were already preparing. George did not like cold ham and tongue. This upset the cook, which upset everybody else, creating a situation which caused Sybil to remark in the bar when she heard the gong sullenly pounded: 'Thank God. I guess we're lucky to get anything to eat at all to-night.'

Miss Garnham's second reason was that although she had moved her table all over the bedroom, seeking the light like a moth, she still could not see to type. Her third reason was that her room was cold; her fourth that the pipes behind the wall knocked like a bevy of plumbers whenever anyone took a bath; and her fifth, desperately added when she saw that she was getting nowhere, was that she was worried about her parents and thought she should return to them.

Sybil did not believe this. Knowing the business of all her guests, she knew that Miss Garnham had received no letters or telephone calls. Miss Garnham tried to be firm, but Sybil overrode her with impregnable bonhomie. She would not hear of Miss Garnham going. My goodness, anything that was wrong could be put right in a matter of moments. No trouble at all. She wanted everybody to be happy, and Miss Garnham, the famous author, must be the happiest of all.

Miss Garnham could not get a word in edgeways. She took off her heavy glasses and blinked in perplexity. The scene was taking place in the lounge, with everybody listening over the dregs of their chicory-laden coffee. Miss Garnham had tried to get Sybil alone, by saying: 'May I speak to you for a moment, Mrs Vernon?' but Sybil had merely patted the sofa beside her and said: 'Speak away, my dear. I'm all ears.'

So was everybody else. Miss Garnham felt that they were on Sybil's side, except possibly Louise, who looked as though she might understand. She was fighting a losing battle. Her resolution to leave in the morning buckled beneath the onslaught of Sybil's unanswerable hospitality. Miss Garnham should move to a better room, for the same price, and should have a coal fire burning all day in the grate, and all night too if she wanted it. Sybil sent for Goldie to see about this immediately, before Miss Garnham could draw breath. She should have Sybil's own desk lamp, and a tin of biscuits and a bowl of fruit, and right at this moment, she should come into the bar with Sybil to celebrate the happy outcome.

'It's your temperament, I expect,' Sybil told her forgivingly. 'I know what writers are. Up one minute and down the next. You just take it easy. You'll be as happy as a grig here. Everybody is.' She sounded like the matron of a girl's reform school, soothing a recalcitrant inmate. Miss Garnham, looking hunted, followed her out to the bar, abandoning all hope of work that night.

'Coming, Lou?' Sybil turned at the door. 'A little snifter will do you good. You've lost all your pep since I saw you last.'

Mrs Maddox cleared her throat juicily, and dealt her patience cards with angry slaps. She did not approve of snifters, or any other kind of drink.

'Shall I ask them to send something out here for you, Mrs M.?' Sybil asked, winking at Louise.

'No, *thank* you.' Mrs Maddox decimated the knave of hearts. Sybil went out humming. Mrs Maddox's uncongenial presence and reluctance to have any extras on her bill were more than compensated for by the rate she was charged for her room.

Miss Dott and Mrs Arbuthnot were already in the bar, whither they had adjourned when the conflict in the lounge cooled to defeat, and there was no further entertainment to be had from it. They sat at one of the low tables, drinking *crème de menthe* and smoking filter-tipped cigarettes. They could not sit on the high stools at the bar, because they were both stiff-bodied and tightly corseted. They were the same shape, with the same blueish hair set in a hundred spiral curls. People often mistook them for sisters.

The pale young man, who was introduced to everyone as Johnny, so that no one knew his other name, was with them, drinking stout reluctantly, for his health. The two ladies had met him in the corridor and swept him into the bar between them, determined to be nice to him, because he looked lonely. Johnny was too polite to refuse, although he had been on his way to his room to read. He drank his stout as quickly as he could swallow it, fretting to get away to his books, for he was trying to catch up with the work he was missing at Oxford.

When Sybil entered, she was greeted with acclaim from the bar, where several of the local regulars were leaning or perching. There were always at least half a dozen people in the bar every night, and in the summer it was crowded, and thick with chatter and smoke. 'Let's nip down to Sybil's,' they said. 'Best pub on the island.' Or: 'Think I'll just pop over to old Sybil's for half an hour, dear,' to a wife who sighed, and stayed with the children, and knew that her husband would not come home before closing-time.

Sybil ordered brandy for Miss Garnham and Louise, without asking them what they wanted, and was absorbed into the jocular group along the bar. She climbed on to a stool with great agility, although she was nearly the same age as Louise, locked her hideous legs round it and settled down with a contented sigh, like a man coming home to his favourite chair. The barman, a glum young man, who was under notice, had been there long enough not to ask what she would have. He set a glass of gin before her without a word. Sybil stroked its rounded sides. She did not need to drink it for a moment. It was satisfying just to have it there in front of her.

Louise and Miss Garnham took their drinks over to one of the little tables, which had pictures of drunks clinging to lamp-posts set into the surface. Sybil had gone to town to buy a new carpet for the first floor landing, and had bought the tables instead, unable to resist them.

The brandy ran like fire down Louise's unaccustomed throat. She usually refused it at Miriam's, so as not to feel embarrassed when Arthur periodically complained about the wine merchant's bill. It was a double brandy. When she had finished it, tipping back her head like a bird to get the last drop out of the awkward glass, she felt more reassured than she had for days. Perhaps, after all, she was silly to worry so much about her family. However much she worried from the other side of the Solent, it would make no difference to them. They would carry on their lives without her, pausing now and then, she hoped, to say: 'I wonder how mother is getting on.' The winter would pass, and perhaps when she went back, everything would be all right.

Not Ellen, though. Ellen would never be all right. I must not die before she's grown up and married, Louise thought. Whatever happens, I must not die and leave her. She cared for Ellen more than she had ever cared for any of her children, and she knew, guiltily, that Ellen loved her better than her own mother.

'Let's have another,' Miss Garnham said. 'The evening's all gone to pieces, anyway. We might as well tear it right up.' She went to the bar and ordered two more brandies. 'What will you have, Mrs Vernon?' she asked.

'How sweet of you,' Sybil said, and the barman silently brought her another glass of gin.

'I hope you're not too worried about your parents, Miss Garnham,' Louise said, when she came back to the table. 'I suppose they'd have to be dying before Sybil would let you go.'

'One way to run a hotel. Please call me Ruth. No, I'm not too worried, really. It's just that they're old, and they're so used to having me with them that I feel a little mean coming off on my own like this ; but my publisher has set a date for me, and I have to get the book finished. But it congeals on me. I've been at it so long, I'm beginning to hate it.'

'Oh, surely not.' Louise envied her for having something so important and definite to do. Even if not many people would read it, at least it was going to be published, and would be a concrete thing, with covers and a jacket.

'I have a friend who writes books,' she said, thinking of Gordon Disher crouched over the table in his room under the roof, stabbing the typewriter with his thick fingers. 'Thrillers. He writes them in two weeks.'

'I've been on this thing nearly two years,' Miss Garnham said gloomily. 'That's why I came down here. It's impossible trying to write at home with Mother and Father coming in all the time and asking me how I'm getting on, and have I forgotten that the shops will be closed if I don't go out soon. They're darlings, but they don't understand.'

'You live with them, then?'

'Yes, I look after them. They haven't anyone else. I've got a temporary woman in for them now, although they don't like her, I'm afraid. A permanent housekeeper would be expensive, even if I could find one they could stand. And I think they'd be hurt, if I said I wanted to go and live on my own. I've been with them for so long, you see.'

'I see.' Louise paused, and then said: 'Parents are quite a problem, aren't they?'

'They can be. But then one loves them, you know, and when they've looked after one at the beginning of one's life, the least one can do is to see them through the end of theirs.'

'I suppose so.' Louise sighed over her brandy. The re-assurance which the first glass had brought her was evaporating. She pictured Miriam, or Eva, or Anne, talking to a stranger in a bar about having a duty to their mother. She began to feel sad, and hoped it was only the brandy.

'I think I'd better go up now, Ruth,' she said. 'I may be getting a little drunk.'

'I feel delightful,' Miss Garnham said. 'I begin to see why people like hotel life. Insidious though.'

Sybil, enjoying herself with her friends, had remembered them, and was offering them another drink.

'Heavens, no.' Louise got up and made two passes at her bag before she picked it up. 'We're going to bed.'

'Bye-bye, then.' Sybil waved gaily. 'See you in the morning, loves,' she said, although it was doubtful whether anyone would see her before noon. She looked as if she was settled in for the night, her fingers grown round the glass like a vine.

George had not appeared at dinner. He often had his meals brought to him by Goldie in the sitting-room. Louise did not see him until she left Ruth Garnham, after helping her to find her new room, which involved surprising the Colonel in bed without his teeth. She groped her way along the corridor. The light was out, and she could never remember where the switch was. The lights were always turned out much too early, or left wastefully burning all night.

A figure came round the corner of the passage, and she stepped to one side and stood against the wall. Her head was undoubtedly whirling. The sooner she reached her room the better. How disgraceful at my age, she thought, but rather nice for a change.

The figure brushed past her and stopped by the corridor window, tall, with hunched shoulders, and powerful, hairy hands seen in the misty moonlight. It was George, locking up the windows.

'Hullo, George,' she said. 'It's me. Louise.'

'Hullo,' he said flatly, and walked on.

Louise would not have been surprised to hear him say: 'You here again?' She could never think why Sybil had married him. It had been a mystery at the time, when Louise had gone to see her school friend married for the third time, and George had glowered at the guests, and been unable to produce a word when called on for a speech.

It was a mystery now, but it appeared to work out satisfactorily. They seldom saw each other, but Sybil seemed content, and between them they were running a profitable hotel. Sybil had a separate room, for which Louise did not blame her. She would not like to find herself alone in a bedroom with George, even if she were married to him.

Louise's days at Driffield Court dawdled by, but there were

too many of them, and they crawled too slowly. The winter stretched before her in meaningless eternity, broken only by the prospects of Christmas at Miriam's. She tried to fill her days with reading, walking, writing letters, but it was hard to find any purpose to life beyond appearing punctually at meals, and keeping her room tidy to help the raw young maid.

Phyllis, the little maid, was a local girl in her first job. When Goldie was not hectoring her, and stalking her round the bedrooms to pounce on her mistakes, Ellen was scoffing at her downstairs and telling her that she did not know she was born, the barman was leering greasily, and the cook was incessantly asking her: Who did she think she was?

Phyllis was very unhappy. Each week, she bicycled home to her parents, and was always in tears when she returned. Louise, taking a late stroll after dinner, found her weeping in the bicycle shed.

'Come up to my room, Phyllis,' she said, 'and I'll make you a cup of tea.' Goldie had found a battered electric kettle somewhere, and had bequeathed it to Louise, with a small teapot and a packet of tea stolen from the rationed hotel stores. Miss Garnham was jealous of the kettle and the teapot. It was just what she needed to revive herself when she had let the fire go out, and her hands and feet were numb from sitting too long at the typewriter; but she understood that she could expect no favours from Goldie until she had worked her apprenticeship as a hotel guest. Goldie never committed herself to kindness until you had been there at least two weeks.

Phyllis did not think that she ought to go to Louise's room, and once there, she did not feel that she ought to sit down. She stood gawkily, warming her grubby, childish hands round the teacup, her big, tear-misted eyes looking nervously round the room, as if she did not see it every day when she came in with her hated mop and duster.

She was only sixteen, and looked a child. She reminded Louise of her grand-daughter. In olden times, this could have happened to Ellen. A brutal father, refusing to keep another man's child under his roof, and a mother ashamed of her folly might have turned her out, even at eleven years old, to drudge amid dust for a pittance, and cry herself to sleep in an attic.

'You're cold, dear,' she said to Phyllis. 'You haven't enough on for bicycling on a night like this. You should have a jersey under your coat. Have you got one?'

'No'm,' Phyllis said tonelessly.

'Look here, I've got one I never wear. It's the wrong colour for me, and too small.' Louise went to a drawer and took out the cardigan that Eva had given her for her birthday, which she had never worn, because it was too nice for anything except a special occasion, and she was still waiting for the special occasion. 'You take it. I'd like you to have it.'

Phyllis looked in wonderment at the soft wool and the glorious cherry colour. She shook her head.

'Yes, please.' Louise took the cup from her and thrust the cardigan into her hands. 'To please me.'

'Yes'm. Thank you very much.' Phyllis turned and bolted out of the door. She heard creaking shoes on the stairs and knew that it was Goldie, coming with the hot-water bottles.

The next day, Phyllis wore the dashing red cardigan under the bib of her apron.

'Where d'you get that?' Ellen pounced on her at breakfast. 'That's a fancy item for a chit like you.'

'I bought it then,' Phyllis said defiantly.

'That you never did, of that I'm sure,' declared the cook, bringing the fat, brown teapot to the kitchen table. 'On your salary? Who do you think you are?'

'Knocked it off, did you?' Ted, the barman, who claimed to have worked in a West End hotel, was an unpleasing sight in the morning, with his oil-matted hair uncombed, and his mouth full of bread.

'I did *not!*' Phyllis hoped that she was not going to cry. She had cried once before in the kitchen, and knew how they would mock.

Goldie removed the top of her boiled egg suspiciously, as if she expected to find it bad. She and the cook were the only

ones who had eggs. 'Perhaps someone gave it to her,' she
suggested. She had looked through Louise's drawers, to see
what the poor lady had to put on her back, and had seen the
cherry-red cardigan. She knew where Phyllis had got it, but
wanted to hear it from the girl's own lips.

'Well, and if they did?'

'Who did? Who gave it you? One of Them?' Ellen jerked
her head towards the swing-door that led to the dining-room.
'What a cheek! Who was it?'

'Who was what? What's going on?' Mrs Peace, one of the
daily women, came through from the scullery in her coat and
hat, with the large leather shopping bag that came to work with
her every day, and often went home with rolls or cake inside—
'Can't be served up again. Too good for the pigs.'

'What's the trouble now?' she clamoured, afraid of missing
something.

'Young Phyll's been toadying round the guests, that's what,'
the cook said, resting the fat arm that held her knife on the
table. 'I'll lay I know who it was. It was that Mrs Bickford, or
whatever she calls herself. She's as soppy as they come.
Give her last penny to a blind beggar.' She spoke with more
disdain than admiration. The cook had no patience with
anybody who did not know how to look out for Number One.

Goldie nodded sagely, and Ellen blew out her pasty cheeks.
'Well, what a sauce! Why should she favour Phyllis over the
rest of us? I always said the upstairs maids get all the pickings.
Where do we come in, I'd like to know?'

'You mind your tongue, miss,' Goldie said sharply. 'I've
seen you tee-heeing round a guest—oh, ever so sweet—when
they were packed up to go and you couldn't wait to get your
great red hands on the tip.'

Mrs Peace sat down heavily, with a sigh of relief for her
varicose veins, and accepted the cup of tea which the cook
poured for her. 'Well, I never.' She would sit now and savour
this affair for quite a long time before she took off her outdoor
clothes and went to work.

'I'll not stand for it,' Ellen announced, getting up. 'I'll go to Mrs V.'

'You'll go to the dining-room and get your tables cleared and laid up for lunch, that's where you'll go,' Goldie told her. 'And Phyllis, you get on upstairs. It's laundry day, and you'll be caught before the man comes, like you were last time. Ted, I heard Mr V. calling round the place for you ten minutes back. What's that burning, Mrs Ellis?'

'My potatoes, I dare say.' The cook got up with a sigh. 'No peace for the wicked.'

Having disposed of everybody, Goldie poured herself another cup of tea, and sat with Mrs Peace to enjoy it at leisure, as was her right as queen of the kitchen.

Ellen went into the dining-room, made a face at the crumb-littered tables and crumpled napkins, and went straight out of the other door to find Sybil.

Sybil was very nice to Louise about the cardigan. 'I know you meant it kindly, Lou,' she said, 'and it was generous of you when you're not so flush yourself. Phyllis is rather pathetic, but I do wish you wouldn't do things like that. It upsets the others, and God knows I have enough trouble with them already.'

Louise felt foolish. She had been pleased with herself for her benevolence, although she was beginning to regret the beautiful cardigan, and to wonder what she would say at Christmas when Eva asked why she did not wear it.

'You'll have to take it back, I'm afraid,' Sybil said. 'That's the only thing that will satisfy them.'

'I can't do that. I gave it to her.'

'Well, tell her to hide it then, or something. If she hadn't been such an idiot, she wouldn't have paraded round in it. But do something, for God's sake, before they all march out on me with the week-end coming.'

Embarrassed, Louise told Phyllis to hide the fatal cardigan until she could take it home, but Phyllis had already taken it off and hidden it under her mattress.

'I've given it back,' she announced in the kitchen at lunch, and the others nodded their heads triumphantly. Only Goldie, who had looked in Louise's drawers again, knew that she had not returned it.

After six weeks at Driffield Court, Louise had read all the readable novels that had been left behind by the summer guests. It was too cold to take her favourite walk down the narrow, winding lane to the sea, and she did not feel like taking bus rides round the island by herself. She had done it last year, and there seemed no point in going to the same places again. She went once to Godshill, and walked about, hoping to see J. B. Priestley, but a woman in a sweet-shop told her he was not there, so she sheltered under a yew tree from the chilly rain, and caught the bus home again. It had at least passed the afternoon.

She wrote to her daughters that she was very happy, but time hung heavily. One could not sit and talk in the lounge all day among the old magazines, and often there was no one to talk to, except the Colonel, who was so gentle and humble and anxious to please, that he fell over himself to agree with everything you said, however futile.

Sybil was busy in the hotel most of the day, or out on her affairs about the neighbourhood. Miss Dott and Mrs Arbuthnot were out all day, and on Sundays they played golf. Mrs Maddox seldom wanted to talk, and when she did, her conversation, unlike the Colonel's, was devoted to proving Louise wrong on every point that was raised. Johnny had caught another cold, and was forced to lie in bed and be nursed by Goldie. Ruth Garnham, now quite resigned to staying, was closeted in her room with the clacking typewriter, emerging only for meals, looking as if she had smoked too much.

Coming in one evening to warm her hands by the fire in the lounge, Miss Dott found Louise looking listlessly through the advertisements for houses in a three-year-old copy of *Country Life*.

'At a loose end?' Miss Dott asked briskly. She was never

idle herself, and it disturbed her to see someone else unoccupied. 'There isn't much to do here in the winter, is there, unless you have a career, like Edith and me.' They always called the shop their career. They took it very seriously. 'It's different for you ladies of leisure, of course. I'm surprised you don't start some knitting, or some embroidery.'

'I can't embroider,' Louise said, 'though I made a patchwork quilt once. It fell to bits at the laundry. I don't knit very well, either.'

'And you the mother of three bonny daughters? I'm surprised. You could knit. It's simple. The patterns tell you exactly what to do, and I could help you. I'm a great knitter. Make all my own woollies. You go into Ryde and get a pattern and some wool, and I'll start you off. What shall you make?'

'I could make some little things for my youngest daughter, perhaps. She's going to have a baby, you know, and I don't suppose she's got anything yet.'

'Capital! Just the ticket, Granny. It will set you up no end. You know what they say about idle hands.' Miss Dott rubbed her own firm hands vigorously before the fire, and gave a short laugh of pleasure at having organized somebody into doing something.

Louise went to Ryde the next day. Sybil ran after her as she was going down the hotel drive to the bus stop on the main road. 'If you're going into town, be a love and pick up a couple of chickens for me. They'll be ready at the butcher's. And the station's just rung up to say there's a parcel there for me. You might collect it, to save me going in. Oh, and if you see any decent cakes knocking around, buy a few. Mrs Ellis has all those extra people for dinner, and Goldie's got the pip.' Sybil never let anybody go to Ryde without giving them some errand. If anyone was so bold as to sail the sea for Portsmouth, they usually found themselves spending half the day hunting for some shop which sold something that Sybil absolutely must have, but whose whereabouts she had been unable to explain coherently.

Louise staggered to the bus stop in the town with her bag of wool, some cakes, the chickens, which were moistening the bottom of the parcel, and a bulky package, for which she had had to pay three and ninepence at the station. She hoped that she could get it back from Sybil. Sybil was far from mean, but casual about money.

The bus would not stop at the hotel drive. It insisted on stopping a hundred yards down the road, as though it thought that if you could afford to stay at Driffield Court, it would do you good to walk. By the time Louise reached the drive gates, the parcels were heavier and more awkward than ever. She flung everything but her bag of wool and needles down in the hedge for someone else to collect. In the drive, she found George, sawing a dead branch off a tree.

'I got some things in Ryde for Sybil, and I've left them by the gate,' she said. 'Perhaps someone could fetch them.'

'It's going to rain,' George muttered, sawing with a set jaw. He was wearing a pair of corduroy trousers and a thick turtle-neck sweater. He looked more like a retired prize-fighter than ever. 'I should have thought you could have carried them down the drive,' he said. He was always very rude to Louise.

'I couldn't. They were too heavy.'

'So you thought I might as well carry them? Well, I'm busy. They've probably been pinched by now, anyway.'

'Look here, George.' Louise thought that it was time she made a stand. 'I know you don't like me being here, and you think Sybil's an idiot to let me have the room so cheaply, but I don't see why you always have to be so rude.'

George turned and looked at her as if she were a gnat, the big saw hanging ominously from his hand. 'Don't get excited,' he said, in his toneless, muttering voice. 'I'm not rude. It's Sybil's affair if she wants to clutter up the place with all her hangers-on.'

Louise turned on her heel and marched up the drive, boiling with rage. She would have liked to say: I'll go to-morrow, but she had nowhere to go to. How would Miriam like it, or Eva, or Anne, if she suddenly turned up on their doorstep when they thought she saw safely in the Isle of Wight for the winter?

'Oh, dear,' Miss Dott said, 'You shouldn't have chosen such a complicated pattern. However, we'll have a bash, as they say.' She cast on the stitches for Louise, and explained the tactics of a matinée coat as patiently as if Louise herself were the baby.

Louise was glad of the knitting, although it often tormented her. She sat in the lounge in the afternoons, hoping that some-one would come in soon and light the fire, clicking away at the intricate mass of greying white wool—'Pink or blue would have been more dainty,' Miss Dott has said—and holding it up now and again to see if it was beginning to look like what it was meant to be. Often, when Miss Dott came home she had to unpick all the work that Louise had done to pick up the dropped stitches.

Sometimes, after dinner, when there was no one amusing in the bar, Sybil would play Backgammon with Louise. 'Let's have a game to-night, Lou,' she would say at tea-time, and Louise would sit in the lounge with the board and counters set out on the card table, wondering whether Sybil was going to come, or whether she should go up and get her knitting.

Sometimes Sybil did not come. Sometimes she came in late, when Louise had given up hope, and cried: 'Oh, Lou darling, I forgot all about you. I got involved with somebody. What a beast I am.'

'It doesn't matter,' Louise would say, feeling Mrs Maddox jeering silently from the high-backed chair. 'I didn't want to play, anyway.'

'That's good,' Sybil said easily. 'Come and have a drink instead. You're going to bed? Oh, you old fogey. I could stay up all night. Well, bye-bye, love. See you in the morning.'

At weeks ends, Sybil had less time for Louise than ever. There were usually extra people staying, and dinner parties and lunches for people who could not find enough food for them-selves or their guests at home. Sunday lunch at Sybil's was a popular pastime. Goldie and Phyllis both had to help in the dining-room, and the lunches often went on until after three o'clock, leaving the harassed staff hardly time to turn round before the Sunday teas began.

When the hotel was full, Sybil was vivaciously on hand for everyone's pleasure. Unlike George, who was seldom seen at week-ends, Sybil was everywhere about the hotel; in the bar, the dining-room, the lounges, fraternizing exuberantly with all-comers, ladling out the informal camaraderie that gave the hotel its free-and-easy attraction.

Mrs Maddox and Mrs Arbuthnot, who could have become a vinegary character without the sweetening influence of Miss Dott, often complained that Sybil neglected the regulars for the fly-by-nights. At week-ends, Mrs Maddox retired into her shell like an ancient turtle. She brooded all day in her corner of the lounge, her fierce ebony stick beside her at an angle designed to trip anyone who came near.

On Thursday night, Sybil went to Louise's room in some embarrassment, which was unusual for her. Her jolly, coarse-featured face wore a small frown under its fuzz of hair, from which all the life and natural oils had long ago been bleached.

'Lou,' she said. 'I hate to ask you this, but I'm in a bit of a fix for to-morrow.'

Louise looked up from her letter.

'I'm a bit pushed for rooms, darling,' Sybil went on. 'I've some Americans booked, and now they want to bring another couple with them, and honestly, I haven't got a decent room to give them. I want them to get a good impression. They're at the Embassy, and you know how those sort of people spread the glad word around.'

'You want this room? Well, of course, Sybil. I don't mind at all. I feel bad about having it, anyway. Where do you want me to go?'

'That's the point. There's only that horrid little room on the third floor where the roof leaks sometimes. Let's just pray it won't rain.

'I'll put my umbrella up,' Louise said. 'I don't mind at all.'

She could not afford to mind. She could only hope that the Americans were only staying for the week-end and that Sybil would not forget to move her back to her pleasant room.

Goldie helped her to move her things. Goldie was put out. 'I don't hold with it, and I told her ladyship as much,' she said, thrusting clothes down into a suitcase as if she were pressing out wine. 'I don't approve of having my regulars disturbed for these easy come, easy go characters. But she won't listen to me. You know how she is about Americans. Dollar conscious. Americans! I know them. The drinking water's too hot, and the bath water's too cold, and empty whisky bottles in the wardrobes when they're gone.'

The Americans arrived in an enormous Embassy car, with a pile of bags and golf clubs that stood about on the steps all morning waiting for someone to take them in. On Saturday afternoon, they set out to do the island. Sybil went with them, abandoning her other week-enders. She never could resist the lure of Americans. They personified for her all that was best in life—large cars, quick drinking, extravagant spending, and a conviction that the world was not meant to be wept for, but to enjoy.

All the lounges were used at tea-time, but the regular guests kept to their own room, drawn together in an introverted group, like soldiers eyeing the new draft.

'Quite taken up with them, hasn't she?' Mrs Arbuthnot said, as a noise of laughter and banging doors heralded the return of Sybil and the Americans. 'Now I suppose we shall never get our tea, till they've been served. I sometimes wonder, Dotty, whether we wouldn't be wiser to look for a place of our own.'

'Don't be so impulsive, Edith,' Miss Dott said. 'You know it suits us very well here. It solves all our problems. Now you never hear good Mrs. Bickford complain, and she has to wait her turn like the rest of us.'

Louise murmured something. It was embarrassing to be lauded in public, especially by Miss Dott, who did not mean it.

Ellen flounced in eventually, took an affronted look round, and sent one of the extra waitresses in to give the old fossils their tea. No tips to be had among that lot. They would probably not even see her right when they finally packed up their traps and left. Although I'll be gone long before them, thought Ellen, slouching off to get lemon for the Americans, and what they would think was cream, although it was only the top of the milk.

By Sunday afternoon, the staff were all as bad tempered as Ellen. It had been a hectic week-end, and was not over yet, with the sun being so inconsiderate as to shine brightly enough to bring people out for a run in the car and a hotel tea.

Last night, Sybil and the Americans had not come to dinner until nine o'clock, and had kept the barman up until long after closing-time, which, he boasted next morning, he was going to make known to the proper authorities. Goldie had gone to bed at midnight and risen before six. There had been ham sandwiches asked for at the dear knows what hour last night, and all the breakfast trays to carry up to the rooms this morning. Goldie, usually as resilient as a tough piece of steak, was feeling her age. She vented her fatigue on Phyllis, who could do nothing right, and had dropped the last of the tartare sauce on the dining-room carpet last night.

There was a crowd for Sunday lunch, with hungry parties waiting in the bar until they could get a table. Sybil always told the waitresses never to hustle the first batch of eaters. 'People have a right to enjoy their meal in peace,' she said, but the staff knew that she liked to keep the others spending money in the bar within the limits of their endurance. She knew the exact moment when a man would not order one more drink, and would leave the hotel if he did not get some food. She would then miraculously produce a table in the dining-room for him and he would forget the long wait in his gratification at being especially favoured.

Johnny, who was a Catholic, had taken Louise to church in his battered little car, which made a noise like a lawn-mower. It was a long time since Louise had been able to go to Mass, and the familiar words and ritual had soothed and refreshed her. She felt happy to-day. She had received a delightfully affectionate letter from Eva yesterday, and coached by Miss Dott, she had turned the heel of a baby's boot at last. It distressed her to see the staff running themselves ragged on a Sunday, when they should be at leisure, like the people for whom they were running.

When she said this to Miss Garnham, with whom she shared a table at lunch, to save space, Ruth had looked at her queerly, and said: 'Are you a Socialist? Don't worry about them. They get paid for it,' which sounded odd coming from the biographer of a social reformer.

Louise kept out of the way all afternoon in her poky little room which never saw the sun, was always either too stuffy or too cold, and, with its gurgling cistern and its view of the Driffield Court dustbins, had obviously been designed for a Victorian servant. When she came downstairs and saw Ellen and Phyllis and the extra waitress pushing their way about, red-faced, among the little tables, with loaded trays for the people who doubtless had only recently eaten a good lunch, she could not bear to go into the residents' lounge and expect one of the girls to bring a tray to her. Why be such a drone? Perhaps she was a Socialist at heart, although it would kill Miriam to hear it. She made her way through the crowded hall, and pushed through the swing-door into the kitchen quarters, nearly knocking a tray of hot-water jugs from the hands of Ellen on the other side, who stared at her agape.

Goldie was cutting bread and butter like a fury in the pantry, her long knife flailing, and the soft butter slapped on in lightning strokes.

'If you've come to see what's happened to your tea,' Goldie said, in a voice that showed she was reaching the end of her tether, 'you can get right back in there and wait, same as everyone else.'

'Don't be cross, Goldie,' Louise said. 'I just came out to see if I could help. You're all so busy. I hate to sit and do nothing.'

'Busy is less than right,' Goldie said, flailing and slapping without pause. 'Don't ask me why we stand for it. There's

G

cook and Mrs Peace off their heads in there with all the boiling
of water. No wonder their rock cakes wouldn't rise. Now go
away, madam, do, and let me get on with my work.'

'But I want to help,' Louise insisted, refusing to be deterred.
'I could put out the cakes and biscuits for you, couldn't I? I
know how many go to a plate. Or shall I start washing-up?
There seems to be an awful pile of it.' The staff had come many
a time in deputations to Sybil to ask for a mechanical dish-
washer. She intended to get them one, but always the money
she had put aside for it was used for something else.

Goldie shrugged her shoulders, and passed a buttery hand
over her cloud of white hair. 'Please yourself,' she said, 'but
don't get in my way.'

Louise found an apron and tied it round her chubby waist.
With enjoyment, she ran hot water and added soap powder,
and started to plunge in the dirty plates and cups. She had
not been near a sink since she was with Miriam. She remembered the time when she had washed-up when the Cobbs were
there, and Miriam had been so cross.

'What's *she* doing here?' Ellen came in with a tray, and
tipped the crockery from it untidily on to the laden draining-
board.

Goldie did not answer. If there was going to be a row, she
was too tired to be dragged into it.

'I'm helping.' Louise looked up with a smile, her wrists
in the soapy water. 'You're so busy, I thought you'd be
pleased.'

'It doesn't do,' Ellen said darkly, clattering clean crockery
on to her tray.

When she came back with more dirty china she deliberately
pushed against Louise. 'I'm sorry, madam,' she said viciously,
'but you're in my way.'

Stepping aside, Louise accidentally splashed some water on
to Ellen's apron. With a face like thunder, Ellen snatched the
dish-towel from her and rubbed at the mark with exaggerated
care, although the apron was already far from clean. Louise
turned back to the sink and pretended not to notice her.

'What's she doing here?' The extra waitress came into the pantry. She was Ellen's friend, and copied her manners.

'Says she's helping,' Ellen grunted. 'If you please.'

'Well, I don't know.' The other girl stood with a tray on her hip, and considered Louise's toiling figure disparagingly. 'They didn't tell me there would be this sort of thing going on when I agreed to do the Sundays.'

Louise was so annoyed at their rejection of her kindness that she could only go on washing-up without a word. To take off her apron and leave would be an admission of defeat she was not prepared to make.

Ellen had fetched the cook to see what was going on. 'That's my apron,' Mrs Ellis announced. 'I was keeping it clean for to-morrow.'

Louise took off the apron, and continued her work without it.

'Does Mrs. V. know about this?' the cook asked ominously.

'No, of course not!' Louise said, her temper rising. 'She wouldn't have let me if I'd asked her. It was my own idea. I wanted to help you.'

'When we want help, we'll ask for it,' Ellen said.

Phyllis had come in now, and was standing with her mouth open, trying to take in what was afoot. Bells were ringing from the lounge, but the staff remained to fight this out.

'What's going on?' Mrs Peace, deserting her bubbling kettles loomed in the kitchen doorway, and was advised of the situation.

'I never heard of such a thing,' she said. 'When I was at the *Castle*, the guests knew their place and respected the privacy of the staff. This is a rum concern, I must say.'

'A damn sight too rum,' Ellen said. 'I've had just about enough of it.'

'Now, Ellen,' said Goldie, who had finally ceased to cut bread and butter, and was eating it unthinkingly, cramming the thin slices into her mouth, with a strenuous working of her lean jaws, 'we've heard enough about your giving notice to last us a lifetime. All talk and no do, that's you.'

'Is it then?' Ellen snapped. 'Don't think I couldn't walk out of here to-day and get a job ten times better. I've had offers, don't think I haven't. And from somewhere not a hundred miles from here, at that.'

'The *Dragon Arms*, I suppose,' Goldie said. 'That hole. I wouldn't be seen dead there.'

'It's a sight better than this dump. They treat you right in the kitchen there, that's all I'm saying. My friend Ida works there. They get the breasts of chicken, that's what they get.'

Mrs Ellis puffed out her bosom. 'If you are insinuating, young lady, that I don't feed my staff correct——' she began, and so it went on, the acrimony hurled about the pantry like flurried snow, and Louise, the cause of it all, still standing by the sink, washing and rinsing, washing and rinsing, not daring to turn round lest she should scream at them.

It was a full-scale row. Ted, who was off duty, heard the voices through the window, and came down from his room over the garage to join in. When Phyllis was in tears, although no one had spoken to her, Ellen hysterical, the cook puffed out like a balloon about to burst, and Goldie standing up and pointing at everybody with the finger that had a wart on the end of it, Sybil breezed in to see what had happened to the teas.

They told her, each clamouring to get in their word. Louise tried to tell her, too, but could not make her voice heard.

'Shut up, everybody!' Sybil shouted. 'I'll fire the lot of you if you don't get back in there and do your work.'

'You need not bother.' Ellen suddenly dropped her voice to one of great refinement. She untied the strings of her apron with fingers that were fastidious, as if they were handling mud. 'I'm leaving now.'

'You can't,' Sybil said practically. 'There isn't a bus.'

'You forget, I have my cycle,' Ellen said with dignity. 'You can send my things after me. I'll forward my address. My sister's, at Eastbourne.' She made Eastbourne sound like Paradise. 'How about you, Alice? Are you going to stay and be made a fool of?' The other waitress untied her apron strings without a word.

'All right, Mrs Ellis,' Sybil said challengingly, 'aren't you going, too? Oh, no, I forgot. Your bicycling days are over.' Mrs Ellis gave her a filthy look, and banged through the door to the kitchen, taking Mrs Peace with her.

'Ted, you're off duty, I know,' Sybil said, with a dazzling smile, 'but be a dear and get your white coat and help finish the teas. I'll make up your time off to-morrow. Phyllis can manage if you help her, can't you, dear?'

'You bet'm.' Phyllis squared her thin shoulders. Perhaps she would be taken off the upstairs and be made head waitress now that Ellen was gone. She piled a tray enthusiastically with more than she could carry, and staggered out through the swing-door.

'Goldie,' Sybil said, 'I'm surprised at you, letting this happen.'

'I didn't,' Goldie retorted. 'It wasn't my fault. Why do you always pick on me?'

'Because you're the only one with any sense.'

'One thing I will say,' Goldie said, sitting down, slightly mollified, to cut bread and butter again, 'we're a sight better off without those two. Nothing but trouble, though I'll allow they didn't start it to-day. It all began when——'

'Oh, shut up, you old fool,' Sybil said. 'If I hear another word about it, I'll scream. Come along, Lou. Whatever you were doing, stop it, there's a dear.' Gently she took away the mop which Louise was still holding distractedly. 'I'll get the keys of the bar and we'll go and have a little drink to quiet our nerves. We'll forget it ever happened.'

She did forget, or at least, she did not mention it again, for which Louise was undyingly grateful. For a while, she felt self-conscious whenever she met any of the staff, but the atmosphere simmered down, a new girl came, and left in two days with Miss Garnham's handbag, another girl was found, and the hotel settled down to its normal state. Louise would be leaving soon to spend the Christmas days with Miriam, and she hoped that when she came back, her *faux pas* would be completely forgotten.

The Americans had left, but since Sybil would be needing Louise's first-floor room while she was away, it was not worth while for her to move. She stayed in her cramped little room upstairs, knitting industriously, so that she would have something to give to Anne when she saw her.

She imagined Anne saying: 'Good God! What am I supposed to do with these? They're much too small.' Anne appeared to have no idea what the baby would be like, nor how she was going to deal with it. Louise could only hope that she would allow her to stay at the Stone Farm for a while after the baby was born, so that she could help her to care for it. She would enjoy that. Miriam had always known exactly what to do with her babies, and would never let Louise interfere.

The night before Louise left the Isle of Wight, Sybil climbed the narrow stairs to talk to her in her room while she packed. She had brought her a bright yellow spotted silk blouse and a purple angora sweater. 'Here,' she said, throwing them down casually, 'you can startle the family with these. No, go on—take them. Don't be silly. I don't want them. Just old rags.'

Louise wondered whether Phyllis had felt like this when she offered her the cherry-red cardigan: glad to accept, but sorry to have to be glad.

'What a beastly little room this is, Lou,' Sybil said, sitting down on the bed, since there was nowhere else. 'Never mind, you shall have your other one when you come back. You were awfully good about being pushed up here, but then you always are good about the things that happen to you. Wish I could say the same for myself.'

'Why? What's happened to you now?'

'Oh—nothing unusual. Just Christmas Eve to-morrow, and nine people coming—God knows why they can't be sensible and spend Christmas in their own homes—and Ted has taken umbrage and declares he'll leave before New Year's Eve, and the extra waiter hasn't turned up yet, which probably means the bastard isn't coming at all. Pity you can't stay and help in the kitchen.'

Louise looked at her and saw that she was smiling, and smiled herself in relief. This was the first time that the incident had been mentioned, and it was just like Sybil to bury it once and for all with a joke, so that it could leave no rancour.

'I'll tell you what it is, Lou.' Sybil lay back on the bed, with her head on Anne's baby clothes and her skirt pulled up above her thick calves. 'I'm beginning to wonder if it's worth staying open in the winter at all.'

Louise stopped folding her clothes, and stayed motionless, bending over the suitcase with her hands among the garments.

'It's true, I've always got the regulars and the week-end people, but that only just about makes it pay. It's always more difficult to get staff, and I tell you, although everyone thinks good old Sybil is in her element, being the life and soul of the party the whole year round, is honestly beginning to get me down. I'm not as young as I was.'

'I've never heard you say that, Sybil. You always seem so young and gay.'

'The clown with a breaking heart, that's me. Passing it off with a sprightly laugh when the cook walks out and the guests complain and the china gets broken quicker than I can replace it. God! I get so sick of it sometimes. I'd like to pack up for the winter and go away somewhere like the South of France, if I could ever get Georgie uprooted. I could face the summer then. I think I'll do it next year. We'll have to put the poor old Colonel in a home, or something. Old Ma Maddox can go on the streets for all I care, and Dotty and Edith can pull their socks up and find themselves a flat. I'm tired of running about after people who are too lazy to look after themselves.'

But what about me? Louise's frightened heart clamoured. The girls think I'm safe to come here every year. What could I say to them?

She managed to compose her face before she turned round and said with a forced smile: 'I think that's a wonderful idea. It would do you a world of good.'

'But, oh Lord.' Sybil sat up with her straw-like hair on end. 'What about my poor old Lou? That would make things a bit tough for you, wouldn't it?'

'You needn't worry about me,' Louise said stoutly. 'It's been wonderful coming here these two winters, but I'm not going to hang round your neck for ever.' She thought of what George had said that day in the drive—'Sybil's hangers-on.' How she disliked that man!

'But where would you go, love?' Sybil asked. 'I know how pinched you are, thanks to that bloody Dudley. Yes, I *will* speak ill of the dead, and you're either a saint or an idiot not to curse him to heaven yourself.'

'There's always the girls,' Louise said uncertainly. 'I've always got the girls. They're wonderful to me.'

'Don't kid. I know you hate it badly enough being passed round from one to another of them all summer long, like a mangy cheese. It wouldn't be much fun having to do it all winter as well. I tell you what, Lou. I can't think why you don't get yourself a job. That's what I'd do if I'd been left with the dregs of the drink like you have.'

'But what could I do?' Louise asked, as she had so often asked herself. 'I can't do anything.'

'Oh, shucks, nor can I, and look at me. Busy as a bee all day long, and making money to boot, though George always wants to plough it all back.'

'Well, but—it's different for you.' You had some capital. You had something behind you, and a man as well. You weren't alone, Louise thought, but she said: 'You're capable. You can run things. Catering and all that—why, I wouldn't even know how many cabbages to order for dinner.'

'We never have cabbage. Mrs Ellis can't stand the smell of it cooking. I'm not suggesting you run a hotel. I wouldn't wish that on you. But there are thousands of jobs you could do.'

'Who would employ me? I'm not trained for anything, and I'm too old. No one can get a job when they're my age.'

'Of course they can. Think of Mrs Ellis, if we must think of her. She's as old as you.'

'But she can cook. I can't.'

'That's true, but you could—well, you could serve in a shop, or something. Any idiot can do that.'

'In a shop?' Louise's mind flew to Gordon Disher. 'I wonder if I could. The girls would be horrified, but plenty of nice people work in shops. Very nice people. Oh, no, Sybil.' She shook her head quickly. 'I'd never get taken on, and if I was, I'd never be able to cope with it.'

'You're hopeless.' Sybil swung her legs off the bed. 'Scared to death of yourself. You always were, at school. Remember how you ran off the platform at the concert because the piano looked at you? Have some guts, woman, and don't be so middle-aged. You're not finished yet.'

'Oh, Sybil,' Louise cried impulsively. 'You always do me good. I do love you.'

'Here, here. Steady on. No pashes here. I'm not the gym mistress.' They both laughed at the memory of Miss Baggott, with her vast bloomers.

'How silly I was,' Louise said, remembering the thrills and the despair. 'I would have died for her.'

'Soft,' Sybil said. 'Now with me, it was always boys.'

'Do you think they'd take me on in your shop?' Louise asked Mr Disher, calling through the doorway to the bedroom, where he was getting the teacups from underneath the wash-basin. He had written to her once at the hotel, saying: 'When am I going to see you?' and so she had arranged to have the afternoon in London before going on to Miriam's.

'Do I think what?' he asked incredulously, coming into the room.

'That I could work in your shop. Selling things, like you. Oh, not beds, of course. That takes experience; but the kind of things on the ground floor that women sell.'

He seemed a little flustered. He put down the cups and went

to plug in the kettle. 'No—oh, no,' he said. 'That wouldn't do at all.'

'Why not? I feel I ought to try and find a job. I'm so useless.'

'No, please. It wouldn't be right.' He came to stand in front of her, and she looked up at him, bulking large over her, with his kind face folded into unusually troubled lines. 'You shouldn't work. You——' He moved his hands, fumbling for words. 'I mean, you haven't been brought up to it. It wouldn't be the thing.'

'You mean, I'm too old?' Louise asked. 'I'm no older than you, and look at you.'

'Yes, look at me.' He passed a hand over the bulge of his shabby waistcoat, and sat down heavily. 'You know I don't mean that. I mean, it's because—well, you're a—you're a lady.' He brought the word out with difficulty.

'Oh, how silly,' Louise said. 'I'm not, and even if I were, what difference does it make? Couldn't you ask someone in the firm at least to give me an interview?'

He shook his head. The kettle began to roar gently. He put his hands on the arm of the chair, but Louise said: 'Don't get up. I'll do it.'

She made the tea and poured it out, and handed him his bread and butter and his dry biscuits.

He leaned back in his chair and looked at her, without touching the food. 'A woman pouring tea,' he said slowly. 'What is there about it that looks so right? It always looks silly when a man does it. I even feel silly when I do it for myself when I'm alone.' He paused and then said: 'I want to ask you something.' He said it so solemnly that Louise thought: Heavens! but all he asked was: 'May I call you by your first name?'

'Of course. I can't think why you haven't done it ages ago. Shall I call you Gordon?'

'If you like.'

'I do like. Of course, when I work in your shop, I shall call you Mr Disher when we meet among the haberdashery.'

'Please don't keep harking back to that. Louise.'

'What?'

'I was just trying it out.' He did not say her name again that afternoon. He did not go back to calling her Mrs Bickford, but he did not manage to call her Louise again.

'There's something else I wanted to say to you,' he said, when they had finished tea. He got up and stood by his untidy work-table, looking out at the sharp roofs across the street. 'That day you came to the shop. You were in some trouble, weren't you?'

'Yes, I was.'

'I was afraid so. I wanted to write afterwards and say how sorry I was that you couldn't wait, but then, I didn't like to interfere.'

'I wish you had written,' Louise said. 'I thought you just weren't interested. The worst part was having no one to tell about Eva.'

'Eva?' He turned round. 'That's the one who has the flat, isn't it?'

'Yes. You've met her. She was in trouble, only she didn't know she was, and she wouldn't let me help her. But perhaps it's straightened itself out by now. She hasn't said a word about it in her letters, but I may find out when I see her to-morrow.'

'Find out what?'

'Whether she and David are—— Oh, I'm not going to bore you with it. You don't want to hear my family troubles.'

'I do,' he said, and she believed him, and told him about her scenes with Frances Graham and with Eva. Some of the words that had been spoken had reiterated themselves so often in her mind since, that it was a relief to speak them out loud.

'I'm sorry,' he said, when she had finished. 'I'm not surprised you were upset, but I'm sure you did all you could.'

'No, I didn't. I said all the wrong things to Eva. I lost my chance to help her. You see, for so long, my girls haven't been used to taking advice from me. It's always they who give me advice. They almost treat me like the child, instead of the mother. It's comical, really. Goodness, is that the time? I must go if I'm to catch my train.'

'I'll come to the station with you.' He helped her to her feet.

'Please don't bother. It isn't necessary.'

'It's Christmas Eve. The streets are crowded. You should have a man with you.' They were standing by the door. He took down Louise's coat, but instead of holding it out for her, he suddenly clutched it to him and began to speak very quickly, almost under his breath, so that Louise could hardly hear. 'You're too much alone,' he said. 'I don't think you're happy. You shouldn't be thinking about a job. It's—it's pathetic. I won't let you be pathetic, and I won't get you an interview. That's not what I want for you.'

He stopped speaking and gazed at her anxiously. What was he waiting for her to say? For a crazy moment, Louise thought that he was asking her to marry him. Then she saw a picture of herself in her mind, looking her age, and realized the absurdity of the thought. But what did he mean? How could she answer him without making a fool of herself if she did not know what he meant?

Embarrassed, she said something trivial, and then nervously, before she could stop herself, she laughed.

He made an odd little noise, and in the quick glimpse of his face before he turned away, Louise saw that she had hurt him.

He stood behind her and helped her on with her coat. 'If you don't mind,' he said, 'perhaps I'd better not come to the station with you after all. I've had a slight cold, and it's raw out.'

He hurried her out of the door as if he could not wait for her to go. Louise walked alone down the cold linoleum of the stairs, baffled and miserable, and hating herself for having hurt him, and for not knowing why she had hurt him.

* * *

Christmas at Miriam's was much the same as it had been last year: the children noisy and over-excited, with one of them in tears before bedtime, and the grown-ups alternating between merriment and irritability. In a million homes all over England, the same moods were prevailing at approximately the same time. The tolerance towards early-waking children, the unusual good humour at breakfast, the sedate party to church and the resolution that this year one really would go again before Easter, the excessive lunch, with the gaiety and seasonal sentiment rising to its peak when someone rose in an unbecoming paper hat and made an inept little speech, and everyone smiled at each other with love, and thought how good it was to be a family after all.

And then the let-down, the terrible Christmas afternoon, with the children quarrelsome and tired already of their new toys, and the grown-ups heavy with food and drink and the desire to get away from everybody and go to sleep.

Arthur went up to his room. He said he had to finish some work. 'On Christmas Day?' the others protested. 'Yes, on Christmas Day,' he said, but Miriam knew that if she went upstairs, she would find him lying on the bed with his shoes off.

Frank would have liked to do the same thing, but lacked the courage. When the children had been sent away and forbidden to reappear until tea-time, he went into the drawing-room with the women, and sat in an uncomfortable chair while they talked. Because Anne had refused to travel alone, he had for once risked leaving his livestock in the care of old Harry. While the women's conversation drifted about him, his mind was in his yard, thinking of all the things that Harry would undoubtedly neglect. The old man would never refuse a drink at Christmas-time. He was probably outside the pub now waiting for it to open, while the pigs and chickens and goats protested their abandonment with despair.

I should have never come, Frank thought, trying to keep his eyes open; but Anny wanted it, and I can't refuse her at a time like this. He looked at his wife, enormous already, and wearing bulky clothes that made no attempt to conceal her shape. It's good for her to be with her family, he thought. Livens her up. Bit slow for her, it must be at times, living with me. That Eva, she's a gay one. Quick as a whistle, too. Funny how the girls are all so different.

Eva was being particularly gay this Christmas. The lines of her pointed face were all tilted upward. She did not seem to have a care in the world. She mentioned David once or twice, with casual bravado, ignoring the lack of response his name inspired among her family.

Was it possible, Louise wondered, that Frances Graham had been wrong, and that Eva and David would eventually be married after all? If that was the only thing that was going to make Eva happy, it would have to be swallowed, although it would be difficult now to receive with open arms a son-in-law whose wife she had met and liked. I shall not say a word though, Louise decided. If Eva and David come to me and say: We are going to be married, I must not cry: Oh, no, you can't! I shall have to smile, and not do anything to spoil Eva's happiness.

Eva was once more excited over the play about the prostitute turned faith healer, which was actually in rehearsal at last, and was to be produced in London in February. 'This is what I've been waiting for all my life,' Eva told her family, talking rather extravagantly, and with fluid movements of her hands, as actresses do when they talk about the theatre. 'It's the biggest thing that's ever happened to me. You'll be proud of me yet. You wait. I am Eva Bickford's sister, Miriam will say, and doors will open for her right and left; and Mother shall have a fur coat. Gosh!' She leaned forward with her bare arms between her knees—Eva never dressed warmly enough in the winter—'I just hope I can do it. I think I can. When I read the part right through for the first time, everyone said it was wonderful. Don't think I'm conceited. Maybe I am, but this is my biggest chance. If I can pull it off, I'll be talked about, written about, people will know my name. I've already been interviewed by a magazine. There's going to be a story about me and the play, with lots of pictures. It's absolutely my part. Everybody says so. One of the boys has got some ghastly woman hanging around—Myrna Laurie. Mother may have seen her way back in her heyday. She thought she was going to get the part, but she never had a hope. She'd be vile in it, and she's much too old, but you know what these *passé* actresses are. They never give up hope.'

'It sounds like a hell of a play,' Anne said, 'from what you've told us.'

'You wouldn't understand it, dear. It's not written for people like you.'

Anne grunted, and shifted her weight. She had indigestion. She often had indigestion these days. She could not think why any woman deliberately set out to have a baby. It worried Frank when she complained of this and that new discomfort every day, but when he was solicitous, she rejected him with: 'Don't fuss. I'm pregnant; not dying.'

Louise had left the drawing-room to fetch the baby clothes she had knitted.

'Good God,' Anne said, dangling a tiny vest from her fingers. 'What am I supposed to do with these? They're much too small.'

'I knew you'd say that,' Louise said placidly. 'I could hear you saying it while I was knitting them.'

'Well, aren't you going to thank your mother for making them, Anny?' Frank had woken up and began to take an interest in the conversation, when the baby was mentioned.

'That's all right,' Louise said quickly, seeing the glare Anne gave him. 'I enjoyed doing it. It gave me something to do. I'll make some more when I go back, Anne, if you'll tell me what you want.'

'Good Lord, I don't know,' Anne said. 'I thought one just wrapped the thing in shawls.'

'Oh, Aunt Anne!' Ellen had come into the room, and was picking over the baby clothes with delight. 'Don't you know anything about babies? I'll have to come over and show you. I used to do a lot of things for Simon and Judy, didn't I, Mummy?'

'You children were all told to leave us in peace until tea-time,' Miriam said.

'I know, but Simon has taken my books, and Judy won't let me play with the doll's house.'

'Well, you can go up and fetch the bundle of clothes on my bed,' Miriam said. 'I put some of my baby things together for you, Anne. I don't imagine I'll ever need them again.'

'Lucky devil,' Anne said.

'I don't know,' Miriam said thoughtfully. 'I'd love to have another baby, as a matter of fact.' To have a baby at thirty-five might make one feel that one was getting younger again, instead of older. Miriam hated the lines that were beginning to appear on her face, although no one else could see them under her careful make-up. Sometimes she felt that the best part of her life was over, the gaiety all gone. She thought back more often to the days of light-hearted excitement. The days of Philip, whom she might have married, and who had been killed in the war, still unhappy about her. The days of Colin, when emotions were everything, and common sense a quality not yet painfully acquired. When she had sorrowed on her last birthday about the passing years, Arthur had said: 'It's natural for you to feel restless. The change of life begins in a woman as early as thirty-six. I read it in a book,' which had made her feel worse.

Arthur did not want another baby, but Miriam felt that it would be the making of her. She would know then that she was not finished.

'Another baby?' Ellen was saying. 'Oh, that would be wonderful. Do let's have one, Mummy. Do let's.'

'Would you like it?' Miriam smiled at her.

'More than anything in the world. Don't let's give our baby clothes to Aunt Anne.

'We'd better.' Miriam sighed. 'Run up and get them.'

Louise went back to the Isle of Wight two days later. She minded going more this time than she had in October. Then, she had been almost glad to get away from her troubled family. Now she hated to leave them. Both Miriam and Arthur had been nice to Ellen. Eva was on top of the world about the play, and happier, apparently, about David—why, Louise did not know, but at least she was happier. Anne was not smoking so much, and seemed very well, in spite of her grumbling. Going to Sybil's the first time had been quite exciting ; a change of scene, a totally different kind of life. Now it was all too familiar. She had said all she could to Mrs Maddox and Miss Dott and Mrs Arbuthnot and Johnny and the Colonel and Miss Garnham, and the week-enders were never there long enough to make friends, even if they had been the kind of people who would want to make friends with Louise.

The Christmas days had been a welcome break from the dishevelled monotony of life at Driffield Court. Sheltering in the cabin of the paddle-boat to Ryde, Louise felt as if she were going back to school after a half-term holiday at home. She did not want to go back, but there was nothing else to do. She could not have stayed on at *Pleasantways*, even if Miriam had asked her, for Miriam and Arthur were taking the children to Austria for winter sports after the New Year. Simon and Judy were wild to go, but Ellen was reluctant. She had been once before, and had hated trying to ski, and hurt her ankles trying to skate, and caught a cold with a painful ear infection.

'Couldn't I come to the hotel with you instead, Granny?' she had asked.

When Louise had suggested this to Miriam, Miriam had said: 'Goodness, no, with everything booked. Of course she has to come. She needs that kind of air. She doesn't really want to stay behind. She's just trying to wheedle you into giving her something she can't have. She can't possibly moon around in that crazy hotel for the rest of the holidays.'

That crazy hotel was just as crazy as ever. Sybil was at her wits' end about the extra staff for New Year's Eve. Goldie had a sty, and went about witch-like, with a black patch over one eye, and the other baleful. She had returned Louise to her large room, however, although she had not been told to. Louise unpacked, went into Ryde to buy some more wool, and settled down to pass the raw young months of the new year as best she could.

On New Year's Eve, the bar was crowded. Sybil had managed to charm an extension licence out of the local authorities, and everyone stayed to drink the New Year in. Louise went up to her room after dinner, but she had to come down for a drink at midnight. It would be middle-aged not to. Even Mrs Maddox was there, enthroned in a corner with a glass of the champagne that Sybil had ordered for all her regulars, watching the bubbles rising and breaking on the surface, as if each one held a grain of poison.

Sybil was in her best form. She had been in the bar nearly all evening, and was flushed, with purple veins appearing on her cheeks, and her mascara melted in a smudge along her upper lids. Everyone was toasting her and offering her drinks. A man who always had to organize something wherever he might be, was slipping round among the guests, organizing them into singing *For She's a Jolly Good Fellow*, as soon as *Auld Lang Syne* was over.

At five minutes to midnight, George came in, looking as dressed-up as he always did when he took off his rough country clothes and put on a blue suit. He took a beer from Ted, and stood at the end of the bar with it, nodding to the people he knew without speaking. The clock above the bar pointed to midnight. From the hall came the first stroke of the gong, pounded by Goldie, who was to sound eight bells.

While she pounded, everyone was quiet, holding a glass, and wearing the reverent face they assumed for the two minutes' silence on Armistice Day. Just as, on November the eleventh, people try to remember the fallen with gratitude, but find their minds wandering, so now they tried, in a blurred way, to realize the significance of the moment when the mistakes and petty sins of the old year could be forgotten in the hope that the new one would bring them all they wanted.

As the last note of the gong reverberated into silence, Louise found one hand grasped by Johnny and the other by Miss Garnham, and was swept into the swaying, unbearable sadness of *Auld Lang Syne*. The motley crowd of people were emotionally united, although in cold blood, most of them had little use for each other.

Glasses were raised. A toast was drunk. Louise's glass was empty, but she tipped it back with the rest.

'Now!' cried the man who loved to organize. He waved his arms. 'For she's a jolly good fellow——' a woman started, much too high, and the others turned towards Sybil and joined shrilly in.

Sybil threw back her head and laughed with pleasure. Suddenly her head dropped on to her chest, her glass smashed to the floor, and she doubled up and toppled slowly from her stool, while the singing died, and the voice of someone who had not seen, quavered: 'and so say all of us.'

'Passed out,' someone said quite clearly into the silence, and wished he had not said it.

'Don't be a fool.' The local doctor pushed his way through the gaping crowd. 'It's a heart attack.'

'Get out of here! Clear out everybody!' George raged at his speechless guests. 'Don't stand there staring like a pack of fools. The party's over. Get out before you're thrown out, and leave Sybil alone.' They went, in umbrage, and in disappointment that they could not stay to see what was going to happen. Would old Sybil kick the bucket, or what? 'Poor old girl,' they said, as they went subdued to their cars. 'You can't go on drinking like that for ever and get away with it.'

Louise stayed in the bar. George had not noticed her. She stayed far off and wished that she could take to herself some of the pain that was racking Sybil. Goldie was kneeling on the floor in tears, with her eye-patch pushed up on her forehead, clutching Sybil's hand. Neither the doctor nor George sent her away.

Sybil looked up, her eyes sunk like a very old woman. 'A damn pack of horses,' she gasped, through her struggles to breathe. 'Like a damn pack of horses on my chest.'

'Don't try to talk,' the doctor said.

'And cart-horses, at that,' Sybil whispered, defiantly trying to make a joke.

Two days later, George told Louise that she would have to

go. He needed her room for his sister, who was coming to help him while Sybil was in the hospital.

The hotel was a miserable place now, with nobody caring to smile or raise their voices, nor daring to ask George how Sybil was when he returned, dour-faced, from his visits to the hospital. Louise, however, had to say: 'I don't think I can go just yet, George. It's not very convenient. Couldn't I move up to the little room I had before?'

'I'm shutting all the rooms on the third floor. No sense giving the staff extra work.'

'But surely there's a room somewhere——'

'There are rooms for those who can pay our terms,' George said tersely.

'I can't. You know I can't!' Louise left him before he could humiliate her further. She went in despair to Miss Garnham's room, ignoring the rebuffing sound of the typewriter.

When she learned what George had done, Miss Garnham stood up at once, her eyes full of pity. 'That devil,' she said. 'He can't do that to you the minute Sybil's back is turned. I'm going to talk to him.' She kicked off her slippers and put on a pair of shoes.

'No, please,' Louise said, 'don't do that. You'll only make him worse.' Miss Garnham was already out of the door. Louise followed her along the passage and down the stairs, vainly pleading for her to come back.

Miss Garnham, looking very unlike her usual mild self, marched into George's office, and said directly: 'Look here, you can't turn Mrs. Bickford out. It isn't fair.'

'What's that to you?' George went on adding up figures in his ledger, his heavy shoulders rounded, and the back of his neck as thick as a tree trunk.

'I like her, and I won't sit by and see her treated like this. How can you be so beastly, with your wife ill and everyone upset?' Miss Garnham had hardly spoken a word to George since she came to the hotel, but she was not afraid of him.

George swivelled round in his chair and looked coldly at

Miss Garnham standing foursquare, with her fists clenched, and Louise hovering apprehensively in the doorway.

'This is my hotel,' he said, 'and I'm running it. Sybil must do as she likes when she's here, but she's not here now, and I'm not going to have the place cluttered up with people who can't pay their way.'

Louise had never told Ruth Garnham that Sybil allowed her to stay for very little. She was painfully mortified. 'Please, George,' she begged. 'Don't let's say any more about it. I'll go, if you really want me to. I'll go as soon as I can make other arrangements. It will only take a few days. I don't want to be a nuisance.'

'You are a nuisance.' George turned round to the desk, and gave them the back of his head again. 'I didn't say go in a few days. My sister's coming to-day. You'll have to hurry with your packing if you're going to catch the afternoon boat.'

'Now look here, Mr Vernon.' Miss Garnham strode closer on her small feet. 'That's too much. You can't turn her out all in a moment like that. Why, it will be evening before she gets to London. Where do you think she's going to go?'

'That's her affair,' George grunted. 'Now please go away, both of you. I've got a lot of work to do.'

'Come on, Ruth.' Louise took Miss Garnham by the arm. 'Come away. Please don't say any more. I'll go and pack. I don't mind. I'll be all right. As a matter of fact,' she raised her voice for George's benefit, 'I shall be thankful to get away. I don't think I could stand this place without Sybil.'

George's solid back gave no sign that he had heard.

Goldie waved Louise mournfully away from the doorstep, as if she were seeing off a funeral. The gardener drove her to Ryde in the station wagon. He was by nature an uncommunicative man, but his silence during the drive made Louise think that he knew she had been turned out in disgrace. She felt like a maid caught thieving, turned out into the snow without notice.

Miss Garnham had sworn that she would leave, too, but she had gone back to her typewriter when Louise went to pack, and

Louise thought she would forget about going. In a few days time, everyone would have forgotten about Louise, and ceased to wonder what had happened to her.

What was going to happen to her? She did not know yet. There had been no time to telephone any of her daughters from the hotel. When she reached Waterloo, Louise was tired and hungry from the turmoil of her parting, and the wretched journey in the slow train. She wanted to sit down somewhere with a cup of coffee, but she must know where she was going first, and get over the awkwardness of having to ask one of her daughters to take her in. She had never had to ask them before. They had always invited her, or at least it had been tacitly arranged among them who was going to have her next. What would they say when they heard of her plight? They would surely understand that it was not her fault. How silly, she thought in the telephone kiosk, to be nervous of talking to Miriam. Her hands were shaking a little as she dialled the operator.

The telephone rang a long time before anyone answered it. 'Who is that?' Louise asked, not recognizing the voice. 'Oh, Mrs Match. Hullo, it's Mrs Bickford. I didn't expect to hear your voice. Is there a dinner-party or something?'

'No, madam. Mr and Mrs Chadwick are away for the week-end. Didn't you know? I've come to clean round a bit. You wouldn't have caught me now, only I thought I'd work late and get the kitchen finished.'

'Oh. I see. What about the children?'

'They're staying with Mrs Matthew, at the Priory. Quite excited about it, they were. I should have thought they'd have told you.'

'No,' Louise said bleakly. 'They didn't. Well, thank you, Mrs Match. I'm sorry to have bothered you. No, it's all right. No message. It was nothing.'

Louise hung up the receiver, found some pennies, and dialled Eva's number. There was no answer. She tried again, in case she had a wrong connection. There was still no answer. Eva was probably out to dinner, unless she was at the B.B.C. There was no knowing what time she would get home. If she were out with David, she might not be back until one or two o'clock, if, Louise thought, unwillingly, she came home at all.

She went to the bookstall to get some change, and came back to the kiosk to telephone Anne. After some discussion between operators in London and Bedford, it was revealed that Anne's number was out of order.

It was now nearly nine o'clock, and Louise was alone in London without any money. She stood in the kiosk, looking at her distraught face in the little mirror, trying to arrange her thoughts calmly, while a man who was waiting to use the telephone pressed his nose against the glass outside, trying to provoke her into hurrying.

Louise came out and stood by her luggage on the platform, looking into her handbag. Miss Garnham had lent her money for the train fare, but after making the telephone calls, she now had only six shillings in her purse. Her small monthly draft from the bank had been held up by the holiday.

Where could she go? Who would help her? She began to panic a little. Her legs felt weak, and she sat down on her largest suitcase, abandoned and miserable, like a child who has got lost on a church outing.

She thought of her few friends in London. She did not know any of them well enough to arrive on their doorstep *in extremis*. Then she thought of Gordon Disher. Could she run to him and ask for help? He had been so queer when she left the last time, but perhaps he had not been feeling well. He was her only hope. He would understand. He always did. She would have to tell him the whole story of her shame and distress, and he would know what she ought to do. But whatever would he think of her turning up at this hour? No, I can't, Louise thought, and went back into the telephone kiosk, as the impatient man came out.

There was still no answer to Eva's telephone. Louise called Broadcasting House. No, said the cultured voice at the reception desk, Miss Eva Bickford was not there to-night. Louise put her luggage in the cloakroom, since she could not spare the money to take it with her in a taxi, and went down into the Underground to get a train for Fulham.

The front door of the ugly, narrow house was not latched. Louise pushed it open and toiled up the four flights of stairs. She stood outside his door for a moment, rehearsing what she was going to say.

She knocked timidly. There was no answer. Could he be asleep already? He might have gone to bed early, since he was not strong. She knocked again a little louder, wondering what he would look like, shuffling to the door in his dressing-gown and slippers, and whether he would be embarrassed for her to find him thus.

There was still no answer. He was not there. Once before, when she went to him in her distress about Eva, he had not been available. Now he had unknowingly let her down again. That did not seem right. Louise had always thought of him as so dependable, the kind of person who was always there when you needed him.

She went slowly down the stairs, feeling hopeless and unwanted. The hotel she had left only this afternoon seemed hundreds of miles away, a remote, unobtainable world. She thought of Miriam's house, with the fire lit in the drawing-room, and the children chattering over their supper in the kitchen. She thought of Eva's flat, and Eva in strange, gay clothes, humming about the kitchen while she threw a casual sandwich together. She thought of Anne's kitchen, with the dogs stretched out on the red tiles, so that you had to step over them to get to the cupboards or the door. Funny, Louise thought, pausing on the ground floor with her hand on the banister, how you invariably thought of kitchens when you pictured comfort and security.

A door along the passage behind the stairs opened, and a head in a hair-net looked out.

'Looking for someone, dear?' asked the owner of the head, a tiny, neat woman, with a face like a mouse. Louise remembered Mrs Dill on the ground floor back, who was so kind about the sugar biscuits. 'God bless her. She always obliges,'

Mr Disher had said. Mrs Dill was friendly with him, and might know where he was.

'Come inside, my dear,' Mrs Dill said, when Louise asked her. 'You're the lady that comes to take tea with Mr Disher sometimes, aren't you? Don't you know what's happened?'

'No—what?' Louise asked apprehensively, standing in Mrs Dill's tiny, cluttered sitting-room, where Mr Dill, in his socks, nodded heedlessly in a leather chair among the photographs and potted plants.

'Taken to the hospital,' said Mrs Dill, sucking in her lips. 'Poor soul. What do they call it? A coma, that's it. Mrs Fagg found him so Christmas Eve, when she went up to get his rent. No one but Mrs Fagg would collect rents Christmas Eve, but there it was, and it was a good thing she did, as it turned out.'

'Christmas Eve?' Louise said. 'But I was here to tea that day. He seemed all right.'

'Ah, no doubt he was—*at the time*,' Mrs Dill said meaningly. 'But later, I dare say he got to thinking about it being the festive season and him having no one to share it with. I had asked him down to share our Christmas dinner, but he said he wouldn't impose. Always the gentleman, Mr Disher was.'

'Was?' Louise cried. 'You don't mean—he's not—dead, or anything?'

Mrs Dill shook her head. 'Deserves to be, Mrs Fagg says, knowing as he did that he should never touch a drop in his condition.'

'But I don't understand. He never drinks anything.'

'Well, he did that night, that's all I know. They found the bottle. And it affected him, you see, being the sugar, and that. Out like a light, Mrs Fagg said he was.'

'Have you a telephone?' Louise asked. 'I'd like to ring the hospital and find out how he is.'

'We don't,' Mrs Dill said, 'but there's a box on the corner. Worried about him, aren't you, dear? You look quite upset. Well, I'm not surprised. He was a lovely gentleman.'

At the hospital, all they would say was that Mr Disher was 'fairly comfortable.' No, he was not allowed visitors yet.

Louise tried to puzzle it out. Had he taken a drink that night because of whatever it was she had said that had offended him? Whatever it was, it could not have upset him all that much. He was too sensible, and had lived too long with his complaint to take a foolish chance like that, unless he was half crazy with unhappiness. It must have been, as Mrs Dill said, because it was Christmas, and he was so lonely.

Oh, poor Mr Disher! Her heart bled for him lying there in the hospital, with probably no one to visit him, even if they were allowed to. The people in the shop would not care. They made jokes about him. He had told her that the first day they met. She would send him some flowers, as soon as she got some money. She would write to him. She would help him, if she could. She was sure that he would have helped her to-night if he had been there.

But he was not there, and she still had nowhere to go. She rang Eva's flat again, but there was no answer. Through the window of the telephone box, she saw a policeman move into the light of a street lamp, and out into the shadows again. In desperation, Louise opened the door and ran after him.

'Excuse me,' she said, and he stopped, and turned slowly round to look at her. He was a young policeman, with red hair and a square jaw. 'I need help,' Louise blurted out. 'I have nowhere to go and no money, and I don't know what to do.' She kept her eyes on the ground, because she was ashamed.

The policeman was not as surprised as she had expected him to be. 'You'd better let me take you along to the station,' he said calmly.

'Oh, no!' Louise looked up in fright. Did they lock up elderly ladies who were found wandering in the streets with nowhere to spend the night? 'I just wanted you to advise me. I thought perhaps there were hostels, or something like that, where one could get a bed for a few shillings.'

'There are,' the policeman said, 'but not for people like you. Better come along with me,' he put his hand under her elbow, 'and we'll see if we can't find someone of your family to come and fetch you.'

Louise pulled away from him. 'You think I'm drunk, or insane, or something, don't you? Well, I'm not. I'm just in a fix.' She told him of her unsuccessful attempts to contact her daughters. 'I won't go to the police station,' she concluded. 'I wish I'd never spoken to you.'

The policeman was not offended. His square young face was serious in thought. 'This daughter of yours that has the flat in Kensington,' he said. 'If it's a block of flats, there's a night porter there, surely. Wouldn't he have a master key and let you in to your daughter's place, if he knows you?'

'He knows me all right, unless it's a new porter. How clever you are. That's the obvious thing to do. I can't think why I didn't think of it straight away, but I was so flustered. I'll be quite all right now. I can't thank you enough.'

'I'll come along to the flats with you,' the policeman said.

'You needn't. I'm not an impostor.'

'I didn't think you were.' The policeman smiled. 'I just thought you needed company.'

'That's kind of you, but please don't. I wouldn't like the porter to see me arriving in custody.'

'Ah, I dare say. Well, I'll say good night then.' The policeman nodded at her and moved off steadily along the deserted street.

It was a blissful relief to go into Eva's warm flat, and to take her things off in the familiar safety of her own little back room. How foolish I've been, Louise thought. I could have saved myself all that worry. Wait till I tell Eva that I almost got as far as spending the night in a doss-house. She'll laugh, but we'll have to keep it from Miriam. She went into the kitchen to make herself some coffee and see if she could find something to eat.

It had been raining heavily for the last hour. When Eva came in at midnight, she was very wet. 'Oh, darling!' Louise cried, running into the hall to greet her. 'How silly of you to go out without a coat and hat. You're drenched.' Then she saw Eva's face under the soaked wisps of her short hair. 'Why, whatever's the matter?'

'Nothing.' Eva shrugged her off, and went into the sitting-room to get a cigarette. 'What are you doing here, Mother?'

Louise told her, trying to make a good story of it, to cover up the unpleasant memory of what had happened at the hotel, and the absurdity of her panic when she arrived in London. She did not tell her about going to see Mr Disher.

Eva appeared to be only half listening. She did not even smile when Louise told her about the policeman and the doss-house. 'Wasn't I a goose?' Louise said, 'not to think of getting the porter to let me in? I kept ringing your flat, but there was no answer. Where have you been?'

'Walking.' Eva humped her shoulders and stared at the floor.

'In this weather? You must be crazy. Who were you with?'

'Nobody. I went out by myself. I wanted air.'

'Darling.' Louise came to sit beside her. 'Something is the matter, and you must tell me. Please don't put on that shut-in face. I won't say anything silly. I won't say a word, if you don't want me to, but if you'll only just tell me, I'll try and understand.'

Eva looked at her. Her eyes, fringed with wet lashes, were enormous. Her face was beautiful in its sadness. 'Well—I lost the part,' she said heavily.

'You mean, the play is not coming off?' Louise forgot that she had promised not to speak. 'I wouldn't worry about that. They've postponed it so often before. They'll——'

'No, no, it isn't that,' Eva said patiently. 'The play's going to open all right, but I'm not. They've chucked me out, don't you understand? Given the part to that cow Myrna Laurie. They said it was because I was too young for it, but I know it isn't that at all. I was exactly right. But Myrna sleeps with the right people. I don't.'

'Well, my darling, you mustn't mind too much.' Louise tried to ignore the last remark. 'I know you'd set your heart on this play, and I think it's a dirty trick to put you out of it, but there'll be other chances for you, plenty of them. You're so clever and attractive, you'll get something much better.'

'I'm going away,' Eva said.   'I'm joining a small rep.

company up in the north. It's a dud one, but I must get away.'

Louise was going to protest, when Eva's face suddenly seemed to crumple, its still melancholy breaking down into unashamed despair. 'Mother!' she cried out, like a child fighting a nightmare, 'Mother, I have to tell you. It isn't only the play. I don't even care much about that now, now that— now that——' She took a deep breath, and said quietly: 'David has gone back to his wife. He isn't going to marry me. He never meant to. I'm not going to see him any more. Well?' She looked up, as Louise remained silent. 'Aren't you going to say: I told you so?'

Louise took her into her arms. Eva rested her wet head on her mother's shoulder, but she would not cry. They sat there for what seemed a long time, feeling each other's breathing.

'When you were a child,' Louise said at last, 'I always thought you'd be the happiest one.'

'So did I.' Eva raised her head, and twisted her mouth into a smile. 'It got away from me.'

CHAPTER SEVEN

WHAT was to be done with Louise? The question was troubling the rest of the family as much as it troubled Louise herself.

'I'll get a job,' she told them. 'I don't want you to worry about me.'

'But what could you possibly do?' they asked, as she knew they would.

'I'll find something. I might work in a shop. I could sell things. Plenty of women my age do it. Look at poor Miss Pitt, Miriam, where you always get the children's shoes.'

'Oh, Mother, really,' Miriam said. 'You're not poor Miss Pitt.' She would not hear of Louise having a job. What would people say? It would look as if her daughters had cast her off to fend for herself. And her ridiculous ideas about working in a shop ! Really, Mother was a little touched sometimes. There was Arthur's position to consider. Barristers who were rising to the top of their profession did not have mothers-in-law behind the haberdashery counter.

'And to be quite frank, Mother,' Miriam said spikily, 'I don't quite see how you'd ever manage to get a job, much less hold it down.'

'Why shouldn't I?' Louise protested. 'I'm not such a fool as you think I am. Why do you always belittle everything I try to do for myself? You're bossy, Miriam. You always were. It used to be on all your school reports.'

'Please don't let's quarrel about this, Mother. We're merely trying to do what's best for you.'

As if I were a child, Louise thought. Packed off willy-nilly to old Nanny, or Auntie someone, because it isn't convenient to have him in the house. But a child has more right to a say in the matter than I do. I have no right to be anything but grateful and amenable. I mustn't get like Ruth Garnham's mother. A difficult old lady. Nothing worse. Better be shot than that.

There was a great deal of telephoning back and forth among the sisters. They agreed that it was inconvenient of Sybil to have a heart attack at a time like this. Eva was due to go up to her repertory company in a few days. Miriam was off to Austria, and Anne was feeling ill and cross, and flatly refused to have her mother to stay.

'Why should I?' she asked Eva. 'You and Miriam go gallivanting off and leave me to hold the baby—and that's not meant to be a joke. I can't have anyone in the house just now. I just can't. I'm supposed to rest, and you know what Mother is. She fusses so.'

'Damn lucky to have anyone wanting to fuss over you,' Eva said. 'I think you're a pig, Anne.' She gave her the insult mechanically. She could not care about Anne's troubles. She could not think about anything these days, except fighting her dismal battle against the humiliation of her heartbreak. The fact that she had known all along that David would break her heart did not make it any easier to fight. Eva could only run. She must run away where no one knew her. Away from London and the flat, with its memories of David in every corner. Away from the theatre people who said: 'Bad luck about the play. The foulest luck for you, darling,' and: 'Where's David these days?' Away from the well-meant sympathy of her mother, and the tactfully disguised relief of Miriam and Arthur that the unfortunate affair was over.

Miriam talked to Anne sternly. 'Listen,' she said, 'I don't care how you feel. You've just got to have Mother while we're in Austria. Otherwise, she'd have to go to a hotel, and you know who'd have to pay. Why should Arthur have to fork out for that, just because you're so selfish? Mother will have to come to you, at least until we get back. After that, I suppose we'll have her. I haven't broken that to Arthur yet. He'll have to put up with it.'

Miriam was telephoning in her bedroom. She did not know

that Louise was in her bathroom, cleaning the bath for her, and had heard the conversation.

Afterwards, Louise came to Miriam and said: 'I don't want to go to Anne's.'

'Why not? You'll have to, Mother. There's nowhere else for you to go. You know I'm shutting this house up, and Eva has let a friend have her flat.'

'I'll think of something. I'll get a living-in job as a companion, or a housemaid, or—or anything.'

'Oh, Mother, *please*. We've been into all that. You can't start working at your age. A housemaid! That's not even funny. What do you think this family is? I wish you'd think of our side of it sometimes.'

'I'm trying to. I hate to be a nuisance.'

'Oh, what's the good of talking about it?' Miriam said irritably. 'There's too much talk about everything in this family.'

'That's what your father used to say. He often said he wished he had a son, instead of all the chattering women in his house.'

'He was probably right,' Miriam said. But if she had had a brother, he might not have been any help. Brothers usually married disagreeable girls who resented having mothers-in-law thrust on them.

When Miriam was out of the house, Louise rang up Anne. Frank answered the telephone. Anne was lying down. Could he take a message?

'I just called to say I shan't be coming to stay with you,' Louise said. 'I'm—I'm making other arrangements.'

'Oh? Well, I'm sorry,' Frank said. 'We were looking forward to having you.'

'Oh, Frank.' Louise felt that she had to speak the truth to him. 'Don't pretend. I know Anne doesn't want to be bothered with me now. No, it's all right. I don't blame her. I know what it gets like towards the end, when you're so tired of waiting.'

'Where will you go, Mother?'

'I don't know yet, but I'll think of something. I just can't be dependent on the girls any longer. It isn't fair on them, and—here's a thing that nobody's thought of yet—it isn't very easy for me, either.'

'I've often thought that,' Frank said candidly. He could speak more easily on the telephone than when he was face to face with someone. 'Poor Mother,' he said. 'I'm darned sorry for you. Wish I could help. Look here, you'd better come to us. I'll talk to Anne.'

'I can't.' Louise gripped the telephone and spoke rapidly, her pride collapsing under his rugged sympathy. 'Oh, Frank, I don't know what to do. Miriam says I can come here when they get back, but I'm sure they don't want me, and I don't want to come. I just can't go on like this for the rest of my life, never knowing where I'm going to be, always packing and unpacking. Don't think I'm ungrateful. The girls have been wonderful, but I hate it, Frank. It's so—Frank, are you there?'

'Right here.' His voice came surprisingly loud from the silent receiver. 'I was thinking. Listen, Mother, I've got an idea. Not much of a one. You'll think I'm crazy, I expect, so jump down my throat if you want to. There's a chap near here —I talked to him the other day, and he mentioned this. Said anyone could have it cheap.'

'Have what? A house? But you know I——'

'Well, it isn't exactly a house. It's a—oh, no, you couldn't. Let's forget it.'

'But what is it? Tell me.'

'Well,' said Frank hesitantly. 'To tell the truth, it's a caravan. Do you hear what I said? A caravan. Decently fitted out, and that. This chap had it for the extra people he took on when he bought more land. He's got a pre-fab up now, and he wants to rent it. Needs a lick of paint, of course, and some touching up inside, but I could do that. I was thinking, we could park it in the field the other side of the cold-frames. Nice big tree there to give you shelter. It's got a heater and Calor gas for cooking, and I could put you up a water tank and things like that.' His voice had grown enthusiastic, but he

H

broke off and said: 'But you couldn't, though, could you? It wouldn't do.'

'Why not? It would be a home. I'd love it. I'll have a dog. A cat, too, perhaps. A crazy old woman living in a caravan, that's what I'll be. A sort of local hermit. Children will come and stare, and run away in terror if I look out.' She laughed. 'Whatever will Miriam say? There she is now, Frank. I'd better run down and break it to her before I lose courage. Go and tell the man that we'll have it.'

'Granny.' Ellen put her hands on her hips, and looked round the narrow space, no wider than a railway carriage. 'It's heaven.'

'Not quite,' Louise said, stumbling over the suitcases and wondering where on earth she was going to put everything, 'but we'll try and make it so.'

For once in her life, some good luck had come to Ellen. When Mrs Match's grandson had German measles, Ellen had gone to him and ordered him to breathe at her, until she felt she must be sucking in a fog of germs. The day before the family was due to leave for Austria, a rash appeared, and Ellen could not go. Simon and Judy had had German measles. They had sensibly had nearly everything, while Ellen, annoyingly, had not caught diseases when she was young, and could be relied on now to fall sick at the most inconvenient times.

Miriam had been furious when Ellen came sheepishly with her pyjamas unbuttoned, to show her the rash. The child was not sick enough to be sympathized with. Miriam began to be martyred about having to stay behind with Ellen, while Arthur went on with the other two, but Louise said: 'Leave her with me. She can come to the caravan.'

'Hardly the place to have measles, I should have thought.' Miriam raised her eyebrows.

'Miriam, dear, it's not a tent. You go off and enjoy your holiday, and let me look after Ellen.'

Miriam had to agree, although she did not approve of Ellen going to the caravan. The child was *farouche* enough as it was. She did not approve of Louise going there, either, although it certainly solved the immediate problem of what was to be done with her.

When Miriam rang up Eva in Lancashire to tell her of the extraordinary way their mother proposed to live, Eva had said: 'Why not? Don't be so stuffy. I think it's a marvellous idea. I'd like to do it myself.'

'No doubt you would. *I* think it's most unsuitable.'

'Most unsuitable,' Ellen said, mimicking what she had heard her mother say. 'Most unsuitable, Arthur, and quite mad. Oh, Granny, to think of those others,' she exclaimed, 'sitting in that awful train, and being told not to fidget, and getting out into that terrible snow, with people running about red in the face and saying how glorious it is. It isn't glorious.' She shuddered. 'It's cold. And everyone wants to rush off all the time and *do* things. I hope they break their legs.'

'Now, Ellen,' Louise said. 'Why be spiteful? You've got everything you want, haven't you?'

'Yes.' Ellen collapsed on to the lower bunk with a sigh. 'Everything I want.'

When Louise grew accustomed to living in the cramped space, and cooking on the tiny stove, and fighting with the oil heater, which Anne prophesied would suffocate them both as sure as hell, she found that she, too, had everything she wanted. She was alone with the person she loved best in the world. She had her own home, without the ordinary cares of housework, for there was not much you could do in a caravan, except to keep it as tidy as possible. If you did not put everything away, you became silted up in a surprisingly short time.

'I don't see how you stand it,' Anne said, the first time she visited them, several days after their arrival. She had refused to come and help when Frank was painting and cleaning the caravan, saying that if her mother wanted to go crazy, she could do it without any assistance from her.

'I'll make you a cup of coffee,' Louise said proudly, being a hostess for the first time since Dudley died. 'Then you'll see how nicely my stove works, when it does work. Harry made me a new chimney out of a piece of drainpipe. Sit down. There, on that bench behind the table. There's nowhere else, except the bunks.'

Anne manœuvred her spreading bulk with difficulty behind the table, and sat with her arms on it, glowering round the caravan. 'Those curtains look familiar,' she said.

'They should. Frank got them out of your attic, and Ellen and I cut them down. We haven't hemmed them yet, but we will, when we get a needle. I hope you don't mind. Frank didn't think you even knew they were there.'

Anne grunted. 'What's that door?' she asked.

'A cupboard.' Ellen opened it eagerly to show the tiny space which held the few clothes that she and her grand-mother had brought. 'Isn't it neat? And look—here's our shelves for china and tins—we practically live on baked beans—and please note the carpet. Uncle Frank bought it for us at an auction.' Whatever the shortcomings of the caravan, to Ellen it was perfect.

'But what do you do all day?' Anne asked. Louise never went up to the house, unless she was asked. She was determined not to be a nuisance to Anne, just because she was living on her land. If she ran out of milk or bread, or needed an extra blanket, she would go without it sooner than ask Anne, and if the water tank needed filling, or the stove went wrong, which it frequently did, she would wait until she could find Frank in the yard to ask him to fix it.

'Oh, there's masses to do,' Ellen said. 'We help Uncle Frank and Harry, you know, when it's not too cold. Granny gets a bit blue if she stays out too long in this weather, and I've got chilblains, but then I always do.' She showed Anne a red and swollen finger. 'Then we sit in here with the heater going and get up a terrific fug. You ought to see how the windows steam up. We play the wireless, and we read. It's heaven at night, with the tree tapping down on the roof, and the wind trying to get at us from outside. The caravan fairly rocks sometimes.'

'Sounds entrancing,' Anne said, making a face over her

mother's coffee. Louise had never been able to make coffee, and tinned milk did not improve it. There was no shop in the village, and a bus only once a week to the little town.

'And we learn bits of poetry,' Ellen went on. 'Granny's got a surprisingly good memory for it. Isn't that funny when she forgets so many other things?'

Louise had begun to read and learn poetry by heart after she was married. Dudley never read anything except newspapers and magazines, and often, when he was at home, he did not talk to her for hours on end. She had found that learning poems was a soothing way to take her mind off the disappointment of her marriage, a disappointment that had crept in before the honeymoon was over, and whose extent she did not dare to admit, even to herself.

When her daughters began to reach a sensible age, she had tried to read poetry to them, and to inspire them to learn it, but they had shut their minds to it, half through embarrassment, half through doubting that their mother could have anything worth while to offer. Then Louise remembered regretfully how, when she was a child, her father had tried to convey his own love of poetry to her, and she would have none of it. How sad it was to be a parent, and have your children only discover after you were dead the things they might have shared with you. But how delightful to be a grandmother with a responsive grandchild, who opened her heart to you without embarrassment, because she had no one to talk to at home.

Ellen usually wanted to learn sad poems. She spoke them dolefully, and sometimes snivelled a little, as she still snivelled happily over the picture: 'Good-bye, Old Friend,' which she had brought with her to hang in the caravan. She was a morbid child, delighting in old-fashioned stories with sadly moral endings, and finding no pleasure in the modern children's books, which ended so brightly, with the children coming out triumphant, and the grown-ups worsted.

Sometimes she insisted on learning love poems. She dwelt on lines like: *The paradise of your imperfect lover*, repeating it over and over again in fascination. She desperately wanted a lover, although she did not quite know what it was.

'Has Mummy ever had a lover?'

'Of course not.' Louise caught her breath. 'Happily-married people don't.'

'A pity in a way. It might have been exciting for her. I don't suppose Daddy ever wrote poetry to her. He's too busy. Once, I saw her looking at a photograph of a man, but when I came into the room, she put it away in a drawer, and turned round, looking cross. Odd, wasn't it?'

'Well, perhaps——' Louise was at a loss. What instinct brought the poor child so perilously close to the truth?

'Poor Mummy,' Ellen said. 'She's really rather pretty without her glasses. Perhaps you were too, at one time. Did you ever have a lover, Granny?'

'No, dear.' Louise was thankful to steer away from Miriam. 'Oh, well, of course, there was your grandfather.'

'That's not the same. It has to be someone you're not married to, doesn't it? Like Mr Disher.'

'Don't be silly, Ellen.'

'No one could write a poem about him, though. It's sad to be so fat. Why don't you invite him down here for the weekend? He'd never get behind the table, but he could have the camp stool on the other side.'

'And where would he sleep? He's ill, anyway. He couldn't come.'

'Is he still in the hospital?'

'I don't know.' Louise had written to Gordon Disher, asking if she could visit him, but he had not answered. She was beginning to think that he might have died, lonely and unmourned, with only obliging Mrs Dill to go to his funeral.

Ellen was miserable when the time came for her to leave the caravan. She did not want to go home to *Pleasantways*, and hear Simon and Judy tell of their exploits in the snow. She did not want to go back to school.

'But you shall come again in the Easter holidays,' Louise promised her, 'if Mummy lets you. Your Aunt Anne will have had her baby by then.'

' "When the fruit's ripe it will drop," Mrs Match says. I hope she'll let me do things for it. I don't expect she'll be much good at it. She's so funny with me sometimes; I don't think she likes children.'

'She'll like her own,' Louise said optimistically.

'What's she going to call it?'

'She hasn't even thought.'

Louise missed Ellen very much when she had gone. There did not seem much point in doing alone the things they had enjoyed together, like making cakes, and digging a little bed for spring flowers, and taking the bus into town to shop and go to the cinema. Set off in the rough field beyond Frank's yard and his neat rows of cold-frames, the caravan was a lonely place. It stood on the windy side of a slight slope; Anne's house stood on the other, so that at night she could not even see the lights burning, nor feel that there was anything near her except the barren trees and rustling hedges, alive with the mysterious night life of the field. The strange cry of a bird woke her sometimes in fright, and she longed for the small bulge of Ellen's sleeping body in the bunk above her.

It was very lonely at night, and very cold. Louise went to bed with two sweaters over a pair of boy's pyjamas, thankful that she had no mirror to see herself in the ludicrous outfit. Oil for the stove was expensive, and she did not like to burn it all the time when she was alone. Frank wanted to buy oil for her, but she refused. After paying the small rent for the caravan, she could just manage to keep herself, without taking help from anyone.

Frank came to see her when he could spare the time, but Anne came seldom. What she called 'the ghastly date' was drawing near, and she sulked in bed most of the day, defeated by the inevitable progression of pregnancy and birth. The last time Frank's mother came, she had filled Anne up with alarming stories of what was going to happen to her, which

Anne chose to believe, rather than the reassurances of her mother and doctor.

Louise wanted to come over and help in the house, which Anne was neglecting, but she knew that Anne would not like it. Frank had to do most of the work himself, wondering why Anne was so different from other women, who, he knew, were impelled to sweep their homes from top to bottom when their time was approaching. He bore with his wife patiently. He was in a quiet fever of excitement about his baby. He had taken to calling it 'his baby,' since Anne persistently referred to it as 'the thing,' and seemed to take no interest in its possession.

Frank gave Louise a cat, a thin, striped female, which roamed back often to its old stamping ground among the corn-bins, but was quite a comfort to her when it stayed in the caravan, biting its claws on Ellen's bunk. Louise wondered what had happened to Mr Disher's cat and whether Mrs Dill had taken it in. If he was really dead, she would have liked to have it.

Dick Bennett came down one day from the village with a mongrel on a piece of string. 'Frank told me you were wanting a dog,' he said. 'My Susie had this one some time ago when she shouldn't have, and we don't really want him about the place. He isn't much, I know. Looks to me as if his father was a fox, but he'd be company for you. It's lonely out here, isn't it? Couldn't stand it myself, but it takes all tastes.'

It was a charming dog. Louise called it Gordon, in memory of Mr Disher, who, dead or not, she did not think she would ever see again. The dog was red and harsh-coated, with a sharp nose, triangular ears, short legs on a barrel body, and an enormous bushy tail, wildly out of proportion to the rest of him. He had been pushed around at the Bennett's, and took to Louise like an orphan needing a mother.

Louise loved him, and talked to him a lot. Now I really am getting to be a crazy old woman, she thought. They always talk to their dogs as if they understood everything, and have a cat that seems to be a witch. She looked at the tiger cat, inscrutable on the top bunk, its yellow, slit eyes brooding over the edge in the eccentric shadows of the oil lamp.

One afternoon, Louise took Gordon out for a walk. She seldom let him run outside by himself, because of Anne's rough, enormous dogs. She stepped carefully down the rickety wooden steps, and turned back to look at her home, standing in the field like a stranded hulk under the black winter arms of the old elm tree. It was not a modern caravan, like a holiday trailer with smart cream paint and wheels that turned smoothly. The tractor that pulled it here had had a rough passage with it, Frank said. He had painted it green outside, but it still had a derelict air, like a cross between an abandoned railway carriage and the home of a third-rate circus troop. Harry's rusted chimney poked up from its weatherbeaten roof as drunkenly as Harry himself on a Saturday night.

Louise found the old man in the yard, crabbily scraping the walls of a hen-house. 'Where's Frank?' she asked.

Harry jerked his head. 'Gone to Bedford,' he said. 'Left me to do all the work, as usual.' He worked on, jabbing with his shovel, and muttering under his breath at the hens huddled in murmurous resentment in a corner. 'By the by,' he said, as Louise turned to go, '*she* wants you. She called to me a while back when I was up to the house after the mallet.'

Louise put Gordon in the woodshed behind the house, so that the barking dogs in the kitchen should not set upon him, and went in at the back door. She pushed away the dogs, which clamoured at her skirts. She was not afraid of them now, but it upset Gordon to find the smell of them on her clothes.

'Anne?' she called.

'Upstairs.' Anne's voice sounded strained and odd. In apprehension, Louise ran up the stairs, and found that she was right. Anne was sprawled on the bed, in pain.

'It's starting!' Anne cried out, as soon as she heard her mother's footsteps in the passage. 'The beastly thing's starting. I'm terrified. Why didn't you come before, Mother? You might have come.'

'Harry's only just told me.'

'God damn him. How would he like to have a baby? I told him to get you ages ago. I've been in agony here for hours. It's—oh, here it is again! I can't—it's——' Her voice trailed off into a moan, as the pain gripped her, and drove away all other sense but feeling.

'Hold my hand, darling. Dig your nails in, that's right, if it helps. Don't be afraid. This is what happens. No worse than this, I promise you, and then it all goes, and you won't remember it.'

When Anne relaxed, Louise ran downstairs and telephoned for the ambulance. Between the pains, Louise packed a case for Anne, who had not got a thing ready, and went back to the bed each time that Anne cried out, to hold her hand and suffer with her.

'You promised it wouldn't get any worse,' Anne gasped. 'It does. You think it can't, and then it does. It isn't fair.' She turned her sweating face wildly from side to side on the pillow. 'Oh, God, it isn't fair on women. Who invented this thing?' she asked more lucidly, as the pain receded once more. 'Where are you going, Mother?'

'Just to the bathroom to get your toothbrush.'

'Don't go. Damn the toothbrush. I never want to clean my teeth again. Don't leave me. Stay here. It's creeping up on me again, and I——'

Louise stayed by the bed until the ambulance came. She had never been so close to her daughter, even when Anne was a baby and completely dependent. This was no longer a mother and daughter relationship. It was the closeness of any two women caught in the eternal crisis that is all their own, man's part in it forgotten, the world entirely female. It was the same relationship that Anne would have with the midwife at the hospital, but for the moment it was Louise's to share, and she lived it intensely.

When the ambulance had taken Anne away—'As quick as you can,' the nurse told the driver, after one look at Anne— Louise sat dizzily down in the kitchen, and suffered the largest dog to put its head on her knee and whimper. She felt pleased with herself. She had done her part. She had managed all right this time.

When Frank came home, she told him proudly how she had called the ambulance and got Anne safely off to the hospital. Frank's immediate reaction was one of disappointment. He had thought it would happen at night, and had seen himself dramatically rushing Anne through the darkness to the hospital, and pacing the floors there while the dawn came up, as other fathers did.

He put on his coat again to go to Anne, but Louise said: 'Better telephone first. The way things were going, the baby may be there already, and that will save you worrying on the way.'

Frank nodded and mumbled over the telephone, then dropped it down clumsily, and turned to Louise with a face so white and desperate that her heart jumped in fear.

'What is it, Frank? What's happened?'

'It's a girl,' he said, sitting down weakly and managing a sickly grin. 'A whopping great big girl, my Anny's had. I'm to go and see her.'

Louise stayed at the house while Frank was at the hospital. She felt too excited to go back to the isolation of the caravan, and she wanted to prepare supper for him and to be there when he came home, because he would need someone to talk to.

It was late by the time Frank had talked out his delight and pride. Anne had said the baby looked repulsive, which shocked the nurse; but Frank did not mind. He knew that the baby was perfect, and he was convinced that it would make all the difference to Anne's happiness. 'Give her something worth while to do. She's talked about it so funny all along, but you'll see; she'll love it as much as she does the dogs. They're making her nurse the baby herself. She doesn't want to, but it'll do her good. Nothing like it for a woman's figure. Oh—excuse me. I shouldn't talk that way.'

'That's all right, Frank.' Louise got up and patted his shoulder. 'I'm so happy for you. But I'll have to go now. I want to get up early and cook your breakfast.'

'You mustn't bother. I've been used to doing for myself before I was married—and after, if it comes to that. Perhaps you should stay the night though, as it's so late.'

'I'd better not. Anne mightn't—I mean, she seems to have the spare room all covered up with dust sheets.'

Frank walked back with her to the caravan under a cold, black sky, with the stars like sparkling chips of ice. He raised his voice in song, and Gordon scuttled about with his great plumed tail on high, barking at bushes, crazy with the delight of a night walk. Louise was very happy. She stood in the narrow doorway of the caravan, calling good night to Frank as he walked jauntily away across the field. Smiling, she turned to go inside. The cat crouched on the table, finishing off the remains of a mouse. In the beam of her torch, it met her smile with cynical eyes, unblinking, devoid of emotion.

Louise went often to the house while Anne was away. She cooked meals for Frank, and made his bed, and tried to clean up some of the dirt and muddle that Anne had left, although she knew that Anne would not thank her for it, even if she noticed the difference.

One evening, Louise found the chestnut-haired girl, Freda, perched on a kitchen chair with her slim legs crossed high up, talking animatedly to Frank, who jumped up in embarrassment when Louise came in.

Freda did not get up. She waved towards a chair, as Louise stood nonplussed. 'Make yourself at home,' she said, looking perfectly at home herself.

Frank looked at Louise pleadingly. 'I know,' his eyes said. 'I'm sorry. I can't do anything with her.'

'How nice of you,' Louise said brightly to Freda, 'to come and keep Frank company. But it's rather late. Shouldn't you be getting home?'

'I been out on my own before,' the girl said cheekily. She had no intention of going, and Louise did not know how to get rid of her.

They talked stiltedly for a while, with Freda laughing on a high note about things that were not funny. She was evidently determined to stay until Louise went away. Louise was equally determined not to leave her alone with Frank. Why couldn't he turn the girl out himself? He was so weak and hopeless about it. He should have rid himself of her long ago, when he married Anne.

The conversation exhausted itself. Freda began to hum and waggle her foot. Frank mumbled something about the chickens, and escaped from the room, stumbling over the door-sill.

Freda laughed. 'Old Frank,' she said.

'I thought you told me last time we met that you had a job in London,' Louise said, trying to be polite.

'Did I? Well, I turned it down. I'm still here, you see.'

'Freda,' Louise said bravely, 'I don't think you should come down here in the evening like this when Frank's alone. It isn't right.'

'He's not alone. You're here, aren't you?'

'But you didn't think I would be, and you wish I'd go. Why can't you leave Frank alone?' If the girl was going to be so bold, she would try to be bold, too. 'He's a married man, and it's wrong of you to run after him.'

'I don't have to run. Frank's not backward, as they say. Listen, Mrs What-is-it, Frank and I were friends, if you get my meaning, long before he took up with your daughter. He'd have married me, if she hadn't come along and given him big ideas about bettering himself. Bettering himself!' She looked scornfully round the shabby untidy kitchen. 'How wrong he was.'

'Freda!' Louise stood up, enraged. 'You can't sit there and talk to me like that. You—you just can't. I won't have it.'

'Go back to your old caravan then,' Freda said serenely, 'if you don't like the company here.'

'I won't go until you do. You've no right to be here, and you're not wanted here,' Louise said, gaining courage. 'Frank doesn't want you, or any other woman. Can't you understand that?'

'You don't know our Frankie,' the girl said in a purring

voice, leaning back and running a hand slowly through her glorious hair.

'Get out of this house!' Louise ordered, stamping her small foot, which was still shod in the rubber boot she wore to come through the mud of the yard. 'If you come back again, I'll tell your mother.'

'She wouldn't care.' Freda shrugged her shoulders. 'She always wanted me to marry Frank.'

'Well then, I'll go to the police.'

Freda laughed. 'What for? A person has a right to go visiting.'

'You're not visiting. You're molesting. How can you be so hateful, sneaking in and making up to a man the minute his wife is gone?'

'Don't you think little Frankie can look after himself?'

'He's too polite to tell you what you deserve to be told. And he's foolish. He doesn't realize the sort of talk this could start in the village.'

'Yes, that's right.' Freda nodded. 'They'll talk.'

'Is that what you want them to do?' Louise asked incredulously.

'Why not? You don't think *I* want Frank, do you, now that he's gone so respectable? I can do a lot better for myself, let me tell you that. Don't forget, there's Americans at the airfield now.'

'Then why have you come? Just to make trouble—out of spite because Frank married someone else?'

'Got it in one, lady.' Freda smiled complacently. 'To make a little trouble.'

'I don't understand you,' Louise said slowly. 'You're like a girl in a film, or a magazine story.' Freda took this as a compliment. 'Haven't you any shame? What do you think people will say about you if you carry on like this?'

'Oh, I don't care. They say bad enough about me already. Always have. I had a baby, you know, during the war. That gave them something to talk about. Mum sent it away, but they don't forget. Oh, well,' she got up and collected a bright-red plastic purse, 'I might as well be getting along, now that we understand each other, and since Frank seems too scared to come back. Good night, Mrs What-is-it. See you again.'

'Has she gone?' Frank poked his head round the back door a few minutes later.

'Yes,' Louise said disgustedly, 'and I think you've behaved abominably.'

'I couldn't stop her coming here.' He spread his hands helplessly.

'You know I don't mean that. Freda told me she had a baby. It's terrible. And to think I've liked you, and been pleased about the marriage——'

'What on earth are you talking about, Mother? Do you think it was my baby?' Frank laughed and slapped his knee. 'That's a good one. It was black.'

Louise could not help feeling a little sorry for Freda after this, but she was determined that she should not come down again looking for trouble. Although she knew that Anne would not like it, she removed the spare-room dust sheets, which turned out to be the good bed sheets that Louise had given her when she married, and stayed in the house to chaperone Frank until Anne came home with the baby.

After living for several days in a proper house, even such an uncomfortable house as the Stone Farm, it was hard to return to the caravan when Anne came back. It looked smaller and poorer and less like a home than ever. Frank had been easy, congenial company, and Louise missed having someone to talk to and someone to cook for. The cat, which had returned to the corn-bins when Louise went to stay with Frank, had gone wild, and could not be persuaded to come back to the caravan.

Louise felt more lonely than before. Up at the house, there were the noises and smells of a baby, and strings of wet washing hanging across the kitchen ceiling. There was homeliness there, chaotic though it was, but Louise was not invited to share it. Anne did not mind her coming to see the baby, but she would not let her help with it. It was hard for Louise to keep quiet when she saw Anne doing things all wrong, and heard the baby crying, and longed to pick it up. Anne treated her daughter as if she were about six years old, and should be expected to have some sense. She spoke to her in a matter-of-fact tone of voice, and made disgusted faces at her when she was wet. The baby throve, surprisingly, although it cried a lot. Sometimes, at night, its piercing protests carried right across the fields to the caravan.

When Anne could stand the noise no longer, she would pick the baby up and feed it, at any time of the day or night. She would nurse it wherever she happened to be, sitting in the kitchen with her dress unbuttoned, a magazine in one hand and a cigarette in her mouth, blowing smoke into the sparse black hair of the suckling baby.

Miriam found her like this when she came the first time to see the baby and to visit her mother.

'Really, Mother,' she said, stepping cautiously into the caravan in her fur coat, as if she were slumming, 'Anne is too crude. She's like a peasant woman. I'm sure even Frank doesn't like it, but he's too silly with her to tell her anything. I told her though.

'I'm sure you did, dear. I don't suppose she minded.'

'She didn't.' Miriam looked round the caravan. 'Mother, is this where you *live?*'

'Certainly. It's cosy, isn't it? Gordon and I are very happy here.'

She and Gordon had stuck it out all through the winds and rain of a tempestuous March. Louise was beginning to long for comfort and for company, and a hot bath whenever she liked, instead of once a week, if Anne's geyser was working.

'It will be better in the summer,' she told Gordon, when they came in cold and wet from a walk, and there was nowhere to get dry. But what about next winter? Could she stand another winter here? Louise began to feel that she was getting old.

However, she said to Miriam: 'Take off your coat and sit down. Don't look so discouraged. I like it very well here. I promise you.'

'But you can't live like this.' Miriam sat down on the bunk and kept her coat on, huddling it about her. 'It's—it's so *meagre*. Where do you keep your clothes?'

'I don't need many.' Louise made her voice very cheerful. 'You know I've left most of my things with you. It's all right, Miriam, really. It does me very nicely.'

Miriam's conscience was troubling her uncomfortably. 'We shouldn't have let you come here,' she said, 'only you were so stubborn about it. But you'll be coming to stay with us soon. For Easter if you like, as you did last year.'

'Oh, I don't know, dear. Perhaps I won't come this year. It's different now. I have a home of my own.'

'Home! Mother, don't be ridiculous. This is all right for a holiday, I dare say, though I'd loathe it myself, but you can't live here all the time. I've someone staying in your room now, but they'll be gone soon, and Eva will be back in the summer. She talks about signing a new contract with the B.B.C. Things can go on as they did before.'

Going from one to the other, trying to pass the time and keep out of the way in someone else's house, temporizing with visit after visit, and no roots anywhere—what did other women do, who had been left alone without money or purpose in life? How did they bear this futile necessity to be housed somewhere, like a surplus piece of furniture?

What did they do? If their children would not have them, they went to shabby hotels, or were pushed into old ladies' homes, if they were senile enough. It would be easier for the family, Louise thought, if I were an invalid. Then they could put me away in a nursing home without any qualms.

When she got home, Miriam said to Arthur: 'It's dreadful. Perfectly dreadful.'

'Anne's baby? Poor thing, it can't look like its mother yet.'

'Oh, Arthur, don't. You know I don't mean that. I mean the way Mother is living. We can't let her stay there. We'll simply have to have her here, I'm afraid, when Priscilla goes.'

Arthur stroked his dark-blue chin, wondering how he could

get out of this without appearing unkind. 'Does your mother want to come?' he asked.

'She says she doesn't, but you know what she is. She's being heroic. Oh, dear.' Miriam sat down and patted her neat hair. 'I do feel rather bad about it.'

'I don't see that you need. It's possible that she really doesn't mind living like a gipsy. Everyone isn't as sybaritic as you, remember. She's over the worst part now. She's stood the winter, and the weather will be getting warmer. The out-door life. Some people like it.'

'She certainly *seems* to like it all right. I don't want to rush her into anything she doesn't want to do.' Miriam began to let herself be persuaded, and to make excuses to her conscience, whose prickings were already becoming more feeble. Presently, as the days went by, the pricks ceased to be felt at all. She thought sometimes about her mother in the lonely, pitiful caravan, but she swiftly stifled her misgivings. Eva wrote airily that she did not know when she would be coming back. Anne seemed quite disinterested in what went on in the caravan. If the others could not bother about their mother, why should she be the one who always had to take the burden? It was not fair on Arthur.

The holidays came. Ellen clamoured to go and stay with her grandmother.

'Do you think she ought?' Miriam asked Arthur. 'She'll see hardly anything of Simon. She'll miss all the parties here, and she's unsociable enough as it is. I don't think it's good for her to go off and lead that kind of uncivilized existence. She was terribly uncouth when she came back last time.'

'Oh, let her go,' Arthur said. 'Simon won't care.'

'Nor will you, will you?' Miriam looked at him closely.

'Want me to be honest? Oh, forget it, Miriam. You know we swore right at the beginning that we'd never say any more about it if I agreed to take on the child. It's the only way.'

'Stop being so noble,' Miriam said. 'I know it's not been easy for you.'

'Easy! Good God——' he flared up at her. 'Of course it's

not been easy. What do you think I am? How would any man like having to take another man's brat into his house, and keep quiet about it, and behave as if it was all one big happy family? But I did it. There was nothing else to do, if we weren't to have a scandal. I forgave you then, and I've never brought it up against you. You must give me that. Now shut up about it.'

'Always so forgiving,' Miriam said, half to herself. 'So unreproachful. That's what's made it such hell.'

'What would you have liked me to do?' he asked scornfully. 'Beaten you and turned you out?'

'I don't know.' Miriam shook her head. 'It's all so long ago. I forget what I felt like then. I crawled to you, didn't I, and begged you to understand? As if you could.'

'Oh, Miriam, I said shut up about it.' Arthur turned away. 'For God's sake stop raking up the past in this morbid way. Send the child to her grandmother, and let's have no more talk about it. It gives me a headache.'

So Ellen went to the caravan, and although the weather had not improved, as Louise had promised Gordon it would, she and her grandmother were happy again, as they had been before. Louise tried not to think about the time when Ellen would be gone back to school and she would be alone once more. She did not know whether she would be going to Miriam's, or whether Eva would come back to London and have her at her flat, or whether Anne would ever uncover her spare room again. She lived merely in the present, and tried to give Ellen the happiest holiday she had ever had.

'*Aren't you coming home for your birthday?*' Miriam wrote to Ellen. '*I think you should. You can have a party, if you like.*'

'Oh, Granny, must I?' Ellen showed Louise the letter. 'I don't want to. There's no one I care to ask to a party, and we were going to have my birthday here, with the cake and everything.'

'Write to Mummy and say that I'll be disappointed if you don't stay,' Louise suggested. 'That might get over it.'

Miriam made no more objections. Louise and Ellen took the bus into town and bought the ingredients for the cake that

Louise was going to risk making. Frank and Anne and the baby were asked up to share it. Ellen was making paper decorations for the caravan, and a frill for Gordon to wear. It would be quite a party. They had been planning it for days.

The day before Ellen's birthday, Frank went away for a night to see his brother, who was ill. Anne, who was bored with the baby, and had nothing to do, although there was a pile of dirty washing dumped on the bathroom floor, wandered up to the caravan, and beat on the door with a stick.

Ellen opened the door, her hair like a mop and her face distraught. 'The beastly stove has gone wrong again,' she said. 'It would, just when Uncle Frank's away. Granny's so upset. She wanted to make my cake.'

Louise was bending over the tiny stove, red in the face, and trying to manipulate a pair of pliers, as she had seen Frank do, only she was not sure which pipe he used them on.

'Simple,' Anne said. 'You're out of gas.'

'We're not.' Louise stood upright, and pushed her hair away from her face. 'I checked it. No, it's the same thing that always happens. Frank is the only one who can fix it. Will you tell him as soon as he comes back to-morrow?'

'But that will be too late,' Ellen said mournfully. 'You'll never get the cake made in time for the party. You know how long it takes you.'

'Relax, child,' Anne said. 'It isn't the end of the world. Harry's fooling about in the yard. Why don't you get him to look at it?'

'We did,' Louise said. 'He couldn't do anything. All he did was to tear one of the burners loose and be unable to get it back on again. He lent us this awful thing to cook our lunch on.' She pointed to a rusty contraption in the middle of the floor. 'It's a sort of primus. He uses it when he's got no coal for his range. I'm scared to death of it, but it will have to do us until Frank gets home.'

'I'll tell him,' Anne said. 'You'll blow yourselves up with that thing.' The primus stove rocked as she kicked it. One of its legs was broken.

By lunch-time next day, the gas stove was still unmended. 'Let me go and get Uncle Frank,' Ellen begged. 'I know he's home because I saw the car. It's getting so late. We'll never be ready for the party, even if you make a sponge. Let me go and ask him.'

'No, you can't,' Louise said. 'He's busy, or he would have come straight away. He has so much to do, and I hate to bother him when he's always so kind. He'll come presently. Just be patient.'

Ellen grew more and more despondent as the afternoon advanced, and Frank still did not come. She went out several times to look for him in the yard, but a storm was getting up, and the wind and rain drove her inside again. The sky had darkened. It was like night-time instead of four o'clock.

'How the wind howls,' Louise said. 'I hate it, don't you? It's so relentless, the way it tears and batters at everything.' She looked out of the little window. 'How can the trees bear it, being pushed at and tormented and given no peace? I can't bear to have my hair blown about even for one minute, and this seems to have been going on for hours.' She stayed by the streaming window, watching the lashed and darkened land-scape. At the beginning of the gale, the trees and leafless bushes had bounced and danced as if they were glad to feel the movement. By now, they looked as if it had gone on too long for them. Louise knew how they felt. If only it would stop! The trees moved their petulant heads from side to side like tired children crying: 'Oh, leave us alone!'

'Perhaps they won't be able to come from the house in this storm.' Ellen's doleful voice recalled Louise to the caravan.

'They'll come. Frank promised. And Anne's mad enough to bring the baby out in any weather.'

'But what will they eat, Granny? We can't give them baked beans. Aunt Anne has them all the time, anyway.'

'I'll make some griddle scones,' Louise said, glad to think of something to do to take her mind off the storm. 'I know I swore I'd never light Harry's stove again after what it did this morning, but I'll try. Stand well back, Ellen.'

'I'm getting up here.' Ellen scrambled to the top bunk, taking Gordon with her. They peered over the edge as Louise worked the pump, then, holding her breath, lit a match and jumped back as the stove flared and roared. She stood by and watched it suspiciously until it settled down and began to burn more calmly.

'There!' she said, looking up triumphantly to the top bunk. 'Nothing to it, you see.'

Ellen and Gordon lay on their stomachs and watched the fierce little blue and yellow flames, while Louise mixed the batter for the scones. Outside, the storm seemed to be gaining strength. The caravan creaked like an old ship in a gale, and sometimes it shuddered, as if the wind that struck it were a wave.

Louise had put the frying-pan on the stove to heat. With her tongue between her lips, she was preparing to spoon out the batter. Her hand jerked and the batter splayed over the floor as the full force of the wind slapped against the side of the caravan with a sound of fury. The caravan rocked, gave a sickening lurch, and Ellen and Gordon fell out of the bunk together as it toppled sideways against the tree and stayed there with the floor at a crazy angle.

The stove had slid across to the wall. It tipped over, and instantly the carpet was alight. In a moment the caravan was a box of flames. 'Get out, Ellen! Get out!' Louise screamed. She heard Ellen whimpering as she tugged at the door. She could see nothing through the scorching smoke. She groped to the door, as Ellen wrenched it open and the wind rushed in and fanned the flames to the ceiling. Louise fell out on to the wet grass. The door was on the upper side, and it seemed a long way to the ground.

'Ellen!' she shouted. A window fell in and the black smoke curled out towards her. 'Ellen—run! Get away from it!' Gordon was running across the field, barking hysterically against the wind. There was no sign of Ellen.

Sobbing, choking, Louise climbed back into the inferno of the caravan and found Ellen on the floor, where she had fallen when the wind rushed in. Blindly, with her clothes on fire, Louise plunged for the doorway, and fell out on to the ground with the unconscious child in her arms.

CHAPTER EIGHT

THERE was a knock on the kitchen door. Frank got up to open it. Behind him, the sisters sat in silence. They had said everything there was to say.

Harry was standing outside, shifting from foot to foot. 'What do you want?' Frank asked. 'I can't come up to the yard to-day. You know that. You'll have to manage by yourself.'

'I didn't come for that. It's me dinner-time. I come to know, what about my little stove? I'm out of coal, and I need it.'

'What stove? What are you talking about?'

Harry told him. Without a word, Frank shut the door on the old man and turned back into the room.

'You knew about the stove, didn't you?' He walked towards Anne. 'You went up there while I was away. Why didn't you tell me?'

'I meant to, Frank. I forgot.'

'Forgot.' Frank let his hands fall to his sides. His face was blank and hopeless. 'You girls forgot pretty well everything about your mother, it seems to me.'

Miriam shifted in her chair. 'Oh, be quiet,' she said. 'What business is it of yours?'

'Just that I happen to care about your mother.'

'And we don't, I suppose?' Eva said sharply.

'I'm saying nothing.' Frank turned away and went upstairs to his crying baby.

'She's not asleep yet,' the nurse said, 'but she's drowsy. Don't talk too much, and don't stay very long.'

'Is she all right?'

'She will be. It will take time.'

244

'And the child?'

'That will take longer. She's badly burned. They've taken her to the Children's Hospital.' The nurse opened the door. 'Someone to see you,' she said gently, and Gordon Disher trod shyly up to the bed.

Louise looked at him without speaking. 'Ellen might die,' she said at last.

'She won't. She can't. You saved her life. I read it in the papers. I had to come. Forgive me.'

'Ellen might die,' she repeated, as if she had not heard him. 'They've taken her away.'

'Just to the Children's Hospital. The nurse told me. She said it would take time, but——'

'Time—yes. She might be ill for months. She'll need so much care. And loving. How will she get that from Miriam? How can she live?' She looked at him blankly. 'It was her birthday.'

He nodded, standing over her, out of proportion in his bulky overcoat in the tiny, pale green room.

'I thought *you* were dead,' Louise said, remembering. 'Why didn't you write?'

'I was ashamed,' he said. 'I took a drink, you know, because I was upset about you, though that doesn't excuse it.'

'About me?' Louise frowned under the bandage that came down almost to her scorched eyebrows.

'Yes. Perhaps you don't remember. I asked you to marry me, and you laughed.'

The drugs had taken away Louise's pain. She lay unmoving, floating on a mist between the ceiling and the bed. It was an effort to think back to Christmas Eve, and herself walking alone down the long, cold flight of stairs. 'I didn't know what you meant,' she said.

'I'll have to make it plainer this time. Don't laugh again. I've come to ask you if you will marry me.'

'Oh, no.' Louise lifted her bandaged arm and let it fall despairingly. 'Please don't try to be kind. I'm tired of people having to be kind to me.'

'For heaven's sake, Louise,' he said, and she realized that it was only the second time that he had ever called her by her name, 'I'm not trying to be kind. I'm asking you to be kind to *me*.'

'Thank you.' Louise smiled. Her swollen eyelids fluttered and dropped. 'We could have Ellen with us later on, perhaps,' he said. 'We could care for her. She could be like—like our child.'

Louise opened her eyes for a moment, and the shy eagerness of his face was still behind her lids when they dropped again of their own weight. 'The girls are coming soon,' she said drowsily. 'I don't think I can keep awake for them. Will you see them for me, and tell them what you and I are going to do? And tell them——' Her voice trailed off to a whisper. He leaned over the bed to catch her words. Half in a dream, she saw her daughter's faces—disapproving, amused, incredulous. 'Whatever will the girls say?' she murmured, and fell asleep with a chuckle.

Miriam and Eva and Anne advanced together down the polished corridor, looking at the doors, and trying not to make a noise with their heels. A Sister in a dark-blue dress came out of the kitchen, small and brisk, and absurdly young to be a Sister.

'Mrs Bickford?' she said. 'Oh, yes, her daughters. I'm afraid she's asleep at the moment. She's under drugs, of course. I shall have to ask you to come back later, unless you'd like to wait.'

The sisters hesitated. Each had prepared what she would say to her mother. They felt let down, and could not decide for the moment what to do.

'There is a gentleman waiting to see you,' the nurse said. 'I've put him in my office. Perhaps you could talk to him right away, as he has a train to catch.'

The sisters looked at each other. Who could it be at a time like this? A lawyer? A policeman? What did he want with them?

'Well, come on,' Eva said. 'We'll have to see him.' They went into the small, square office, with the tidily arranged desk, and the drug cupboard, and the tea-tray, and the pictures of Sister in groups with other nurses. Mr Disher was standing in the middle of the room with his hands folded.

'Please sit down,' he said. Miriam took the chair by the desk. Anne and Eva took the straight chairs by the wall, where nurses sat to be told what to do, or what they had done wrong. They sat and looked at Mr Disher, prepared to be a little arrogant with him; but he stood calmly before them, less like a schoolboy before three examiners than like a teacher instructing three schoolgirls.

'My name is Gordon Disher,' he said. 'Miss Eva knows me. You other ladies,' he nodded to Miriam and Anne, 'probably know me, if you know of me at all, as "Mother's friend who sells beds".'

He paused. They did not say anything to encourage him. 'I don't know what you'll think,' he went on, 'but the truth of it is this. Your mother and I are to be married. I hope you don't mind too much. Oh, no,' he said, seeing Miriam's face, 'It's not impossible. I shall have to retire in two years, but we can just manage on my pension, if I keep on writing books.'

'Why didn't Mother tell us this herself?' Anne asked petulantly. 'She should have told us herself.'

'She asked me to tell you. She wanted me to tell you that she would not be a worry to you any more. She wanted me to say how grateful she is for the affection and care you've shown since things have been so difficult for her. She spoke so nicely of you all, and then she fell asleep, smiling. It was very sweet.'

They sat in silence. He twisted his hands, and then said shyly: 'I want to thank you, too, for all you've done. You have been good to her.' He waited for them to speak, but the sisters bent their heads and would not look at each other.